"At last a worthy successor to Ellis Peters.
Mel Starr brings medieval crime to life. He has a brilliant
understanding of the language and nature of the people
of the later 1300s. I really enjoyed this book. An excellent
plot, engaging characters – all in all a superb read."
– **Michael Jecks, author of the *Templar* series**

"A thoroughly enthralling and entertaining
medieval crime novel, full of suspense, action and
delicious historical detail. The medieval surgeon, Hugh
de Singleton, is a worthy successor to Ellis Peter's Cadfael,
and the plot twists are equally as satisfying. I became so
captivated by the characters of Hugh and his wife that I
couldn't wait to go back and read the whole series
from the beginning."
– **Karen Maitland, author of *Company of Liars***

"A delightful treasure trove of historical detail as we
delve into further medieval intrigue with Mel Starr's
thoughtful and endearing Hugh de Singleton."
– **Penelope Wilcock, author of
The Hawk and the Dove series**

The chronicles of Hugh de Singleton, surgeon

The Unquiet Bones
A Corpse at St. Andrew's Chapel
A Trail of Ink
Unhallowed Ground
The Tainted Coin
Rest Not in Peace
The Abbot's Agreement
Ashes to Ashes

Ashes to Ashes

The eighth chronicle of
Hugh de Singleton, surgeon

MEL STARR

LION FICTION

Text copyright © 2015 Mel Starr
This edition copyright © 2015 Lion Hudson

Published by Lion Fiction
an imprint of
Lion Hudson plc
Wilkinson House, Jordan Hill Road,
Oxford OX2 8DR, England
www.lionhudson.com/fiction

ISBN 978 1 78264 113 9
e-ISBN 978 1 78264 134 6

First edition 2015

Acknowledgments
Cover images: Skeleton © manx_in_the_world/iStockphoto.com;
Campfire © Jens_Lambert_Photography/iStockphoto.com

Scripture taken from the New King James Version. Copyright
© 1982 by Thomas Nelson, Inc. Used by permission. All rights
reserved.

A catalogue record for this book is available from the British
Library

Printed and bound in the UK, August 2015, LH26

For Dan Runyon

Acknowledgments

Several years ago, when Dan Runyon, Professor of English at Spring Arbor University, learned that I had written an as yet unpublished medieval mystery, he invited me to speak to his fiction-writing class about the trials of a rookie writer seeking a publisher. He sent sample chapters of Master Hugh's first chronicle, *The Unquiet Bones*, to his friend Tony Collins. Thanks, Dan.

Thanks to Tony Collins and all those at Lion Hudson who saw Master Hugh's potential. Thanks especially to my editor, Jan Greenough, who, after eight books, knows Master Hugh as well as I do, and excels at asking such questions as, "Do you really want to say it that way?" and, "Wouldn't Master Hugh do it like this?"

Dr. John Blair, of Queen's College, Oxford, has written several papers about Bampton history. These have been invaluable in creating an accurate time and place for Master Hugh. Tony and Lis Page have also been a great source of information about Bampton. I owe them much. Tony died in March 2015, only a few months after being diagnosed with cancer. He will be greatly missed.

Ms. Malgorzata Deron, of Poznan, Poland, offered to update and maintain my website. She has done an excellent job. To see the result of her work, visit www.melstarr.net

Glossary

Ambler: an easy-riding horse, because it moved both right legs together, then both left legs.

Angelus Bell: rung three times each day to announce the Angelus Devotional: dawn, noon, and sunset.

Bailiff: a lord's chief manorial representative. He oversaw all operations on the manor, collected rents and fines, and enforced labor service. Not a popular fellow.

Beadle: a manor official in charge of fences, hedges, enclosures, and curfew. He served under the reeve and bailiff. Also called a hayward.

Boon work: the extra days of labor service villeins and tenants owed the lord at harvest and other specific times of the year, beyond normal labor service, which was called week work.

Braes: medieval underpants.

Buck: a male fallow deer, not so large or prized as the stag/ hart, a male red deer.

Cabbage with marrow: cabbage boiled with marrow bones, spices, and breadcrumbs.

Candlemas: February 2; it marked the purification of Mary after the birth of Christ. Women paraded to church carrying lighted candles. Tillage of fields resumed on this day.

Capon: a castrated male chicken.

Capon farced: a capon stuffed with hard-boiled egg yolks, currants, chopped pork, breadcrumbs, and spices.

Chancery Court: a high court with common law functions and jurisdiction over property disputes.

Chapman: a merchant, particularly one who traveled from village to village with his wares.

Charlet: a dish of pork, eggs, almonds, and flour, ground fine, boiled with spices, served cold and sliced when firm.

Chauces: tight-fitting trousers, often of different colors for each leg.

Chemise: a girl's undergarment.

Cotehardie: the primary medieval outer garment. Women's were floor-length, men's ranged from the thigh to the ankle.

Cotter: a poor villager, usually holding five acres or less. He often had to labor for wealthy villagers to make ends meet.

Curia: the space occupied by a manor house and its barns and yard.

Daub: a clay-and-plaster mix, reinforced with straw and/or horsehair, used to plaster the exterior of a house.

Dexter: a war horse, larger than packhorses, palfreys, and runcies. Also, the right-hand direction.

Fallow deer: a small deer, not so prized as the red deer.

Fast days: Wednesday, Friday, and Saturday. Not the fasting of modern usage, when no food is consumed, but days upon which no meat, eggs, or animal products were consumed. Fish was on the menu for those who could afford it.

Fence month: a period of weeks to months when animals, particularly deer, could not be hunted. The time varied with the species.

Glebe: land belonging to or providing revenue for a parish church.

Groom: a lower-ranking servant to a lord, outranking a page but beneath a valet.

Hallmote: the manorial court. Royal courts judged free tenants accused of felony or murder, otherwise manor courts had jurisdiction over legal matters concerning villagers. Villeins accused of homicide might also be tried in a manor court.

Hart (or stag): male of the red deer.

Infangenthef: the right of a lord of a manor to try and execute a thief caught in the act.

King's Eyre: a royal circuit court, presided over by a traveling judge.

Kirtle: the medieval undershirt.

Lammastide: August 1, when thanks was given for a successful wheat harvest. From Old English "Loaf Mass."

Leach lombard: A dish of ground pork, eggs, raisins, currants, and dates, with spices added. The mixture was boiled in a sack until set, then sliced for serving.

Let lardes: A type of custard made with eggs, milk, bacon fat, and parsley.

Liripipe: a fashionably long tail attached to a man's cap.

Lych gate: a roofed gate in a churchyard wall under which the deceased rested during the initial part of a burial service.

Marshalsea: the stables and associated accoutrements.

Martinmas: November 11, the traditional date to slaughter animals for winter food.

Maslin: bread made from a mixture of grains, commonly wheat and a coarser grain like barley or rye.

Michaelmas: September 29. The feast signaled the end of the harvest. Last rents and tithes were due.

Midsummer's Eve: June 23/24.

Page: a young male servant, often a youth learning the arts of chivalry before becoming a squire.

Palfrey: a riding horse with a comfortable gait.

Passing bell: ringing of the parish church bell to indicate the death of a villager.

Pax board: a wooden board, frequently painted with sacred scenes, which was passed through a medieval church during services for all to kiss. Literally, "peace board."

Pottage: anything cooked in one pot, from the meanest oatmeal to a savory stew.

Poulterer: the villager in charge of a lord's chickens and geese.

Reeve: an important manor official, although he did not outrank the bailiff. Elected by tenants from among themselves, with the approval of the lord, he was often the best husbandman. He had responsibility for fields, buildings, and enforcing labor service.

Remove: a dinner course.

Runcie: a common horse of a lower grade than a palfrey.

Shilling: a coin worth twelve pence. Twenty shillings equaled a pound.

Solar: a small private room in a castle, more easily heated than the hall, where lords often preferred to spend time, especially in winter. Usually on an upper floor.

Squab: a young dove or pigeon, about four or five weeks old.

St. Beornwald's Church: today the Church of St. Mary the Virgin in Bampton. In the fourteenth century it was dedicated to an obscure Saxon saint enshrined in the church.

St. John's Day: June 24.

St. Swithin's Day: July 15.

Statute of Laborers: following the first attack of plague in 1348–49, laborers realized that because so many workers had died, their labor was in short supply, and so demanded higher wages. In 1351 Parliament set wages at the 1347 level. Like most attempts to legislate against the law of supply and demand, the statute was generally a failure.

Tenant: a free peasant who rented land from his lord. He could pay his rent in labor, or, more likely in the fourteenth century, in cash. Or a combination of both.

Toft: land surrounding a house, often used for growing vegetables.

Verderer: a forester.

Vicar: a priest serving a parish but not entitled to its tithes.

Villein: a non-free peasant. He could not leave his land or service to his lord, or sell animals without permission. But if he could escape his manor for a year and a day, he was free.

Whitsuntide: White Sunday, ten days after Ascension Day, seven weeks after Easter. Also called Pentecost.

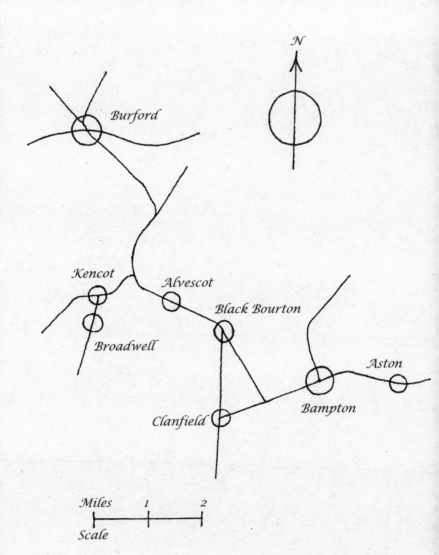

Chapter 1

I had told my Kate for several days that St. John's Day should not be considered midsummer. Roger Bacon, the great scholar of an earlier century, and Robert Grosseteste before him, showed how the calendar has gone awry. Bacon told all who would listen that an extra day is added to the calendar every one hundred and thirty years or so, and so in the year of our Lord 1369 we are ten days displaced. Kate laughed.

"What difference," she asked, "even if 'tis so?"

"Saints' days, and the seasons," I replied, "are out of joint."

"Oh... aye." But she was yet unconvinced, I think, so when men of Bampton began gathering wood for the Midsummer's Eve fire I said no more. We would make merry with others of the town and castle, and celebrate the warm days of summer, regardless of the calendar. I have been wed three years and more. I know when to hold my peace.

The great pile of fallen branches from Lord Gilbert Talbot's forest was raised in a fallow field to the north of the Church of St. Beornwald. For three days fuel was added. I watched the pile grow each day, little suspecting that the daily increase would soon bring me much consternation.

Kate had tied green birch twigs above our door in honor of the summer, so when we departed Galen House at dusk to watch the lighting of the St. John's Day fire I had to duck my head to avoid entangling my cap in the greenery.

I am Hugh de Singleton, surgeon, and bailiff to Lord Gilbert Talbot at his manor of Bampton. I thought that Lord Gilbert might, with some of his knights, attend the Midsummer's Eve blaze. The Lady Petronilla died a year past, when the great pestilence returned, and Lord Gilbert was much distressed. But when he returned to Bampton in the spring, after spending the winter at Goodrich Castle, I thought he seemed somewhat recovered from his great sorrow.

Lord Gilbert did not attend, but several of his retainers – knights, gentlemen and their ladies, valets and grooms – did so. I am not much given to capering about like a pup chasing its tail, so stood aside and lifted my Bessie to my shoulder so that she could better see as others danced about and played the fool, aided in their efforts, no doubt, by great quantities of ale.

Bessie has discovered speech, and exercised her vocabulary as the flames reached into the sky as high as the roof of Father Thomas's vicarage, which stood a safe distance to the east. Kate held Sybil in her arms. The babe is but four months old, is unimpressed by anything inedible, and so slept through the shouts and singing and garish illumination.

Bessie also soon became limp against my shoulder. The merry-making would continue without us. Kate and I returned to Galen House, put our daughters to bed, and fell to sleep with the raucous sound of celebration entering our chamber through the open window.

I was breaking my fast next morning with a loaf and ale when I heard the church bell ring in a solemn cadence. The passing bell. The Angelus Bell had sounded an hour before. Someone in Bampton or the Weald had died in the night. At nearly the same moment a hammering upon Galen House door jolted me from my semi-comatose condition. The pounding ceased and a man shouted, "Master Hugh," in a voice which might have awakened half the residents of Church View Street. It did awaken Sybil, who instantly realized that she was hungry and began to wail. Kate hastened to the stairs to deal with our daughter while I stumbled to the door to learn who was awake so early after such a night.

Father Thomas's clerk, Bertrand Pecock, stood before me, his fist ready to again strike against the Galen House door if I had not opened it.

"Master Hugh, Father Thomas would have you attend him. There are bones."

"Bones?" I replied stupidly. I am not at my best until an hour or so has passed since Kate's rooster has announced the dawn.

"Men gathering the ashes found them."

"Ashes?"

"Aye... from the St. John's Day fire. To spread upon a pea field. They came to the vicarage to tell Father Thomas. He has sent me to tell you of this foul discovery and to fetch the coroner."

"The bones are human?"

"Aye. There is a skull. I have just come from the place."

In past years men would often pitch the bones of swine into a St. John's Day fire so as to ward off sickness in cattle and men. 'Twas thought to do so would prevent aerial dragons from poisoning streams and ponds of a night with their foul froth. But I had not heard of this being done at Bampton since I came to the village. Of course, men might toss a few bones into the pile of wood as a precaution, I suppose, and none know of it.

Kate descended the stairs from our chamber carrying Sybil, with Bessie holding tight to her mother's cotehardie. I told my wife of the discovery and set off for the field while Bertrand hastened to tell Hubert Shillside, Bampton's coroner, of the bones and request that he assemble his coroner's jury.

Father Thomas had notified Father Ralph and Father Simon of the discovery. The three vicars of the Church of St. Beornwald stood staring at the ash pile, their arms folded across their chests as if deep in thought. Who knows? Perhaps they were. But knowing Father Ralph, I doubt it so.

Four villagers by the ashen mound opposite the priests, leaning upon rakes and shovels. A wheelbarrow half filled with ashes stood beside the four.

"Ah, you have come," Father Thomas said. This was obvious to all, so I did not reply. As I drew near the ash pile I saw a familiar shape in the morning sun and crossed myself. Being forewarned, I knew what this must be.

"Bertrand will fetch the coroner," the vicar continued, "but I think Hubert will need your advice."

I did not ask of what advice Father Thomas thought I might supply. Surgeons deal with bones, although when called to do so the bones are generally clothed with flesh. Shillside and his coroner's jury would put their heads together, cluck over some fellow's misfortune, then leave the matter to me. 'Tis what bailiffs are to do: find and punish miscreants. I knew this when I accepted Lord Gilbert Talbot's offer to serve him at his Bampton manor. Good and decent folk prefer to have little to do with a bailiff. So also felons. Most bailiffs have few friends.

I walked slowly about the pile of blackened ashes and felt yet some warmth from what had been six or so hours before a great conflagration. The men scooping the ashes had come early to the work, to gather ashes before others might think to do so. But they had ceased their labor when they found the skull. This was clear, for the rounded cranium was yet half buried, eye sockets peering blankly at me from an upturned face. Well, it was a face at one time.

I saw a few other bones protruding from the ashes, enough that I was convinced that whoso was consumed in the flames went into the fire whole. But to discover if this was truly so I would need to sweep away the ashes and learn what bones were here and how they lay. I would await Hubert Shillside and his jury for that. And the ashes would cool while I waited.

Bampton's coroner did not soon appear. Most of his jurymen had attended the St. John's Day fire the night before, drunk too much ale, and cavorted about the blaze 'till near dawn, and had to be roused from sleep to attend to their duty. A sour-looking band of fellows eventually shuffled into view beyond the church.

When they had approached close enough to see the skull, one and all crossed themselves, then bent low to better examine the reason for being called from their beds.

I stood aside as Shillside collected the jury after each had circled the ash pile. I could have predicted their decision. There was, they decided, no reason to raise the hue and cry, as they could not know if a felony had been done, and even if 'twas so there was no evidence to follow which might lead to a murderer. A man, or perhaps a woman, was dead. The coroner's jury could discover nothing more. They would leave further investigation to me. So said Hubert Shillside as his jury departed to seek their homes and break their fast.

Before the coroner left the place I drew him to where the three vicars of the Church of St. Beornwald stood. I asked the four men if any man or woman had gone missing from Bampton or the Weald in the past few days. They shrugged, glanced toward one another, and shook their heads.

"Perhaps some fellow had too much ale last night, before he came to the fire, and danced too close," Father Simon suggested.

"Odd that no one would see him fall into the flames," Father Thomas said. "Most of the village was here, and in the light of the blaze he would surely have been seen."

"Would've cried out, too," Shillside said. "No man burns in silence, I think."

"Or woman, either," I added.

"What will you do with the bones?" Father Ralph asked. "We should bury them in the churchyard, but must not do so 'till we know that the dead man was baptized."

"And was not a suicide," Father Simon said.

Were there any corpses to be found in England unbaptized, and therefore ineligible to be interred in hallowed ground? I thought not. And I could think of a dozen more acceptable ways to take one's life than to dive into the flames of a St. John's Day fire.

The vicars and coroner fell silent, staring at me. They wanted to know who had died, and whether or not he had perished in Bampton's Midsummer's Eve blaze. I needed to know how the man, or woman, had died, and, if possible, where. If the four men gazing at me expected me to provide answers to these questions, I had best begin the search.

The first thing must be to gather all of the bones. Mayhap there would be the mark of a blade across a rib to tell how death came, or perhaps the dead man had broken an arm or leg in some past accident, and the knitted injury might help to identify the corpse.

But I had no wish to go down on hands and knees in the still-warm ashes to inspect bones. I turned to the men who had found the bones, instructed them to sift carefully through the ashes, and place all bones into their wheelbarrow.

These fellows were not pleased to be assigned the task, but knew that their lord's bailiff could make life disagreeable if they balked.

Unpleasant tasks are best accomplished quickly, and so after a moment of hesitation Lord Gilbert's tenants emptied the ashes from their partly filled wheelbarrow and set to work with spades and rakes to uncover the bones. I had to caution them several times to use less haste and more care. The vicars and Hubert Shillside watched from across the ash pile as the stack of bones in the wheelbarrow grew.

Only a few minutes were required to discover and retrieve the bones. The men continued the work, however, finding nothing more, until I bade them desist. I assigned one fellow to follow me to Galen House with the wheelbarrow and told the others to watch for any bones they might have missed when they continued the work of recovering ashes for use upon their fields.

When Kate agreed to wed a bailiff she did not consider, I think, that her husband would use her table to inspect a skeleton. Marriage may bring many surprises.

I told Osbern, for so the villager who accompanied me with the wheelbarrow of bones was named, to take his burden to the toft behind Galen House. Kate looked up from a pot in which she was preparing our dinner, and her mouth dropped open in surprise as I propped open the door to the toft and began to drag our table through it.

"There is better light in the toft," I explained.

"For what?" she asked.

"Examining bones... human bones."

Kate's hand rose to her mouth. "On my table?"

"They have been through last night's fire," I said.

"You will place roasted flesh upon our table?"

"Nay. There is little flesh. Nearly all has been consumed. Bones remain. No man knows who it was that was in the blaze. I hope to discover some mark upon the bones which will tell who has died, and how."

"Oh. You believe murder may have been done?"

"I have considered why a man, or woman, should be in a Midsummer's Eve fire. Would they place themselves there? I cannot believe it so. Then why would some other lodge a corpse there? The only explanation I can imagine is that the person who did so thought the flames would consume all, flesh and bones, and so hide an unnatural death."

Kate's hens scattered as I dragged the table from the door and Osbern set his wheelbarrow beside it. In a few minutes I had emptied the wheelbarrow, heaped the ash-covered bones upon the table, and set Osbern free to return to his work at the ash pile.

Bessie, I believe, understood something of the nature of the business her father was about, for she stood in the doorway with her mother, clutching Kate's cotehardie and staring wide-eyed at the pile of bones. Kate soon tired of watching me scratch my head and returned to her pot.

I intended to assemble the bones as they would have been a few days past when they held some man upright. As I did so I discovered that most of the small bones of feet and hands were missing. Either they had been consumed in the fire or were overlooked when the four tenants recovered the larger bones from the ash pile.

Several years past, when I was new-come to Bampton, I had stood in my toft over a table like this covered with bones. Those had been found in the castle cesspit, and in pursuit of a felon I had nearly sent an innocent man to the gallows. I breathed a silent prayer that the Lord Christ would turn me from error if I blundered so again.

When I had arranged the bones properly I began my inspection with the skull, and here the examination might have ended. Behind the right ear was a concave fracture. A few small fragments of the skull were missing, and those that remained showed a depression deeper than the width of my thumb. There was no indication of the injury beginning to knit. The victim had surely died soon after the blow was delivered which made this dent. The stroke had killed him, or rendered him senseless so

23

that a blade could be used to end his life, perhaps with a slash to the throat, or a thrust into his heart.

I studied the remainder of the bones, but found no other marks upon them. I did not search these for a cause of death. I believed I had found that. I hoped to discover some anomaly which would help to identify the corpse. A broken limb, perhaps, which had healed, so that some friend or relative of a missing man who knew of a past injury might tell me whose bones lay upon my table.

I turned the skull and examined the teeth. Only one was missing, and the others had few flaws. Here, I thought, was the skull of a young man. I took a femur from the table and held it aside my leg. I am some taller than most men, so did not expect the bone to match mine in length, but was surprised how short the femur was when compared to my own. 'Twas perhaps a woman, I thought, who burned in the fire, or a very short man. How to know?

I puzzled over this as I stood over the bones, and remembered a lecture from my year as a student of surgery at the University of Paris. The instructor had placed before his students two pelvic bones, one male, one female. That of the man appeared larger. Then he placed before us a plaster imitation of the skull of a newborn infant, and showed how a babe's head would pass through the female pelvis, but would not do so through the opening in a man's pelvis, even though the male pelvis seemed the greater.

A movement in the door of Galen House caught my eye. Kate had left her fire to watch my examination of the bones. She held Sybil in her arms.

I called to Kate to bring the babe to me. Sybil is four months old. Her head is larger than when newly born, but not much. I spread my hands about her head to measure, then went to a corner of the toft where mud from recent rain had not yet dried. I fashioned a sphere of the proper size from the mire, then returned to Kate and Sybil and the table of bones.

24

Kate drew back as I approached with the muddy ball. "What are you about?" she asked.

"Watch," I said.

I held out the muddy orb to compare it in size to Sybil's head. It was somewhat smaller, which was as I intended. I turned to the pelvic bone upon the table and tried to pass the mud ball through it. I could not do so. The opening was far too small. 'Twas the bones of a man which lay in the sun upon our table. A small man, who had lost one tooth.

Chapter 2

John Prudhomme has served as Bampton's beadle since Alan was slain in pursuit of poachers. I sought John after visiting Father Thomas to tell him of my discovery and release the bones to him. He promised to send a clerk to Galen House who would transfer the bones to the church. Kate would be pleased to have them away from her toft and hens.

John was one of those who had raised the pile of wood for the St. John's Day fire, and as beadle he walked the streets after curfew to see that all was as it should be. I found him hoeing his onions.

Word of untoward events passes swiftly through a small village. The beadle knew already of the skeleton in the ashes, although 'twas no more than three hours since the find.

"Have you seen any man about the streets after curfew in the past few days?" I asked.

"Richard Hatcher," he replied.

"Was he near to the church, or the meadow where you built the fire?"

"Nay. Had too much of Alvina's ale two nights past an' was wanderin' down Bushey Row seekin' 'is house."

"He lives nowhere near Bushey Row."

"Aye," Prudhomme grinned. "As I said, 'e'd 'ad too much ale, an' Alvina's careful not to water her ale so's to avoid trouble with Ranulf."

Alvina Yardley is one of Bampton's ale wives, and Ranulf Higdon is the village ale taster, a position which he has held and jealously protected since long before Lord Gilbert brought me to Bampton.

"Did Hatcher go to his house? Have you seen him since?"

"Aye. Took 'im there. 'E was at the fire last night. Didn't topple into the woodpile drunk, if that's what you're thinkin'."

"When you worked gathering limbs from Lord Gilbert's wood did you notice anything odd as you piled the branches?"

"Nay. Who would? We collected the wood in Andrew Pritchard's cart, an' when 'twas full we brought the branches back an' tossed 'em on the pile, then went for more. Paid no attention to what we'd already gathered."

"Who would?" I agreed. "I didn't really expect that you'd have seen a man under the pile."

"You think the fellow was put there in the night?"

"Aye. I believe someone did murder, and thought the blaze would consume the evidence. Brought the corpse to the meadow when all good men were abed, dragged some of your branches aside and shoved the dead man into the opening, then covered him over again, so next day, when you brought more wood, you'd see nothing amiss."

Prudhomme crossed himself. "Hope 'e was already dead. Hate to think we might've burned a man what was alive."

"He'd been struck behind an ear strongly enough that his skull was broken. He'd not have been alive when the pile was set alight."

The beadle seemed relieved to learn this.

"I must discover who it was that burned," I said. "Have you heard of any man gone missing?"

"Nay," John shook his head. "Not in Bampton. If I do so I will tell you straightaway."

A beadle knows almost every man's business in a village like Bampton. If he did not know of any man unaccounted for, it was unlikely any others would.

I left John and made my way to the castle. My employer, Lord Gilbert Talbot, would want to know of the discovery. I crossed the drawbridge, greeted Wilfred the porter, who tugged a forelock in reply, then sought John Chamberlain and told him of the bones.

"Heard of it already," he said.

"Does Lord Gilbert know?"

"Don't know," he replied. "I've not seen him since I learned of the business."

"Tell him that I fear a felony, and intend to seek more knowledge of the matter. I will tell him of any discovery."

"I will do so."

St. John's Day passed, and no man spoke of friend or neighbor gone missing. I thought that I might visit nearby villages, Cote and Black Bourton and Alvescot, to learn if some resident of those places had disappeared. 'Twas Saturday when I made up my mind to do this, so put off the travel 'till Monday. But after mass on Sunday visits to these places were no longer necessary. So I thought.

Father Ralph had sent the pax board through his congregation and given a benediction when I saw an ancient crone leave her place and totter toward the altar. Everyone else moved toward the door to the porch, so her direction briefly caught my attention. Some old woman who sought words with a priest, I thought, and dismissed her from my mind.

I did not know this woman, but had occasionally seen her upon village streets. She lived in the Weald, and with her husband worked lands of the Bishop of Exeter. No concern of mine.

We were slow leaving the churchyard, Kate and I, because Bessie wished to walk rather than be carried. The babe will become a lass with an independent nature, I think. Much like her mother. Kate would more likely ascribe stubbornness to an inheritance from me.

The world and all in it is new to Bessie, and she must stop to investigate flowers, insects, and the stones of the churchyard wall. So it was that we had not yet passed through the lych gate when Father Ralph hastened through the porch and called my name – loudly enough that I might hear, but not so as to be unseemly in a churchyard.

I turned and saw the vicar motion to me to return to the porch. I sent Bessie off with Kate to Galen House and returned to the church. On a stone bench inside the porch I saw the grandmother who had sought out the priests while I and others left the church. Father Thomas and Father Simon stood beside her. 'Twas Father Ralph who spoke.

"Here is Herleve Mirk with unpleasant news."

I looked down upon the old woman and waited for her to speak. "Gone three days now," she said. "Never so long before."

"Who?" I asked.

"Peter... me husband."

"You are of the Weald?" I asked.

"Aye. Half a yardland of the bishop."

"She and Peter are villeins," Father Thomas said. "We offered tenancy but they refused. Peter said he was too old to change and intended to go nowhere but the churchyard when his days were done."

"Your husband has been gone three days, you say, and has disappeared before?"

"Aye. Wanders off, does Peter. Comes home on 'is own, or folks seek 'im an' bring 'im back."

"How old is your husband?"

"Dunno," she shrugged. "'E lost track. Older 'n me," she smiled toothily.

The vicars looked at me under frowning brows, their lips thin. Could an aged man be he who had burned in the St. John's Day fire? None wished to be the first to suggest this.

"Folk in the Weald been seekin' Peter since Thursday. Asked Father Ralph what more can be done. Losin' 'is wits, is Peter, though truth to tell 'e never 'ad much wit to begin with. Never went off so long before," she repeated.

"Where did he go when he wandered away in the past?" I asked.

"Often went to the wood toward Cowley's Corner. Said 'e liked to watch the squirrels. An' twice we found 'im sittin' on the bank of Shill Brook, watchin' the water... just watchin' the water."

"Sometimes he would return?" I said.

"Aye. At first he come back before night, but since Easter I've 'ad to send Aelred to find 'im."

"Aelred?"

"Our lad. When Peter didn't return Aelred went out Thursday eve to seek 'im. Two others of the Weald went with 'im. Could find no sign of 'im. I'm fearful 'e's layin' dead in the forest, or fell into Shill Brook an' drowned. Come to ask Father Ralph for help, the vicars bein' the bishop's men hereabouts."

The woman fell silent and looked from me to the three priests. Neither I nor the vicars wished to tell Herleve of what had been found in the St. John's Day fire, and as she had not mentioned it, she likely had not heard of the morbid discovery. Surely there were folk in the Weald who knew of the bones, and also knew that Peter Mirk was missing, and would associate the two facts. If so, no man or woman wished to bear the bad news to Herleve.

The silence became oppressive, and Herleve spoke again. "Why does no one speak? Do you know what's become of Peter? Will no man tell me?"

"You said that Peter was older than you," I said. "How old might that be?"

"Not sure. We was wed the year the old king was done away with."

If it was Edward II of whom she spoke, she had married in 1327. If she was then twenty years or so, she would now be past sixty years of age. Her husband, she said, was older. Old enough to have lost some teeth, likely.

"Was Peter a tall man, or short?" I asked.

"Short... but strong, an' a hard worker was Peter, 'till 'e began to cripple up."

"What of his teeth? Had he lost many?"

"Oh, aye, like most folk what live so long as us. Why'd you ask was Peter tall or short?"

Herleve's description of her husband did not fit the bones found in the Midsummer's Eve blaze. But who else from Bampton and the Weald was gone missing? Perhaps I interpreted the tale told by the bones incorrectly? I have been mistaken before.

I looked to Father Thomas, who is senior of the three vicars assigned to the Church of St. Beornwald, and nodded toward Herleve. She was the bishop's villein. It was the vicar's duty, more than mine, to explain to the woman that her husband might be dead. He did so.

"A man was found yesterday," he said.

"Where? Was it Peter?" Herleve asked. "Where is he?"

"No man can be certain who it was… he was found in the ashes of the St. John's Day fire, when the ashes were all that remained."

"'E was burnt up?"

"Aye," Father Thomas said softly. "Master Hugh has told us that the man was short, much like your Peter."

Herleve crossed herself, looked down at the bench, then spoke.

"Couldn't watch 'im every minute. When I seen 'im wanderin' off I'd fetch 'im home, or sometimes other folk in the Weald would see 'im walkin' away an' bring 'im back to me. 'E had enough wit to know when I might see 'im leave the toft an' when I might not. Was't really Peter found in the ashes?"

The vicars looked to me to corroborate Father Thomas's words. I decided to speak plainly.

"Only bones remained when the fire had died, but the man consumed in the blaze fits your husband's description but for two things. He was missing but one tooth, and I saw no sign of the disease of the bones which can cripple an old man. But no other man is missing from his home."

"Knew one day 'e'd not return," Herleve sighed. "When 'e'd go off I'd fret 'till someone brought 'im home. No need for that now. Where is he? His bones?"

"There is a small box before the church altar," Father Thomas said. "We held the bones there until we knew who it was who had died and whether or not he had been baptized, so we might then bury him in the churchyard was it so."

"My Peter was a Christian man."

"We will bury him tomorrow, now that we know who rests before the altar," Father Simon said. "Return at the third hour tomorrow with your son and others who will see Peter to his grave."

The old woman stood, swayed briefly, from age or grief, then walked from the porch.

"'Tis surely Peter Mirk who was in the ashes," Father

Thomas said when Herleve was beyond hearing. "You think he crawled into the woodpile and perished there?" The question was addressed to me.

"Mayhap he was lost, and when night came he saw the pile and thought to burrow into it for warmth," I said. "But why, then, did he not leave the pile when dawn came?"

"Nights last week were chill," Father Simon said. "Perhaps too cold for one so frail as Peter. If he entered the woodpile, then died of the cold, who would know? Men came next day and piled more limbs upon the stack, so no man would see him buried there."

"Or if he did awaken in the pile," Father Ralph added, "with more wood placed above him he could not shift himself and crawl from his trap."

"Even so," I said, "he might have cried out when he heard men approach the pile with more wood... if he yet lived."

"I hold with Father Simon," Father Thomas said. "There is no felony here. Peter was full of years, and his mind overthrown. He knew not where he was, somehow crawled into the pile at night, and because 'twas cold and he unwell, he perished. When men placed more wood upon the pile next morn he was not noticed, and so nothing but bones of him were found when the fire was reduced to ashes."

"We forget the skull," I said.

Blank faces stared at me, as if to say that I was needlessly complicating the matter.

"Someone delivered a blow to Peter's head strongly enough to crush the bone behind his ear. And Herleve said that her husband had lost teeth, but the skull in the ashes was missing but one."

The vicars were silent, each contemplating how these overlooked facts might be made to fit an accidental death.

"Mayhap a stout limb was dropped upon the man whilst he lay hidden in the woodpile," Father Simon suggested. Father Thomas and Father Ralph nodded agreement, clearly willing to accept any explanation which did not complicate the matter nor include a felony.

"A man's skull is strong," I said, "even in one so full of years. I saw the woodpile before it was set ablaze. In it there was no limb much larger than a man's arm. For such a stick to crush a man's skull 'twould have to be dropped on him from atop the spire of St. Beornwald's Church."

This was not a welcome thought. The vicars were again silent, considering other ways in which a man might suffer a broken head.

"No doubt Peter was unsteady," Father Thomas said, "being of great age. Mayhap he stumbled in the wood to the north of the tithe barn, cracked his skull in the fall, yet managed to rise again and totter to the field where the fire was to be before he collapsed."

Once again I saw nods of satisfaction from the other vicars for this new interpretation. I do not enjoy dissolving other men's beliefs, but if the opinions are flawed, someone must do it.

"If a man catches a toe upon a root in the wood," I said, "will he not fall forward?"

Silence followed, until Father Thomas said, "'Twas the back of Peter's skull was smashed?"

"Aye. Is it likely he would stumble and fall backward?"

"He might," Father Simon said, unwilling to abandon a plausible explanation which did not include murder.

"Then there is the matter of force," I said. "What is there in a wood which, if a man toppled backward onto it, would leave such a dent in his skull?"

"Oak roots are tough," Father Ralph said.

"Aye, so they are. But the oak puts down deep roots. Seldom are they found near the surface, and even so, is an oak root tough enough to crush a short man's skull if he should fall against it? I think not. And, if so, the blow would render him senseless, if not kill him outright. How would he then find strength to rise and seek the woodpile?"

"Are you sure," Father Thomas asked, "that the fracture was severe enough to perhaps end his life, or destroy what wit he yet retained?"

"Nay," I said. "Of this I cannot be certain. I have rarely treated such an injury but for Gerard, Lord Gilbert's verderer, who stood in the way of a falling oak and received a crack in his skull. His sons brought him to me senseless, and I repaired the fracture."

"I remember," Father Thomas said. "You were newly come to Bampton then. Was the blow Gerard received much like the dent in Peter's skull?"

"Not so bad as Peter's, I think," I replied.

"Then if Gerard had to be brought to you unconscious, 'tis unlikely Peter would have risen from such a fall," Father Thomas said, and folded his arms as if to conclude the matter.

I could see that Father Ralph and Father Simon did not wish to accept Father Thomas's conclusion, but neither could think of a rejoinder. Eventually Father Ralph said, "Who would want to slay a witless old man, harmless to all but himself?"

"'Tis what Master Hugh must set himself to discover," Father Thomas said, now evidently convinced that murder had been done.

"Peter Mirk was the bishop's villein," I said. My intent was to require the vicars of St. Beornwald's Church to accept responsibility for discovering who had slain Peter Mirk, if 'twas the old man whose bones were found in the ashes. I had doubts. Many doubts. But this hint did not succeed.

"The man died and was burned upon Lord Gilbert's land," Father Simon said. "If you believe a felony was done, and Peter's death no accident, 'twould be your duty, as Lord Gilbert's bailiff, to seek out the murderer."

Father Thomas and Father Ralph nodded agreement. If asked, Lord Gilbert would likely have agreed. I know when I am defeated. No sense in prolonging a losing fight.

"I must have your cooperation, and that of all the bishop's tenants and villeins in the Weald."

"You shall have it," Father Thomas said. "What will you do first to discover a murderer?"

"Return to Galen House and have my dinner," I said, and departed the porch to do just that.

Chapter 3

Kate had prepared a leach lombard for our dinner, but the flavor seemed off. I attributed this to the image of a soot-blackened, dented skull which continually appeared in my mind's eye.

I resolved to begin the search for Peter Mirk's murderer next day, after his funeral. Most folk of the Weald would attend. So would I. Perhaps some man might seem pleased with the death, rather than saddened. And I had other business upon a Sunday afternoon. King Edward requires that all able men practice at the butts, and Lord Gilbert has assigned this matter to me. Uctred and Arthur, two of Lord Gilbert's grooms, prepare the targets. All I need do is distribute Lord Gilbert's pennies to the winners of the competition.

Henry Warner won the contest this day. He usually does. Henry is no larger or stronger than other men. Why he is so successful with a bow and arrows no man knows. I awarded the fellow his six pence while Arthur and Uctred dismantled the butts.

Father Simon had told Herleve that her husband's funeral would be Monday at the third hour. As that time neared I heard the sound of wailing approach from the south. I went to my door, opened it, and peered down Church View Street to see a small procession appear.

Father Simon and his clerk walked before, then two men carrying a small box. Here, I thought, was the container of Peter Mirk's bones. Sometime Sunday afternoon or evening what remained of Peter Mirk had been taken to his house. For a proper wake, no doubt.

Herleve and two younger women followed the box, howling in grief, as expected of a bereaved spouse and other female family members at such a time. A dozen or more men and women followed the weeping women, likely the son of whom Herleve had spoken, and neighbors from the Weald. A few of the women gave vent to

35

an occasional wail, but their hearts seemed not in it. I closed Galen House door and followed the procession to the church.

The company halted at the lych gate and the mourners fell silent while Father Ralph prayed over the box containing his bones. When he had done, the box was lifted and taken to the church for the mass. I followed.

When the mass was concluded the two fellows who bore Peter Mirk's bones carried them from the church and followed Father Simon to a place near the north wall of the churchyard. Here two villagers stood, leaning upon spades. Father Simon sprinkled holy water upon the grass and the two men set to work digging a grave whilst Father Thomas read a psalm. This was read in Latin, of course, so few who listened knew what was said. How this was to bring consolation to Herleve Mirk I cannot tell.

The grave-diggers' work was not so great as usual, for what remained of Peter Mirk did not require a large hole. The task was soon completed and the box lowered into the small grave. Herleve began again to wail, we others who stood about the grave crossed ourselves, Father Simon spoke the final collect for forgiveness, and the earthly remains of Peter Mirk, villein of the Bishop of Exeter, were interred. Well, someone's earthly remains were interred. I yet had doubts. The grave-diggers began to shovel earth into the pit before I reached the lych gate.

I thought to wait a decent interval, then visit the Weald and speak to Herleve and her children. How many of these she and Peter had produced I knew not, so could not know when I might return to Galen House. Kate prepared a pease pottage for our dinner, and after the meal I set off for the Weald, little expecting what I found there.

There are several vacant houses in the Weald, much like Bampton itself. Some of these are the result of plague, now returning for the third time in twenty years; others are empty because their inhabitants fled to other manors offering lower rents. The Statute of Laborers has fixed rents, and the Bishop of Exeter will not allow his stewards to reduce these in violation of the statute. So three of the bishop's tenants have absconded in the past two years, their now-decaying houses forlorn aside the path.

The first man I saw in the Weald was repairing the leather hinge of his door. He directed me to Herleve Mirk's hovel, which was at the far end of the way, against the wood which had given the Weald its name long ago.

I was yet a hundred paces or more from the dwelling when I saw four men appear from behind a barn which lay across the path from Herleve's house. Two of them bore a pallet. I was not near enough to see what burden these men carried, but such a litter is oft used to transport an injured man.

And that was my first thought. Here was a man wounded at some labor being assisted by his fellows, and likely in need of a surgeon. I had no instruments with me, but could send one of the four to Galen House to fetch them whilst I dealt with whatever injury had put a man upon a pallet. First impressions are often faulty. The man upon the pallet did not need the services of a surgeon.

I did not know this, of course, at that moment, but soon learned it was so. I arrived before Herleve Mirk's door at the same time as the men who carried the pallet. As these fellows approached I heard one call out for Herleve, and she stood in the door as we came near.

This puzzled me, and I held back, curious as to why an injured man should be set down before Herleve Mirk. I thought perhaps 'twas a son who lay upon the pallet.

The figure upon the pallet did not move, and as those who bore it entered Herleve's toft I saw one hand fall to the side and dangle unsupported. The pallet was set down before Herleve and I watched her approach it slowly, then shriek and throw herself upon the motionless form at her feet. I was near enough that her words were plain. "Peter... Peter," she cried.

'Tis common enough for a lad to be named for his father. I thought the woman was distraught because that day she had buried a husband and now saw a son injured so grievously that he must be carried to her door.

Not so. I came near Herleve's toft and when close to the pallet I saw that no injured man lay upon it. A dead man was there, and he was not young. A beard white with years covered the man's chin and his head was as hairless as a pig's bladder.

The corpse was white and bloated, the skin of face, neck, and hands pale and wrinkled. 'Twas then I saw that the dead man's clothing was wet.

The four men who brought this corpse were known to me, even though they were the bishop's tenants and not of my bailiwick. I approached the nearest and asked who it was upon the pallet, although I was nearly certain that I knew already.

"'Tis Peter Mirk," he said with much disbelief in his voice. "Him as who we buried this morning... thought we buried."

"This is sure?" I asked. "His features are distorted."

"Aye. Found 'im in the brook."

"Shill Brook? Who found him?"

"Some lads was playin' in the stream, splashin' about as boys will do on a warm summer day, an' found 'im face down in the water. Gave 'em a fright. My lad was one of 'em. Came runnin' to tell what they'd found. Didn't know who 'twas then."

"Did not men from the Weald search for Peter along Shill Brook some days past, when he first went missing?" I asked.

"Aye. I was one. Never saw 'im. The lads found 'im under the bank, where the brook has cut a deeper channel an' bushes an' such grow out over the water. Deeper there, an' the lads like to swim an' plunge about. A fallen tree is there also, an' we found Peter caught fast against it."

From the corner of my eye I saw Herleve wobble to her feet. Her sobs had subsided. I walked to her side and spoke.

"'Tis truly Peter... your husband?" I asked.

She did not answer for some time, as if struck dumb by events, but eventually said, "Aye... Peter, sure enough. Found 'im in the brook, they say."

Herleve had been staring at her husband while she spoke, but raised her eyes to mine and said, "Who'd we bury this mornin', then?"

38

I had no answer. Prayers had been said for Peter Mirk. Some other man had been interred. But the Lord Christ would know for whom Father Simon prayed even if we did not.

"Liked to sit by the brook an' watch the stream," Herleve said softly. "Likely fell in."

The woman's explanation of events seemed as reasonable as any other. I had already one unexplained death to bewilder me; I needed no other. Unless something untoward was found when Peter Mirk's body was bathed and prepared for burial I would not trouble myself with this additional corpse. And Mirk was the bishop's tenant and had not met his end upon Lord Gilbert's land. Well, probably not. If the vicars of St. Beornwald's Church wished an investigation of Mirk's death they could themselves conduct it. I set off for Father Thomas's vicarage to tell him so.

Father Thomas's first thought was much like Herleve's. "If Peter Mirk lays dead upon a pallet in the Weald, who did we bury this morning?"

I shrugged in reply for want of a better answer.

"Must we dig the fellow up, so you may again inspect the bones?"

"To what purpose? I have learned all I can from them. Enough that I had doubts that an old man's bones were those found in the St. John's Day fire. Allow the man to rest in peace 'till the Lord Christ calls him from his grave."

"I must go to the Weald and comfort Herleve," Father Thomas said. "Will you tell Father Simon and Father Ralph of this?"

"Send your clerk to do so. I am off to the castle to see Lord Gilbert. He wishes to be informed of events in his demesne, and the bishop's lands, also. This is a curious business, and he will be displeased to learn of it second hand rather than from me."

I bid the priest "Good day," even though 'twas not, and hurried to the castle. My route took me past Galen House so I stopped to tell my Kate of the discovery of Peter Mirk. She listened open-mouthed, and understood what the news portended.

"This morning you had but to discover a felon," she said. "Now you must again discover a victim. You believe the dent in the skull is sure evidence of murder?"

"I am not sure of anything," I replied.

"You may be sure of me," Kate smiled.

"A constant in an uncertain world," I said. "But it is of the bones we planted in the churchyard this morning that I speak. Now I am off to the castle to tell Lord Gilbert of this matter."

I found my employer in the marshalsea. One of his best dexters had gone lame and Lord Gilbert was bent over Adam Marshall's shoulder inspecting the beast's hoof.

Lord Gilbert was, before Lady Petronilla's death, a genial man, much given to mirth and ready with laughter at the antics of entertainers employed in his hall. Now I seldom saw him smile, and for a year no laughter had creased his bluff face. And it seemed to me his beard had begun to turn gray rapidly.

"I give you good day, Master Hugh," Lord Gilbert said, rising and placing hands behind his back to relieve the strain of his close inspection of the hoof. "What news this day? Have you learned more of the bones found in the St. John's Day blaze?"

"I have learned less."

"Less?" Lord Gilbert raised one eyebrow, which he did when puzzled by some matter. This was an affectation I had once tried to copy, but eventually gave it over. "How is it possible to know less of some matter?"

"Peter Mirk, whose bones I thought were found in the ashes, is this moment laying dead in his house in the Weald."

"How can this be?"

"Lads of the Weald were frolicking in Shill Brook and found him face down in the water, his corpse lodged under a fallen tree."

"Then who...?"

"Don't know," I shrugged. "We have buried a man unknown to all. Well, known to someone, and to God, but not to any of us of Bampton or the Weald."

"No man of either place is missing?"

"Nay. Tomorrow I intend to visit Alvescot and speak

to Gerard. If he knows of none gone missing I will try other places nearby. Whoever the fellow was he cannot, I think, be of some far place. Who would carry a corpse many miles to see it burnt?"

"The man was dead when placed in the wood pile?"

"So I believe... but I have been wrong about this business once already. I am prepared to be wrong again."

"You will keep me informed?"

"Aye. 'Tis why I have sought you."

"You will ferret out the truth of the matter, Hugh. You have always done so."

With that expression of confidence my employer turned his attention back to his beast. The sun was declining in the west, the day warm and pleasant. I might have taken a palfrey from the castle marshalsea and set off for Alvescot yet this day. Gerard is Lord Gilbert's verderer. He walks the forest every day, and knows all men and their business who live near the village. But tomorrow, I decided, would be soon enough to seek the man.

I left the castle and paused upon the bridge over Shill Brook, as I often do, to watch the flowing stream and gather my thoughts. 'Twas not a significant collection. The brook and Peter Mirk's death so captured my mind that I did not hear John Kellet draw near. Of course, the man goes about barefoot in all seasons, so can approach silently.

Kellet is priest at St. Andrew's Chapel, a short way east of Bampton. He once wished me dead, and for his efforts to cause that end was required to go on pilgrimage. He returned from Compostela a changed man and was sent to Exeter to assist the almoner at St. Nicholas's Priory. There he was so assiduous in seeking the poor that he nearly impoverished the priory. The prior begged the bishop to be rid of him, and as no curate had been found for such an insignificant parish as that of St. Andrew's Chapel, he was returned. He is uneducated in the Scriptures, speaks the words of the mass from memory, resides in a tiny room in the tower, and goes without shoes so as to devote more of his meager income to the poor. Three years past he was as fat as a prize sow. Today there is nothing rounded under his cassock. He is all angles and boney protrusions.

"Master Hugh... I give you good day. You are well met."

I made no reply. If John Kellet was pleased to find me gazing into Shill Brook, who was I to disagree with him?

"I learned this day that bones were found in the ashes of the St. John's Day fire. 'Tis said they were of a man of the Weald."

"So it was thought," I replied. "But I have learned that this is not so. 'Twas thought that Peter Mirk was burned to bones in the blaze. He had gone missing some days past, but this day his corpse was found in Shill Brook. No man knows who we buried this morn in St. Beornwald's churchyard."

Kellet was silent for a moment, looked into the stream, then spoke. "There is another man missing."

"Who?"

"Thomas Attewood."

"The swineherd?"

"Aye, the same."

"Does he not reside in the forest with Lord Gilbert's pigs?"

"Aye, he does. But he always comes to the chapel for mass on Sunday, and yesterday he did not do so."

"Perhaps some of his charges wandered far and he sought them."

"Some of them wandered into the tofts of folk who live about St. Andrew's Chapel. I heard them when I awoke this morning, shouting to drive off the beasts who were rooting about in their tofts. Thomas drives his pigs into a sty each night."

"He has a hut in the wood where he lives in the summer, does he not? Did you seek him there?"

"I did. He is not there."

"Perhaps he is pursuing swine who have fled in one direction, and other of his charges took advantage of his absence to seek a meal in the tofts near to the chapel."

"Perhaps," the priest said, but I could see that he was unconvinced. "Not like Thomas to be absent from mass."

"Thomas is a small man, is he not?"

42

"Aye."

"Of what age, you think?"

Kellet pursed his lips in thought. "Hard to say. Perhaps thirty years."

I thought it likely that Thomas Attewood would be discovered gathering his swine, but there were yet several hours of daylight remaining and finding the pig man at his work would eliminate a possible victim of the St. John's Day fire.

"Show me the man's hut," I said.

Kellet led me through Bampton, past his chapel and the cluster of houses gathered about it, thence across a meadow and into the wood. I knew the place well enough. Two years past the priest and I had found a dying chapman's cart there, and I was yet convinced that somewhere nearby a cache of ancient coins lay buried.

The priest led me several hundred paces into the wood, and so well hidden was the swineherd's hut and sty that we were upon it before I recognized that the collection of boughs was the habitation of a man and swine.

"Just here," Kellet said, and walked around the tiny structure to a door made of slender twigs bound together with vines and hinged with the same. The roof was of reeds cut from a nearby marsh and seemed whole enough to shed rain, but 'twould be no place to spend a winter.

"Does Thomas live here year 'round?" I asked.

"Nay. Once pigs is butchered come Martinmas, 'e takes a boar an' some sows to Lord Gilbert's barn on the way to Witney."

I know of the barn, of course, but there are matters regarding Lord Gilbert's manor of Bampton which I am still learning even though I have been his bailiff for five years. Pigs are more a reeve's concern than a bailiff's.

I peered over the wall of the sty and saw but one pig; a sow with a litter of piglets eyed me suspiciously.

I shouted Thomas's name. The wood echoed back.

"Tried that," Kellet said.

I pushed the door of the swineherd's hut open and entered. Furnishings were few. A crude table and bench, a straw-filled

43

pallet, and a blanket. Upon the table was a wooden bowl and a pewter spoon. There was no chest in which a man might keep possessions. The clothes Thomas owned, he wore.

"Did you seek Thomas in the wood nearby the hut?" I asked.

"Nay. Tried to gather the pigs what was in folk's tofts an' bring 'em back here to the sty. They might obey Thomas, but not me. Gave up an' went to my dinner, then sought you."

The priest looked about through the long shadows of the sun-dappled wood. "No Thomas, and no pigs around, neither," he said.

That was true enough. But if Thomas Attewood's bones now rested in a box under the sod of St. Beornwald's churchyard there might be some sign of struggle near his hut. If some felon struck him down it seemed to me likely that it would have happened where the swineherd spent his days.

But if some man did murder here in the wood, why move the corpse to the St. John's Day fire? Why not leave Thomas in the forest, and sweep leaves over the corpse to hide it?

I answered my own question. Because when his swine were seen rooting through folk's onions and cabbages, angry men would seek Thomas to discover why he had not performed his duty. They would find him dead, for the pigs would have discovered him and chewed at his flesh. They would not devour his skull, and the blow which dented his head would be visible to me if I was called to the discovered remains. I began to think that the missing pig man's bones might indeed be those found in the ashes. But how to know?

The door to Thomas Attewood's hut was low, and Kellet and I stooped to pass through it. When again vertical I pointed toward the setting sun and told the priest to circle through the trees and see if he could find any sign of struggle.

"I will go the other way. Look for some place where the forest floor is shredded and the leaves displaced, or mayhap a drop or two of blood."

"Would not swine cast leaves asunder as they rooted for acorns and such like?" the priest said.

"They might, if any acorns remained from those which fell last year. I have no better suggestion."

"Very well," Kellet shrugged, and set off to the west, his shadow growing long where the evening sun penetrated the grove. I turned and walked to the east.

A goldfinch chirped in a branch high above my head and a squirrel scolded me for invading his domain. A forest is a pleasant place on a warm summer evening.

I did not really expect to see evidence of murder, and did not. But Kellet did. Or thought he did. I heard him call my name in an urgent voice, and bid me hasten to him. I did so.

I found him standing over a small pile of offal. Whether these were the guts of man or pig I could not tell. It seemed that leaves had indeed been spread over the entrails, but swine had surely found the viscera and consumed much of the remains.

Were these the entrails of man or beast? I searched carefully for bones, but found none.

John Kellet had stood silent as I gazed down upon the guts. "Was the swineherd slain here, you think?" he finally asked.

"I think not. If 'twas Thomas's bones found in the ashes, why would his murderers slice open his belly before taking him to be burned in the St. John's Day blaze?"

"Mayhap some other man's bones were in the fire," the priest said.

"Can there be a third man gone missing from Bampton and the Weald?"

Kellet shrugged. "Was a pig butchered here, then?" he said.

"So it seems. See, no bones remain. Even the head is gone. Swine might consume the corpse of one of their dead fellows, but they'd leave a skull behind, surely."

"Then some man has taken one of Lord Gilbert's pigs for his table, you think? Perhaps Thomas did so, and has fled to avoid the penalty."

"Where would a swineherd go?"

"Or a man angry that Thomas allowed pigs to forage in his toft killed one to feed his family."

45

I agreed that such might be true. June can be a thin month for the poor. If they had a pig of their own to slaughter in the autumn, its meat was likely consumed by Whitsuntide, and the harvest was yet a month and more away. A man watching his children wail with hunger might take a pig. Would he also slay a swineherd if he was surprised at the business?

"What'll you do about the pigs?" Kellet asked. "Thomas had near thirty in 'is keepin', what with piglets born recently. They've scattered about the countryside now."

John Holcutt is reeve to Lord Gilbert's manor at Bampton. I told the priest that I would instruct John to organize men to seek the missing swine in the morning. A fat sow or boar is worth nearly three shillings. Lord Gilbert would not be pleased to learn of the loss, if the reeve could not recover them.

Was it Thomas Attewood's bones I had assembled upon my table in the toft? I could not be sure unless I found some evidence that he was dead and not away from his hut for some other reason. I told Kellet that I would return to St. Andrew's Chapel in the morning with the reeve, to search the wood, and I requested his aid.

We passed the swineherd's hut as darkness began to obscure the place. The priest thought to call out the missing man's name once more, and so bellowed "Thomas," then stopped to listen for any reply. 'Twas well he did so.

Chapter 4

The response was so faint that a footstep in the dry leaves would have muffled the cry. Kellet turned to me with questions in his eyes and furrowed brow, as if unsure that he had heard a human voice. The breeze had died, the forest air was calm. No zephyr rustling through the leaves had made the grove speak, or obscured the sound of a voice.

The priest saw me become alert. I turned to face the direction from which I thought the cry had come.

"You heard it also?" Kellet asked.

"Aye. Had I been alone here I might have thought it my imagination. Two men will not imagine the same fantasy, I think."

I looked beyond the sty into the darkening wood. "The cry was weak," I said, "but it seemed to come from the east, toward Aston. If Thomas, or some other man, lies injured in the wood we had best search him out at once. 'Twill be dark soon and we will find no man then."

In our haste we stumbled over roots and the occasional fallen limb. Of these there were few to impede our progress, for folk had gleaned fallen branches in the autumn to warm themselves through the past winter. When we had travelled perhaps a hundred paces I put a hand upon Kellet's arm to bring him to a halt, then called out the missing swineherd's name. The cry echoed through the wood. There was no reply.

"Have we gone the wrong way, you think?" the curate asked.

"We both heard the response come from this direction. If Thomas lies injured somewhere nearby it may be that he is at times insensible. Come. In a few minutes 'twill be too dark to find a man who cannot answer our shouts."

We plunged on, tripping over unseen snares which clutched at our feet. The way led up a hill, and when we reached the top I shouted Thomas's name again. The reply was not much more than a whisper in the still air.

But there was now no doubt that we traveled the proper course, and that a man would be found at the conclusion of our journey. We hastened down the eastern side of the hill, and in the gloomy twilight I saw before us a gully perhaps twenty paces across and half as deep as it was wide. I had no wish to scramble into the declivity if it was not necessary, so halted at the top and called out the swineherd's name again.

It was necessary. A moment after I spoke the name I heard clearly a reply from the dark depths of the gully. "Here... I'm here."

Kellet looked to me, then scrambled down the slope. I followed. The priest called "Thomas!" once again, and again, close by now, came a reply.

A tiny stream flowed at the bottom of the decline. Thomas told me later that he had been able to reach the rivulet with a cupped hand and so survive. Had he not been able to do so, thirst might have ended his life there in the wood.

Darkness so engulfed the place that I could at first see no reason for the swineherd to be supine and seemingly helpless. Kellet found the cause soon enough.

The priest had gone slipping and sliding ahead of me and so reached Attewood first. When he found the man flat upon the ground he knelt, placed his hands behind Thomas's shoulders, and attempted to lift the man to a sitting position. The swineherd's response was a yelp of pain. Kellet backed away, uncertain of what he had done to cause such a cry, and unsure of what to do next.

It was too dark to see what injury or wound had immobilized Attewood. I thought it likely that a broken leg might do so. And the slope was just steep enough that, if he toppled down it, the fall could cause such an injury.

So rather than poke about his body there in the dark, I asked the fellow what hurt he had which brought him to this place.

"Water," he whispered. "Need water."

I cupped my hands and lifted some water from the tiny stream to the swineherd's lips. Kellet saw what I was about and lifted the man's head, carefully this time, so that he could drink.

I brought water to Attewood's lips three times before he sank back against Kellet's hand and spoke again.

"'Twas the old boar," he said.

"What? Did the beast attack you?"

"Aye," he whispered.

I wished to know the tale and learn from him of his injuries, but a darkening wood was no place to discover either. And the man must not spend another night in such a place with his injuries, whatever they were, untreated.

I instructed John Kellet to return to his chapel and rouse the cotters whose houses clustered about the place. I told him to send one man to Galen House to explain my absence to Kate, and to fetch my sack of instruments and pouches of pounded hemp and lettuce seeds. These the fellow must bring to the chapel and await our return with the swineherd.

The other cotters Kellet must bring here, with a pallet of some kind; two poles and a blanket would do if nothing better was at hand. And torches. Kellet must return with torches. The moon would not appear until midnight, and even then a quarter moon would shed little light through the leaves.

"Did you tumble down the slope?" I asked when the priest had scrambled up and away from the gully.

"Aye," Attewood replied.

"You are not able to rise. Is your leg broken, you think?"

"Aye... an' me ribs. An' shoulder, mayhap. Hurts to breathe."

I asked of the boar, and the swineherd told me of how he came to be at the bottom of the gully.

When he awoke Saturday morning he found that his swine had nearly all escaped the sty. One or more of the pigs had pushed through a weak place in the enclosure and the others, but for one sow which had farrowed the day before and would not leave her litter, had made off in the night.

Attewood immediately sought the escaped beasts and followed their trail through the wood, over the hill, to the lip of the gully where he had found most of them rooting about. He had prodded the pigs with his staff to move them back toward the sty, for they were near to encroaching upon the land of Aston Manor. The boar had disliked this method of persuasion and turned on him.

Thomas said that he had attempted to evade the boar's attack, but caught his foot between two fallen trees. The boar struck him and he heard a crack as he felt the pain in his ankle. The blow pitched him down the bank onto the stump of one of the fallen trees, whence came the pain in his ribs and shoulder, thence to the bottom of the defile, where he had lain since Saturday. His fall had ended close enough to the tiny brook that he had been able to cup water in his palm, but to reach for the water had caused him much hurt.

Although we had had few dealings in the past, Attewood knew of me. "Can you patch me up, or am I for St. Andrew's Chapel churchyard?"

"'Tis too dark to know much of your injuries. Did you try to rise and climb from this place?"

"Oh, aye. Thought to support meself with a stick, could I find one, but can't raise myself. Got to me knees, but could rise no farther."

I gently prodded the fellow's ribs through his tattered cotehardie and learned from his groans that several were likely broken. I touched Thomas's shoulder and brought from him a gasp when I pressed upon his collar bone. I then turned my attention to his leg, and made a gruesome discovery. His left leg was so badly broken that the man's foot pointed off to the side.

"Is the pigs back to the sty?" Thomas asked.

"Nay. But tomorrow I will tell John Holcutt of this and he will see that they are recovered."

"Lose my place for this, likely. That old boar is gettin' too wise for 'is own good. Lord Gilbert should roast 'im for Christmas dinner."

I agreed that might be best, and tried to keep the man's mind from his injuries with talk of trivial matters until Father John returned with aid.

Time passes slowly when a man is crouched in a dark wood awaiting assistance. And if minutes became hours for me, for

Attewood the wait for Kellet's return must have seemed endless.

Eventually I saw the yellow light of a torch flicker through the trees above the gully, and I heard the priest say, "Just there," to his companions. Soon the rescuers slithered down the steep slope of the gully, the torch-bearer leading.

Two of the arrivals carried a pallet. "Brought Thomas's bed from his hut," Kellet explained.

Hard men can be gentle. I warned Kellet's companions of the swineherd's injuries, and told them that moving him to the pallet would cause him pain even if they were careful of the hurt. I showed the fellows where it would be best to lift Thomas, and watched in the torchlight as they raised him from the leaves and deposited him upon his bed as gently as if he was a sleeping babe. The swineherd groaned once, but otherwise bore his affliction well.

It was no easy matter to draw the injured man and his pallet up the slope. The bed was jostled several times severely enough that I heard Thomas gasp. But he did not cry out, not even when one of his bearers tripped upon a root when we were nearly to St. Andrew's Chapel and dropped a corner of the bed.

The door from the porch to the church was barely wide enough for the pallet. Those who carried Thomas were required to shift their places from the sides to before and after to slide through the narrow entrance. St. Andrew's Chapel is small, and very old.

John Kellet directed the men to place Attewood's bed before the altar, then hastened about the chapel collecting candles and two cressets. These he placed upon stands and a corner of the altar. Their combined light allowed me to see clearly the ghastly injury to the swineherd's ankle. His bearers saw, also, and turned away rather than gaze upon so twisted a leg.

The cotter whom John Kellet had sent to Galen House was at the chapel before us, and followed us into the tiny building. My sack of instruments and herbs was slung over his shoulder. I took the sack from him and drew from it the pouches of crushed seeds of hemp and lettuce. I asked the priest if he had ale. He nodded, and went to the stairway – little more than a ladder – which leads to his room in the chapel tower. A moment later he reappeared with an ewer and a cup. I filled the cup with ale, then poured in a large measure of the crushed hemp and lettuce seeds. Some surgeons prefer mandrake for dealing with such pain as was likely to assail Thomas when I straightened his foot, but mandrake is a poison, nearly as strong as monkshood, and I will not use it unless no other of God's remedies will suffice.

Thomas drank the mixture gratefully, then lay back upon his bed. It is my experience that the seeds of hemp and lettuce do their work an hour or so after being consumed. This I told Thomas, the priest, and the cotters who yet stood by the altar.

Two of the men I wished to remain, to restrain the swineherd when I put his leg right. I asked if any would do so. All four offered to stay.

These fellows seemed unlikely to flinch when they heard Thomas cry out, as he surely would. I sent two to Shill Brook to cut reeds which I could use to build a splint when I had got the swineherd's foot pointing forward again. The moon was now risen above Aston, so the brook and reeds would be visible in its light.

Two of the candles flickered low before the cotters I had sent for reeds returned. The reeds would hold the swineherd's broken leg in place, but only if they were bound tight to the appendage. For this I needed strips of cloth. Linen would be best, but who of these cotters possessed linen garments? And if they did so, who would give up a kirtle or braes? Some tattered woolen cotehardie must serve.

I asked if any man there had such a garment and John Kellet spoke. "For what use is it needed?"

"I must tear it to strips so as to fix the reeds about Thomas's broken leg."

"I have a robe which will serve, I think," he said, and again disappeared into the dark at the base of the tower. I heard him climb his creaking stairs. A few moments later he reappeared with a black garment over his arm.

52

Here was no tattered vestment but a fine robe, simple in design, as suited a curate, but made of good wool and surely reserved by the priest for wearing on high holy days.

Kellet held the garment out to me. "Are you sure you wish to sacrifice this to the swineherd's injury?" I asked.

"What better use? I have another."

Kellet owned the threadbare robe he wore, I thought, and no other.

"This is unsuitable," I said. "'Tis too heavy to tear into strips. What of the robe you wear? Might you donate that to the need?"

The priest looked from the robe in his hands to the garment which draped his skeletal form.

"This fabric is strong," he said, proffering the richer robe again, "and you will be able to bind Thomas's leg securely with it."

"Poverty is a virtue if a man uses his goods and coin to help others," I said, "but pride is a sin. A man proud of his poverty is as surely a sinner as a man proud of his riches." I did not reach for the robe.

The priest looked me in the eye for some time, then slowly withdrew the proffered robe. "I am well rebuked," he said softly, then turned and walked toward the tower and the stairs to his chamber. When he returned he wore his fine robe and carried the tattered garment. This he held out to me, and I took it gladly from him.

Even this old vestment, being wool, was difficult to tear into strips. I employed my dagger to begin the work, and continued the rips until I had a dozen long black strips ready to bind the reeds to Thomas's leg.

The pounded hemp and lettuce seeds had by this time done their work. The swineherd snored softly upon his bed. He had likely slept little for several days, so fatigue aided my potion. When I straightened his twisted leg he would awaken soon enough.

I assigned two cotters to hold Thomas in place when I turned his leg to its proper shape, and told them to take care for his ribs and shoulder. With my blade I cut ten reeds to the proper length, then with John Kellet peering over my shoulder I set to work on the swineherd's grotesque leg.

I first removed his shoe, and so deeply did Thomas sleep that I was able to do so without awakening him, even though his foot was swollen and it required some tugging to draw the shoe from it. Then, with my dagger, I cut away his worn, dirty chauces the better to see what injury lay before me. Thomas shifted, but remained asleep.

The place of the break was clear, even in the dim light of candles and cresset. Just above Thomas's ankle was a swollen place, discolored red and purple. His foot was turned in such a way that I was sure that both bones under the bulging flesh were broken. 'Twould be difficult under such swelling to be sure the fractured bones were set in proper place so as to heal.

I told the cotters to hold Thomas fast, and from the corner of my eye saw John Kellet cross himself. His lips moved in a silent prayer.

The swineherd came immediately awake when I took his twisted foot in my hand. He gasped, and would have thrashed about, but his friends held him fast.

To spare the man extended pain I wished to do the work of straightening his leg quickly, but too much haste would risk a poor result, and the torment might be greater, although of less duration, than if I worked more slowly. I was conflicted. The instructors in surgery at the University of Paris had not discussed the matter.

Pain might not be the greatest evil to befall Thomas. If I did my work poorly he would stumble about upon a misshapen leg 'till the grave called him. There is purpose in pain, although when under its attack 'tis easier to lament the cause than praise the lesson.

I bent low over the swineherd's face and told him what must be done. I spoke of the happy result if his leg knitted properly, and of the torment which he must endure to make it so. He nodded understanding when I had done, and I saw the muscles of his jaw bulge as he clenched his teeth.

My words did not lessen Thomas's pain, but perhaps made it more bearable. The pounded hemp and lettuce seeds also did their work. The man gasped and moaned as I set his leg straight, but did not writhe about or twitch in such a manner as to complicate my work. The men I assigned to hold him quiet had little to do.

When I had got the leg straight I asked assistance of John Kellet and one of the cotters in holding reeds about the appendage whilst I tied them tight with strips of black wool from the old robe. The night was cool, but sweat beaded upon my forehead and lip before I finished the task.

"What is to be done with Thomas now?" Kellet asked when I stood from the completed work. "Will you also bind his ribs and shoulder?"

"There is little to be done with broken ribs," I told him. "And for a fractured collar bone the only cure is to place the arm in a sling to support it until the break is mended. A man lying abed needs no sling. Perhaps, in a few days, Thomas will be able to rise and move about with the aid of a crutch. Then will be soon enough to learn if he can stand the pain of supporting himself with a crutch, with an arm in a sling."

"He will require care," the priest said. "I will see to him." Then, to the cotters who looked on, "Carry him to the tower... gently, now."

This the fellows did, depositing the bed and its burden at the base of the tower, aside the stairs to Kellet's chamber.

The quarter moon was by this time well over the chapel. I told the priest that I would call in the day to learn how did the swineherd, dismissed the cotters to their homes, then set out for Galen House and my own bed.

Twice I had thought that bones found in the Midsummer's Eve fire were identified, and twice I was wrong. There now seemed no other choice but to travel to villages nearby to learn if any man was missing.

Kate had barred the Galen House door, as I had told her to do when I was absent in the night. I pounded upon it for some time before she lifted the bar and admitted me. She would not hear of returning to bed until I had told her all, and so the sky to the east was growing light before I rested my head upon a pillow. Then, as sleep was nearly upon me, Sybil awoke and decided 'twas time to break her fast. This was no work of mine, but the babe's cries delayed my rest and interrupted Kate's.

If Kate's cockerel announced the dawn I did not hear it. When I finally awoke, the day was well along and I heard Kate below, about the business of managing her house.

Kate rises early, even when her sleep has been interrupted. So she had been to the baker while I slept, and I found a new loaf yet warm upon our table when I stumbled down the stairs. Bessie takes after her mother, and also wakes with the dawn. She gazed thoughtfully at me, munching her loaf, as I drew a bench up to the table and broke my loaf. Kate had also brought home an ewer of fresh ale, brewed by the baker's wife. A man who has been awake most of the night should wince to face the sunlight falling upon his face, but the fresh loaf and ale revived me.

Lord Gilbert must be told that the man whose bones were found in the St. John's Day fire was yet unknown, and I intended to collect a horse at the castle marshalsea. A beast under me would make travel to nearby villages easier and more quickly accomplished.

On my way to the castle I turned from Church View Street to Rosemary Lane and John Holcutt's house. I found the reeve finishing his loaf, told him of the roving pigs, and requested that he gather a few of Lord Gilbert's tenants to collect them, and then assign one of the fellows to tend the beasts until Thomas was able again to do so.

I did not linger this day at the bridge over Shill Brook. When confronted with a riddle, I cannot readily turn aside from it, even to watch the water of the brook flow south to the Thames.

Wilfred the porter greeted me at the gatehouse, and at my request sent his assistant to tell a page that I required a horse forthwith.

Lord Gilbert sat in the solar with his son, Richard, when John Chamberlain announced me. A lord need not rise to greet his bailiff, but as I entered the chamber Lord Gilbert did so. His lad stood also, emulating his father – a thing most children do, for good or ill.

Great men do not like to receive bad news. Lord Gilbert is a great man. I told him of his swineherd's injury, and that no name could yet be assigned to the bones found in the Midsummer's Eve fire. He did not smile, but neither did he frown.

"The swineherd, Thomas… is that not his name?"

"Aye."

"Will he be of use again, or must some other be found for his duty?"

"I have told John Holcutt to take men this day to gather the pigs, and assign one to watch over them 'till Thomas may again do so."

"The swineherd will be whole?"

"I believe so. John Kellet is caring for him in St. Andrew's Chapel. I intend to go from here east to learn if any man has disappeared from Aston or Cote or Yelford, then upon my return I will stop at St. Andrew's Chapel to see how Thomas fares."

I passed through Aston first, then Cote, and sought the bailiffs in each place. Such officers would know if a man of their bailiwick was missing, as I would know of a man absent from Bampton. None was. Yelford was too small, since plague struck, to have or need a bailiff, but I found the reeve and learned that all men under his authority were accounted for.

My return to Bampton took me past St. Andrew's Chapel. I tied the palfrey to a shrub growing from the churchyard wall and entered the dark structure.

John Kellet sat upon a bench beside Thomas Attewood, and stood when he saw me enter the chapel.

"Moans an' thrashes about in 'is sleep, does Thomas," the priest said.

"'Tis to be expected. I should have thought to send more herbs to soothe his pain."

I lifted Thomas's cotehardie to see how fared his ribs and collar bone. Both places were purple and swollen. There was no cure for that but time. It seemed to me that the bulge about the swineherd's leg was some reduced. The reeds I had tied tightly about the fracture seemed loose. I untied two of the ribbons of black wool I had used to bind the reeds to Thomas's leg and retied them more tightly.

"Come with me," I said to Kellet when the work was done. "I have plenty of pounded lettuce seeds which will help Thomas sleep. When he sleeps he will not feel pain."

The priest walked with me to the gate, where I retrieved my palfrey and walked with Kellet to Galen House.

I had few crushed hemp seeds to spare, but provided the curate with a pouch of pounded lettuce seeds and told him to give the swineherd a large thimbleful in a cup of ale twice each day – perhaps at midday so the fellow might rest in the afternoon, and at dusk to help him sleep the night.

"Where will I find a thimble?" Kellet asked.

"Perhaps a cotter's wife will have one. If not, look to your thumb and pour enough crushed seeds into your palm that 'twould fill a small pouch the size of your thumb."

"Oh, aye."

Kellet hurried away with the pouch and I went to my dinner. Kate had not known when I might return this day, so had prepared a simple pottage which would serve no matter when I appeared. There was honeyed butter for the maslin loaf. Bessie licked her lips and asked for more when she finished her portion. So did her father.

The palfrey dozed in the warm sun where I had left her, tied to a post before Galen House door. I poured water into a bucket so the beast might drink, then mounted and set off for Clanfield, Black Bourton, and Alvescot. Somewhere a man must be missing.

Chapter 5

*L*ord Gilbert's verderer, Gerard, lives in Alvescot, to be nearer to the forested lands of Lord Gilbert's extensive demesne. The old fellow walks with a limp, and has since an oak fell upon him. I patched his broken skull only a few months after I assumed the post of bailiff upon Lord Gilbert's Bampton manor. A verderer, even one who totters while upon his rounds, knows every man's business in his parish and also the business of most of those in the parishes bordering his own.

No man had disappeared from Clanfield or Black Bourton, or Alvescot either. So said Gerard. But the bailiff of Kencott was missing, the verderer said.

"How long past?" I asked.

"Heard of it Sunday," Gerard replied. "Don't know how long afore that 'e went missing. Don't think 'twas many days past. Kencott's less than a mile from 'ere. Whatever happens there is known 'ere right soon."

'Tis indeed but a short way from Alvescot to Kencott. The village is small, so every man there would likely know every other man's business. The men likely to know most about a missing bailiff would be the lord of the manor or the village priest. I guided the palfrey to the Kencott church, dismounted, and fastened the reins to the lych gate.

A priest may not always be found in his church late of an afternoon, but the priest of St. George's Church was this day. I found him standing in conversation with his clerk before the altar. When I opened the door from the porch, they stared at me, as men will when they see a stranger in an unusual place.

Neither man moved or spoke as I approached. The declining sun sent shafts of light through the tall, narrow windows which illuminated the church and the dust motes that floated in the still air.

"I give you good day," I said. "I am Hugh de Singleton, bailiff to Lord Gilbert Talbot at his manor of Bampton."

"I am Kendrick Dod, vicar of St. George's Church," the priest replied. "How may I serve Lord Gilbert's bailiff?"

"I am told that the bailiff of Kencott is missing. What can you tell me of him?"

"Randle? Gone from the village, is Randle, but I'd not say 'missing.'"

"What would you say?"

"Why does the bailiff of Bampton manor want to know of Randle?"

"A man has been found dead in Bampton. I seek to discover who he might be."

"When?"

"St. John's Day morn."

I saw the clerk peer from the corner of his eye at the priest. He began to speak. "Randle..." he said.

But the priest interrupted. "Randle often travels, especially in midsummer, when roads are dry, the work of planting is done, and the harvest is yet to begin."

The clerk looked to the priest and said no more. When I caught the man's eye he quickly looked away. There was something odd about the clerk's behavior.

"Where does he go?" I asked.

"Visits a brother near to Banbury, so I'm told."

"And this journey would cause a rumor to reach Alvescot that the man has gone missing? If he often travels to Banbury, why would his absence from Kencott cause men to believe he was missing?"

"Men seek trouble when they have already worries enough to plague them," the priest said.

"When may the bailiff return?" I asked.

The priest shrugged. "Don't know."

"Who is lord of this manor? Surely he told his employer when he would return."

"Sir John deMeaux is lord of Kencott."

"Does he reside on the manor?"

"Aye."

"His house is nearby?"

The priest motioned toward the setting sun and said, "Two hundred paces beyond the church."

I thanked the priest, retrieved my palfrey at the lych gate, and as the vicar promised, I soon came to a large house of two stories, one end of the dwelling freshly whitewashed and well thatched, the other end not so well cared for, as if the lord who lived within had decided 'twas too costly to renew his entire house and was content with the work half done. I saw several uninhabited and derelict houses in the village, as in most places in the realm. And each time plague returns more houses fall to decay. I spoke a silent prayer that Galen House would not become one of these.

A servant crossed from barn to manor house as I drew the palfrey to a halt before the place. He glanced my way, continued toward the house, then turned and walked toward me as if it had just then dawned upon him that a well-garbed stranger approached his master's house.

The man tugged a forelock, bowed, and spoke. "How may I serve you?"

"Is Sir John within?"

"Nay, sir. Gone a-hawking."

"When will he return?"

"Dunno. Soon. Doesn't like to miss 'is supper."

"I have heard that your bailiff has gone to Banbury... to visit a brother."

"Randle?" the servant said, with a question in his voice.

"Aye. Does the village reeve live nearby?"

"Just there," the man said, and pointed to a long, well-kept house.

I thanked the fellow and turned my beast to the reeve's house. It was across the road and but a few paces from the manor house.

The door of the reeve's house was open to the pleasant summer evening. I shouted a "Hello," and stood awaiting a reply. It was not long coming.

A young man left the dim interior of the house, blinked and frowned in the low sunlight which temporarily blinded him, then finally focused upon me.

"I give you good day," I said. "I am Hugh de Singleton, bailiff to Lord Gilbert Talbot at his manor of Bampton."

I forget me how many times that day I introduced myself with the same words. I have learned since joining Lord Gilbert's service that mentioning his name, he being one of the great barons of the realm, can loosen tight lips. Folk would rather not run afoul of such a man's bailiff.

The reeve bowed slightly and I continued.

"I am told that you are the reeve of Kencott Manor."

"I am. How may I serve you?"

"Your bailiff, Randle, is away, I am told... off to visit a brother near to Banbury."

"Aye. If you seek 'im, you've missed 'im by a few days."

"When did he depart?"

The reeve hesitated, scratched the stubble upon his chin, then said, "Wednesday last, it was."

"When will he return? I am told he often travels to Banbury in midsummer."

The reeve shrugged his shoulders and said, "Dunno when 'e'll return. A fortnight, mayhap."

"Sir John is agreeable to these absences?"

"Aye."

"Does the brother live in Banbury, or some village nearby?" I asked.

The reeve hesitated. "Uh... nearby, I think. Don't know the place."

"He never named it?"

"Not to me. Brother has a yardland an' more of some abbey, so Randle has said."

I saw the reeve look over my shoulder, turned, and followed his eyes. A corpulent man upon a horse had halted his beast before the manor house. He held the reins in his left hand, and upon his leather-gloved right hand a hooded hawk was perched.

Two younger men, one a beardless lad, followed close behind. As I watched, one of the youths dismounted and took the hawk. Servants appeared to lead the beast away, and the two remaining men dismounted and entered the manor house.

"Sir John?" I asked the reeve.

"Aye. He'll know more of Randle, where 'e's gone an' when 'e'll return."

The reeve did not ask why I sought knowledge of his bailiff. Perhaps he thought it best to show as little curiosity as possible to Lord Gilbert's bailiff.

I bid the reeve "Good day," although 'twas near to the time one should say "Good eve," then led my beast across the road to the manor house.

Sir John had conveniently provided a rail to which mounted visitors might tie their beasts. I wound the palfrey's reins about this rail, approached the manor house door, and rapped my knuckles against the oak.

The door opened instantly. One of the youths who had appeared with Sir John stood in the opening. His apparel said here was no servant. He wore green chauces, fine linen, a tan cotehardie, and his green cap was complete with a long liripipe wound fashionably about his head.

The lad did not greet me or in any way acknowledge my presence but to stand in the open door staring at me. The silence grew oppressive. I finally spoke, identifying myself and my employer and asking to speak to Sir John. Lord Gilbert's name again worked its magic.

"Please enter," the youth said. "My father is within. I will tell him of your request."

Sir John appeared but a few minutes later. Both of the young men walked behind him, curiosity writ upon their faces. The two lads were not yet men. Although one labored to produce a beard, the effort was mostly a failure. But they were no longer boys. They were nearly as tall as me, broad-shouldered, with a frank look in their eyes which spoke of privilege and self-esteem.

"Alan has told me you serve Lord Gilbert Talbot," Sir John said. "How may I serve Lord Gilbert?"

"Early on the morn of St. John's Day men discovered bones in the ashes of the Midsummer's Eve fire in Bampton. I have come here seeking information of your bailiff. I am told that he has gone missing, and no man knows whose bones have been found in the ashes."

I had also been told that the bailiff was visiting a brother who lived near to Banbury, but I decided to wait for Sir John to corroborate that. I cannot say why. Perhaps I did not trust the fellow. Or perhaps I did not trust the priest or the reeve. 'Tis unfortunate, but bailiffs learn to mistrust most other men. Fair enough, I suppose, as most men mistrust bailiffs.

"Missing?" Sir John said. "Nay. Randle often visits his brother in midsummer. For several years he has done so."

"Whereabouts does his brother live?"

"Near to Banbury. 'Tis a half-brother, actually," Sir John added after a brief hesitation.

"Did you see your bailiff depart? Was he mounted?"

"Aye, to both your questions."

"When will he return?"

"I required of him that he return by St. Swithin's Day."

"If 'twas not your bailiff whose bones were found in the ashes, it must be some other. Have you heard of any man gone missing from any neighboring village?"

Sir John scratched at his beard and pursed his lips. "Nay, but should I learn of such a thing you would like to know of it, I suppose."

"Indeed. One other thing. How tall is your bailiff?"

"Hmmm. Not so tall as you. About my height, I'd say, 'though not so great of girth," he chuckled.

I bid Sir John "Good day," and sought my palfrey. Unless I made haste I would not set foot in Galen House 'till night had come.

I prodded the palfrey to a quick pace, and was soon passing the church, when I saw the clerk cross the road before me. I drew upon the reins and called out to the fellow. He stopped and turned to me. I cannot say why I asked the question of him which I did.

"Did you find Sir John?" the clerk asked.

"Aye, I did so. Your bailiff, Randle... was he a tall man, or short, or of medium height?"

"Short, was Randle. Come up to my chin, no more."

"Thank you," I said, and with a flip of the reins and a cluck of my tongue I continued my journey home.

Here was an interesting disagreement. Sir John said his bailiff was of his own stature, which was about the same as the clerk's. But the clerk described Randle Mainwaring as a short man. The bones found in the ashes were those of a short man. I had set out upon this journey to Black Bourton, Clanfield, and Alvescot to solve a riddle. In Kencott I had found another.

And it was surely odd that the lord of a manor would allow an underling to leave his duties for a fortnight. Even when planting was done there was much to oversee on such a manor. Men would be making hay, shearing sheep, plowing fallow fields, and children and women would be weeding crops. The reeve could not be pleased to have responsibility for all of this with the bailiff away.

My Kate has become accustomed to my odd hours. She had prepared for supper that eve a charlet, which may be consumed cold, and so was ready with both supper and a kiss when I entered Galen House.

Bessie and Sybil were abed, so when we finished the charlet I quietly carried a bench to the toft where we might sit in the quiet of the summer evening and watch the stars appear as darkness ended the day.

"Bailiffs are not esteemed," Kate said when I told her of what I had learned in Kencott. "But for in Bampton," she added with a smile. "Few bailiffs can mend a wound or set a broken bone. Perhaps that Kencott bailiff departed for his brother's village but was set upon by some man he had defrauded. 'Twould not be so far, then, to bring a corpse here to Bampton, and every village has a Midsummer's Eve fire, so a felon might pick any village to dispose of his victim. Bampton would do as well as any other."

"'Tis odd," I said, "that Sir John said his bailiff was as tall as he, but the clerk said that the man was short."

"Could be that a man's stature is relative to another's. A tall man believes most men to be short, whereas a short man thinks most men tall."

"Perhaps," I agreed.

"Will you travel again tomorrow, seeking a missing man?"

"Aye, to Witney and Burford and villages thereabout."

'Twas again near dark when I arrived home next day. No man was missing from Witney, but a man had disappeared from Burford some weeks earlier, before Easter. The man who told me this had also an explanation. The man's wife, he said, was a shrew. I thought it unlikely that a man who had been missing since April would be found in the ashes of Bampton's Midsummer's Eve fire, but sought the man's wife to learn more of his disappearance. I learned that the informant spoke true. The woman was a termagant. I heard her scolding a child while I was yet thirty paces from her door. Ten minutes of conversation convinced me that her husband was missing for good reason. Had I made the mistake of wedding such a woman, I might have departed as well. Even the cold winters of Scotland would seem appealing to a man who was the target of this woman's hot tongue.

Once again I carried the bench to our toft and told Kate of the day.

"Is there any place else you might travel to seek a missing man?" she asked.

"I cannot think of any other. None nearby. A murderer would not haul his victim many miles, I think. If I expand my search to Oxford or Abingdon or some such place, I might be upon the roads 'till Michaelmas seeking a missing man."

"What, then? Will you quit the search?"

"It has been fruitless so far, and I see no sign of success if I continue."

"What of the bailiff from Kencott?"

"His lord said that he would return in a fortnight. Perhaps I will travel there about Lammastide. That will give the fellow plenty of time to return. If he has not done so, then mayhap they are his bones we buried in St. Beornwald's churchyard. If he has returned, then I will put this incident in my mystery bag."

"Mystery bag?"

"Aye. When something untoward happened which seemed beyond explanation, my mother would say that she was putting the matter in her mystery bag, and when she met the Lord Christ in heaven she would open the bag to Him, and He would explain all."

"How many items have you in your mystery bag?" Kate asked.

"A few."

"Tell me of them," Kate smiled. "Which is the greatest?"

"Hmmm. The greatest? That, I think, would be the mystery of how a slender village bailiff with a large nose won the hand of the most beautiful maid in Oxford. A lass who had her choice of handsome, wealthy young burghers and scholars."

"I saw beyond your nose," Kate laughed. "And saw behind it a kind man who would be a good husband and father."

"'Tis a wonder you could see past such an impediment."

"I will solve a mystery for you," Kate said softly. "When I watched you deal with my father's wounded back I was certain that you were the husband I wished for. When you departed for Bampton and did not return to Oxford for many weeks I thought I had lost you. My love is no mystery."

"Nor mine," I replied.

Kate rested her head upon my shoulder and our conversation ended. So also, reader, does this account of that evening.

Chapter 6

Haying was nearly done. Men had been in the meadows since before St. John's Day, swinging their scythes, their wives and children following to turn the hay so it would dry evenly. Soon the dried hay would be gathered into stacks.

No sooner was the hay cut than it was time for shearing. While men worked at this, women and children rid the fields of weeds, cutting dock and cornflower from fields of rye, and dead-nettle from pea fields.

All this, of course, is a reeve's business, and John Holcutt needed no advice from me. I have few duties in midsummer, so long as villeins and tenants meet their obligations to Lord Gilbert. Some do not, and must be persuaded. Robert Wroe sliced the heel of his hand whilst shearing and I stitched the wound. Remarkable how tough and calloused a man's hand may become. I bent a needle attempting to pierce the skin of Robert's hand. 'Tis a wonder the leathery hide would yield to any blade.

The only remarkable event in the weeks after St. John's Day was the arrival of two black-robed Benedictines from Eynsham Abbey. One of these carried a sack across his shoulders. In it was the Bible I had been promised for discovering the felon who had slain a novice of that house.

"Abbot Gerleys begs pardon that the work was not completed by St. John's Day, as Abbot Thurstan had promised," one of the monks said.

I assured him that the delay was of no consequence and invited the fellows to share our dinner before they returned, with my thanks, to Eynsham.

By St. Swithin's Day Thomas Attewood was able to hobble about upon a crutch John Kellet had made for him. He seemed to have little pain, so to preserve my store of lettuce seeds I told the fellow his convalescence must continue without more of the physic.

By Lammastide I found myself rarely thinking of the bones found in the ashes of the Midsummer's Eve fire. Some days the matter did not cross my mind at all. But whilst Kate and I and our daughters marched with others of the village to St. Beornwald's Church for mass to thank the Lord Christ for a good wheat harvest, I remembered that it had been my intent to return to Kencott at Lammastide to learn if the bailiff of the village had returned to his duties.

Lammasday fell upon a fast day, but Kate provided a feast for the celebration even so. There were fresh wheaten loaves and a fruit and salmon pie.

The day was warm, my stomach full, and I would have preferred to doze in the sun. But I needed to inform the marshalsea that I would require a palfrey on the morrow, and had not told Lord Gilbert of developments in the search for a missing man since I returned from my first visit to Kencott. There had been nothing to tell.

So it was just as well that Lord Gilbert was, along with some visiting knights and gentlemen, out hunting. Fence month was but a fortnight past, and Lord Gilbert, who enjoys the chase, was surely eager to follow his hounds in pursuit of a hart or a buck.

Perhaps, I thought, after visiting Kencott I would have more to tell of bones and a missing man.

Kencott is but four miles from Bampton. There was no need to start early next day for the village. The sun was well up when I rubbed my eyes, washed my face, greeted Kate, Bessie, and Sybil, and consumed a loaf to break my fast. The apostle wrote that those who wed must not be unequally yoked together. By this he surely meant that Christian folk must not wed unbelievers. But Kate and I *are* unequally yoked in some small way. She rises with the dawn, or before it when winter comes, whereas I prefer to bury my head in a pillow 'till the sun illuminates our chamber.

"You are off to Kencott today?" Kate asked.

"Aye. If the bailiff has returned you will see me for dinner. If he has not, then there are folk of the place I must visit."

"If you find the bailiff, what then of him who was buried unknown in the churchyard?"

"He will never be known, I think… but to God."

"You will be content with that?"

"Nay, not content, not with ignorance. I am content with what I have and where I am, but I am not content with ignorance. Of any matter."

"Then you will continue to seek who was burned in the Midsummer's Eve fire?"

"I will not lay abed past midnight puzzling over the matter," I replied. "But if some new clue appears I will follow where it leads."

"All depends, then, upon the bailiff of Kencott," Kate said.

"It does, which is why I must be away."

I kissed Kate and Bessie and hurried to the castle. Wilfred the porter had already lowered the drawbridge and raised the portcullis, so I was able to go directly to the marshalsea where a page had a palfrey ready for me. Less than an hour later I entered Kencott and saw there a disagreeable sight.

A man dangled by the neck from a crude gibbet. This gallows had not been erected when I was previously in the village.

Carrion crows had consumed the dead man's eyes. He stared sightless over my head. The man had not been hanging there long, I thought, or the crows would have done him greater injury. Why is it, I wonder, that birds will feast upon a dead man's eyes? At Lord Gilbert's Christmas feast no man seems tempted to pluck out the boar's eyes for a treat.

My first thought upon seeing the corpse was that Randle Mainwaring had returned to his post and discovered some felon amongst his lord's villeins. A free tenant may only hang with the sheriff's consent and a finding of guilt by the King's Eyre.

I passed under the corpse and drew the palfrey to a halt at the manor house. Sir John could tell me of the hanged man. Although matters upon his demesne were no affair of mine, Lord Gilbert's influence reaches far – to Kencott, at least.

A servant answered my rapping upon his master's door and invited me to enter while he sought Sir John. I do not know where the knight was, perhaps yet abed, but he did not soon appear and when he finally did so made no apology for his tardiness.

"How may I serve Lord Gilbert?" he said after we had exchanged greetings.

"The man we buried in St. Beornwald's churchyard is yet unknown," I said. "Has your bailiff returned from his travel?"

"Nay. He never traveled."

I peered at Sir John with a puzzled expression, and he explained.

"Randle did not return in a fortnight, as he said he would. After three weeks I sent my lads and two grooms to Bloxham to seek his return. His brother said he'd never come."

"You said you'd send word if you learned of some missing man," I said.

"Oh... aye, so I did. We've settled the matter, so you've no concern on that score."

Sir John's words caused me to remember the hanged man I had passed upon the road. "Was your bailiff slain?" I asked.

"Aye. Likely 'twas his bones you found in the Midsummer's Eve fire. Bailiffs are not popular, as you will know. Randle ran afoul of one of my villeins and the fellow murdered him. Found the man with Randle's horse, tryin' to sell the beast in Burford but four days past."

"The man now hangs from a gallows near the church?" I asked.

"Aye. Them as see 'im there will think twice before they try to flee Kencott or do felony to their betters."

"Why did your villein slay his bailiff?"

"Randle caught 'im twice stealing away from Kencott, seeking some manor where the lord would not ask questions an' he might gain a tenancy. Told 'is sister he'd like to slay Randle, an' did so. Knew he was to be upon the road, so lay in wait for 'im. Probably draped Randle over his horse an' took 'im to Bampton in the night to dispose of him."

Sir John's explanation of events and motives seemed reasonable. But for one thing.

"When was the felon found in Burford, selling the bailiff's horse?"

"Three days before Lammastide. 'Twas fortunate he was seen, else Randle's murder would be unavenged."

"Who saw the fellow?"

"Henry Thryng."

When I made no reply Sir John explained. "Another of my villeins. Good worker is Henry, not like Bertran."

"I wonder why the fellow waited so long to try to sell the bailiff's beast, and where he hid it for a month," I said.

Sir John shrugged. "Who can know? But when we found Bertran with Randle's horse we did justice for the bailiff."

"Do you want Randle to rest here, in your own churchyard?"

"Nay. One churchyard's as good as another. He'll not care," Sir John laughed.

The matter of bones discovered in Bampton's Midsummer's Eve fire seemed closed. I bid Sir John "Good day," and set out for Bampton and my dinner. But two issues nagged me, and so halfway to Alvescot I halted the palfrey and returned to Kencott.

Why did one man describe Randle Mainwaring as of average height, while another said he was short? And why would the hanged villein have kept the bailiff's horse hidden from St. John's Day 'till nearly Lammastide before attempting to sell the beast?

'Twas the clerk who had told me that Randle Mainwaring was short. If it was the bailiff whose bones now rested in St. Beornwald's churchyard, then the clerk spoke true, and Sir John spoke false. Why? If I wished to know more I thought it likely I would learn more from the clerk than Sir John. I re-entered the village resolved to seek him.

Two women and a man left the church porch as I approached. One of the women carried a babe. The priest had evidently just then completed a baptismal and these folk were the godparents. The babe was a lass.

The village priest, when I had first encountered him some weeks past, had not seemed helpful in the matter of a missing man. He would now know that the village bailiff had not traveled to visit a brother. I thought the clerk seemed more ready to speak of village affairs than the priest. I tied the palfrey to a convenient post and waited at the porch until the clerk might appear.

'Twas the priest who departed the church first. He glanced in my direction, bid me "Good day," then hurried across the street to his vicarage. He gave no sign that he remembered me. No doubt his cook had his dinner ready. The thought made my stomach growl. I wonder if Lord Gilbert appreciates the inconvenience of serving him and keeping the peace of Bampton?

I entered the church and looked about the dim interior. The clerk was busy at his duties, locking the font as I approached. He looked up, startled to see me near. Perhaps he thought me a witch seeking holy water for use in some black art.

I bid the clerk "Good day," and introduced myself. His eyes spoke recognition when I gave my name.

"When first we met I sought the name of any man missing from this village," I reminded him.

"I remember."

"Your priest said that no man was missing, but just now I spoke to Sir John and he told me that the corpse which hangs from yon gallows is that of a villein who did murder of the village bailiff."

"'Twas not known, when you first came here, that Randle had been slain."

"He went each summer to visit a brother, I was told, who lives near to Banbury."

The clerk was silent for a moment, then replied, "So 'twas said."

Here was a strange answer. "So who said?" I replied. "I was told this by your priest, the reeve, and Sir John himself. You seem to have doubts."

"I have served Father Kendrick only a year. I know little of the village and folk in it."

"I need to know of but one man of Kencott: the bailiff. Since you came here has he left the place to visit a brother, until this year?"

"Nay... he may have done in years past."

"You heard folk say as much?"

"Nay. But if Father Kendrick now speaks of it, it must be so."

"When did you first learn of his travel? Was it many months past, when you first came to Kencott?"

"Nay. No man spoke of it 'till St. John's Day or thereabouts."

"This year? Not last year, when you were new to the village?"

"Aye."

"The man who hangs over the street..."

"Bertran Muth?"

"Aye. Sir John said he'd tried to leave Kencott twice and Randle found him and forced him to return. Men heard him threaten the bailiff for this apprehension."

"So 'twas said."

"Did you ever hear the man speak of doing harm to the bailiff?"

"No more than any other. Randle was not much liked. What bailiff is?"

"Had Bertran family? A wife? Children?"

"Never wed. That's why he thought to flee, I suppose. No one for Sir John to take vengeance upon but for 'is sister."

"What of the bailiff? Was he wed?"

"Nay."

"Where does Bertran's sister live?"

"You'd pass 'er house on the way to Alvescot. 'Bout a hundred paces beyond the church. She an' Richard have a half yardland of Sir John."

"Tenant or villein?"

"Villein. Sir John doesn't much like the new ways... has but few tenants, does Sir John. Most upon his lands are villeins."

"Has the sister, or her husband, ever tried to flee Kencott?"

"Dunno... not since I've been here. Beatrice an' Richard have four children. Not easy to set off for some new place with such a brood."

I agreed, thanked the clerk for his time, and left the fellow to his duties. As Beatrice and her husband lived along the way I would take to return to Bampton, I decided to pay the woman a visit. She would likely be found tending a pot, preparing to feed her family.

So she was. I walked before my palfrey a hundred paces, turned to the house I found there, and as I approached two children tumbled from the open door. The lads halted, peered up at me, then retreated to the safety of the house. I heard one call out to his mother that a man stood at the door.

No other announcement of my presence was necessary. A woman appeared from the dark, smoky interior of the house. She carried an infant upon her hip, a spoon in the other hand, and blinked from sunlight and the smoke of her cooking fire.

The woman glanced from my cap to my shoes, then peered at me with suspicion. Few men dressed as I was, with a fine woolen cotehardie, parti-colored chauces, and a cap with a long liripipe, ever came to her door. And if such a man did, it would not likely bring her any benefit. More likely such a visitor would bring trouble.

"You are Beatrice?" I said.

The woman did not reply, assuming that if I knew her name no response was called for.

"Your brother, I am told, hangs from the gallows just beyond the church."

She remained silent, but I saw a tear begin to well up from an eye. No more reply was necessary.

"He slew the bailiff, 'tis said, and was discovered with the man's horse in Burford."

"Aye... so 'tis said."

"Your brother attempted to flee Kencott twice, Sir John said, and the bailiff caught him both times."

"Aye, he did. Randle fined 'im. Six pence first time, ten second. Who are you to care?"

I introduced myself to the woman, and explained my interest in her brother and Randle Mainwaring. "And so he wished to slay the bailiff, and did so?" I concluded.

"May have wished to. Don't know 'bout that, but 'e didn't do murder."

"Did you ever hear your brother speak of vengeance against the bailiff?"

"Only man I ever heard Bertran speak harshly of was Henry."

"Henry? Henry Thryng?"

"Aye. You know 'im?"

"Sir John said 'twas him who saw your brother in Burford, attempting to sell the bailiff's beast."

"Aye, 'twas Henry's word what got Bertran hung."

"You said that your brother did not like Henry."

"Nay. Two years past 'e caught Henry shearin' one of 'is sheep after dark, to steal the fleece. Last year Henry tried to steal a furrow from Bertran. Reeve made Henry keep to 'is own bounds. Was Bertran likely to slay anyone, 'twould've been Henry."

"Did you speak to your brother after he was accused of murder?"

"Only when 'e was took to the gallows. He seen me an' Richard as they was liftin' 'im to the cart."

"Did he speak?"

"Aye. Said 'e'd done no murder, but found a beast in the wood an' took it to Burford to sell."

"The animal was not his. If this was true, would he not know that it was a stray, and belonged to some man?"

The woman hung her head. "Should've, I s'pose. A man can get himself hung for thievin' as well as murder."

"There are empty houses in the village. Would Sir John see a man hang for theft when he has lost so many villeins? Would he not fine him and let him live to labor upon his demesne?"

The woman looked over her shoulder through the open door of her house, then to the spoon she held in her hand.

"Got to mind the pot," she said. "But Sir John wouldn't need to search far to find folk glad of Randle bein' slain. Have to hang half the village."

I thanked the woman for her time and she hastened to deal with her dinner. I mounted the palfrey and set out for home, late for dinner, and confused.

Why would a man keep a horse hidden, in a wood or elsewhere, for a month after he murdered the beast's owner? Where would a poor villein find coin enough for oats? The beast could not have been allowed to graze in a meadow, else it would have been seen and likely recognized.

The marshalsea had provided me with a beast with a leisurely gait, so I knew that another cold dinner awaited me when I returned to Galen House. But the palfrey's slow pace provided time to consider the perplexing matter of the bones in the ashes and the slain bailiff and the murderous villein. I could make little sense of the business. As I passed through Alvescot I was nearly convinced that Sir John's view of the matter must be correct for want of any better answer.

Chapter 7

A mile east of Alvescot the road narrows and passes through a copse of trees, a part of Lord Gilbert's forest. Thoughts of bones and slain bailiffs had given way to a drowsy peace as the palfrey plodded on toward Bampton. I was not asleep, but nearly so, paying no attention to my surroundings, allowing the palfrey to carry me home at its own pace.

The beast suddenly shied and so drowsy was I that I nearly tumbled from the saddle. I regained my balance, then saw the reason for the beast's behavior. Mounted men closed upon me from both sides, appearing suddenly from the verdure which bordered the road in that place. One grasped the reins, yanked them from my hands, and brought my horse to a stumbling halt. The man on the other side had in his hand a large club – not that at that moment I saw it, but it must have been so. My attention was drawn to the rider who had seized the reins, so I did not see the blow coming which unhorsed me and brought me to the mud of the road. But I felt it.

I managed to lift myself to hands and knees, but to rise higher was impossible. The mud of the road swirled before my eyes like a leaf caught in Shill Brook.

"You'll be advised to keep to your own bailiwick," a voice said. "Kencott can deal with its own. No help from you wanted. An' just so you get the message..."

The fellow delivered a kick to my ribs. Message received. I rolled in the mud, trying to make of myself as small a target as possible. 'Twas then I saw that what I had assumed was two assailants was four. And each man seemed determined to strike more blows and kicks than his fellows. One of the attackers wore a shoe which had been torn and mended. I saw the repair clearly as the man delivered a kick to my cheek.

From the corner of my eye I saw the man with the club lift it high above his head, this fellow having given up on kicking me.

Perhaps he had injured his toe. The club descended and I saw all the stars and planets in their orbs. Then I saw nothing.

If any man saw me wounded there in the road he passed by on the other side, and no Good Samaritan found me nor cared for my injuries.

I know not how long I lay in the mud, but when I awoke, my attackers were away. I managed to rise to my knees and saw my palfrey cropping grass at the verge of the road some fifty paces distant. At least, fifty paces for a man in his right mind, able to stride out in robust steps. I was neither. When I finally stumbled near to the beast she took fright of the apparition which approached and trotted another fifty or so paces away. At least the beast traveled toward Bampton.

I spoke soothingly to the palfrey through thickening lips and managed to catch her bridle before she could again draw away. I gained the saddle after only three attempts, which, under the circumstances now that I look back upon it, was a commendable achievement. Although I try not to look back upon the event any more than necessary.

With my heels I prodded the palfrey into motion and watched the world sway past. The beast knew the way to the castle and little more than half an hour later turned into the forecourt with no guidance required of me. Wilfred tugged a forelock as I passed under the portcullis, then I saw his eyes widen. But for the mud on my garments my appearance then was a mystery to me. My features evidently amazed the porter.

I drew the palfrey to a halt before the marshalsea and set about the business of descending from the beast's back, which seemed likely to be as troublesome as rising to the saddle had been.

Dame Fortune chose that moment to smile upon me. This was proper, as she had been frowning upon me for several hours past.

Arthur Wagge, a groom to Lord Gilbert and my assistant in several matters in recent years, walked at that moment from the hall, saw me about to topple from my perch, and hastened to catch me before I planted my face upon the cobbles of the castle yard. Arthur assisted me from the saddle. I thanked him and stood leaning against the palfrey.

"Master Hugh," he said with some shock in his voice, "what has happened?"

'Tis awkward to try to speak through lips swollen the size of a large man's great toe. I opened my mouth to explain my condition, but before I could do so Arthur saw a page crossing the castle yard and shouted to the lad that he must fetch Lord Gilbert.

"Four men," I managed to say.

"What? You were set upon by four men?"

I nodded. Moving my head brought an ache, but less so than speaking.

"Whereabouts? Where have you been?"

"Went to Kencott."

"You were attacked in Kencott?"

I shook my head "No" – but gently. "Near to Alvescot... returning," I said.

"Brigands wanted your purse? I'll gather some lads an' we'll be after the fellows."

I shook my head "No" again. This was becoming a disagreeable experience.

"They didn't get your coin? You fought 'em off?"

Again I shook my head "No," and held up a finger to indicate to Arthur that he should be patient.

Speaking slowly, I told the groom of the advice I had received, delivered with kicks and club, that any further investigation of events in Kencott was not desired. When I had done, Lord Gilbert arrived, followed by two visiting knights.

He asked many of the same questions as Arthur, and the groom, understanding my indisposition, answered for me.

"Have you seen these men before?" Lord Gilbert then asked.

"Nay."

"You are close to uncovering a thing which some men wish to remain hidden, I think," Lord Gilbert said. "Else why would men attack you so?"

Here was a fair assertion and a good question. But I was not so close to revealing some hidden thing as some men thought. The beating I had received surely had something to do with the death of Randle Mainwaring and the discovery of bones in Bampton. Some men thought that I was near to finding the hidden truths of the matter. They were wrong. This did not make my wounds less painful.

"A man's bones have been found here in Bampton," Lord Gilbert continued, "and it seems the solution to the matter will be learned in Kencott. Why would men desire you be ignorant of the business? Because," he answered his own question, "they are guilty of murder... or know who is."

I told Lord Gilbert then of the villein hanging upon the gallows in Kencott, and the evidence against him. My employer raised one questioning eyebrow as I haltingly concluded the abbreviated tale.

"If a murderer has already been punished for his felony, why would men care what questions you asked in Kencott, or what answers were given? There is something rotten about this business," Lord Gilbert said.

I had been standing beside my palfrey, leaning upon a stirrup, whilst Arthur and Lord Gilbert plied me with questions. This support was suddenly withdrawn. The palfrey grew impatient, I think, for her stall, and so moved a few paces toward the marshalsea. I tried to move with the beast but found myself upon the cobbles, looking up to concerned faces above me.

Arthur was at my side in an instant, and raised me to a sitting position. Lord Gilbert turned to a page and ordered him to seek grooms and a pallet.

"You are in no condition to walk to Galen House," he said. "Nor are you fit to speak more of this matter now. But," he continued, "more must be said. I will call at Galen House on the morrow and we will consider what response will be made to this outrage. No men will deal so with my bailiff and escape justice."

Two grooms appeared with a pallet and lifted me upon it. With Arthur leading the way, I was delivered to Galen House. The grooms rested my pallet upon the ground whilst Arthur smote the door with his fist and I tried to stand so as to appear whole when Kate opened it. In this I failed, and managed only to rise to a sitting position.

Kate opened the door, saw three men standing before her, one of whom she knew well, and then her eyes fell upon me. She dropped to her knees before the pallet. Questions poured from her mouth and tears from her eyes. I had not thought my appearance so dreadful, although now that I consider it, my looks must have reflected my affliction.

Arthur understood her need and my incapacity. He told Kate what I had told him of the cause of my injuries, and when he had done she attempted to lift me to my feet. With Kate at one elbow and Arthur at the other I managed to stand upright. Indeed, the world seemed remarkably stable compared to an hour before. With this assistance I stepped across my threshold. Kate guided me to our table, where Arthur drew up a bench. I sat and rested my elbows upon the planks of the table.

My sleeves were caked with mud and blood, as was the front of my cotehardie. A button had been torn away. I must seek Hubert Shillside, I thought, and buy another. Odd, the thoughts which pass through a disordered mind. Kate returned me to my senses.

"I will cleanse your wounds," she said, "but then you must tell me what next to do." Turning to Arthur, she said, "Go to the castle and bring an ewer of wine. Hugh always bathes a wound with wine."

I heard Arthur reply that he would do so and a moment later his heavy footsteps passed from Galen House.

"Wait here," Kate commanded. Where did she think I was about to go?

I turned my head – slowly – and watched as Kate poured water from a bucket into a basin. She brought the basin to the table, then turned and walked out of the door to the toft behind Galen House. A moment later she reappeared carrying one of Bessie's linen chemises which she had earlier washed and laid out upon a bush to dry. It would need to be washed again, for she dipped a corner of the garment in the basin and began to dab at my cheeks and forehead. The water in the basin soon became brown with filth, and she emptied it into the toft, filled it again, and continued the work.

Kate was silent all this time. This was worse than had she berated me for being so careless as to allow myself to be surprised along the road. Sometimes 'tis worse to guess another's thoughts than to know them.

The water in the basin turned dark more slowly this time. Kate finally straightened from her labor and at that moment Arthur plunged through the door. In his hand was a small stoppered flask.

Kate held out her hand for the flask, withdrew the stopper, and poured some of the wine on a clean corner of the chemise. This she then applied to my cheeks and forehead.

I have done the same to wounded men before I closed their cuts, and watched them wince as the wine touched flesh. I now know why they did so. Why wine applied to a wound will aid its healing is a thing no man knows, but 'tis so.

When she had finished with my lacerations Kate again soaked the corner of the chemise with wine and placed it against my mouth. I sucked upon the wet linen and felt the sting against my split and swollen lips. When Kate took the cloth away I saw upon it red stains which were not from the wine.

"What is now to be done?" Kate asked.

"Mirror," I mumbled.

When we wed, Kate brought with her from Oxford a small mirror, little larger than the palm of my hand. It was a prized possession of hers. The glass would tell me of my wounds and what further treatment was required.

Kate hurried up the stairs to our chamber, where I heard her exploring the contents of her chest. A moment later she reappeared and handed me the mirror. I held it before my face and saw then why Wilfred, Arthur, Lord Gilbert, and Kate had been so troubled by my appearance.

A kick had laid open my forehead above my left eyebrow, and a flap of skin as long as my thumb lay loose. Both cheeks were lacerated. Two small cuts disfigured my right cheek and one, deeper, angled from nose to ear across my left cheek.

The cuts upon my cheek were just above my beard. They, and the slash across my forehead, would have to be sewn together. Kate would have to do the work, but she would not be required to trim away my beard.

Kate was not much pleased to learn that she must take upon her the role of surgeon. When I told her she looked to Arthur, who had remained after delivering the wine, as if she wished for him to ply the needle and put my face together again.

Arthur evidently also thought her glance an entreaty, for he raised his hands before him and said, "Nay, Mistress Kate. I'm no tailor."

My Kate is talented with a needle and thread, and she put the skill to good use. So well did she stitch up my face that by Michaelmas a man would have needed to examine me closely to see the scars.

I told Kate to get needle and silk thread from my instruments box, peered again into the mirror to closely examine my wounds, then with Bessie's chemise dabbed away blood and told Kate to begin with the laceration upon my forehead.

She has seen me stitch wounds together, and so with delicate fingers she drew the edges of the cut together and I felt the prick of the needle as she began the task.

"How many stitches must I make?" she asked.

"The scar will be the less if you make many small stitches," I replied through thick lips. "Ten or twelve."

"Twelve, then," Kate said, and I watched her frown in concentration as she plied the needle.

I heard her say, "Thirteen," and then she straightened from the work and put a hand to her back. Sweat glistened from her upper lip.

I lifted the mirror and saw a neat line of silk sutures above my eyebrow. When next I must close a wound I should ask Kate

84

to work the needle. Her work was much finer than any I could do.

With the stained chemise I dabbed drying blood from my cheeks, and with a new length of silk thread Kate labored to close these wounds. She worked slowly, again making many small sutures. When she was done I again raised the mirror to inspect her work.

"Well done," I mumbled, then moved the mirror to better see my mouth. My lips bulged and were turning purple. In several places their skin was split. There was nothing to be done. I slid my tongue carefully across my teeth and felt one of them move. It did not seem very loose. Perhaps I would not lose it. Time would tell.

Arthur had watched silently while Kate put me back together. He now spoke.

"Lord Gilbert will ride to Kencott on the morrow with 'is knights an' some of us grooms. Plans to tell Sir John what happened to you, if Sir John don't already know, an' tell 'im that you're not to be molested whilst you are upon 'is business. Furious about this, is Lord Gilbert. Seldom seen 'im so wrathful."

I had been molested often enough whilst upon Lord Gilbert's business: beaten, tied with Arthur in a swineherd's hut, shot through by an arrow. 'Twas enough to make me consider my employment. I would not like to abandon Galen House, but Kate's father had given as dowry a house in Oxford. We might live there and I practice my trade as surgeon. No man in Oxford was likely to lay about my head with a club or pierce me with an arrow or dagger.

"Will you take some herbs?" Kate interrupted my melancholy thoughts. "You oft give such stuff to injured men. Will you take some pounded lettuce seeds in a cup of ale?"

I nodded my head and Kate left the bench for the chamber where I keep my herbs and instruments. She returned with the pouch of seeds, set it upon the table, then from our pitcher poured a cup of ale.

"How many?" she said, while tipping the pouch so that crushed seeds fell into her palm.

"Enough," I said. Kate emptied her palm of the seeds into the ale, then offered the drink to me. I swallowed most of it. 'Tis not easy to drink through lips made as round as a fat pike from the mill pond.

Kate found a clean place on the stained chemise and wiped from my beard the ale which had not passed my lips. "Will you eat? A loaf, perhaps?" she said.

I shook my head. I wished most to lie down, but the thought of mounting the stairs to our bedchamber filled me with dread. I envisioned reaching the topmost stair, then pitching backward if my legs refused to obey my commands.

"I'll be off, then," Arthur said. "Lord Gilbert said we'll set off for Kencott soon after dawn. When we return I'll visit and tell you how matters stand. Unless you want to travel with us?"

I shook my head.

"Didn't think so," Arthur said. "Can me an' Uctred find who did this, they'll wish for mercy before we've done with 'em."

I thought to speak then to Arthur of forgiveness, but my lips were in no condition to make any long theological discourse. And, to be frank, the thought of Arthur and Uctred avenging me upon my assailants was not unpleasant. I thought this might be a sin. I would confess it to Father Thomas and do penance if it was.

With Arthur grasping my arm, I carefully mounted the stairs to our bedchamber. I discovered then that pain will not keep a man from sleep if he has had a large dose of crushed lettuce seeds. Such a man may sleep, but he will not sleep well.

Chapter 8

I slept fitfully, and when I did I dreamt of clubs and kicks and bloody linen. Toward dawn I fell to deeper sleep, and was not awakened 'till Kate's rooster crowed. Kate's place in our bed was empty but warm. She had just arisen to begin the day, but did so silently so as not to disturb me.

She must have heard me place my feet upon the planks, for a moment after I did so I heard her scrambling up the stairs and she shouted for me to await her arrival.

I had removed my bloodied, mud-stained cotehardie and chauces before seeking my bed. The kirtle and braes I slept in were also foul. When Kate entered our chamber she found me bent over my chest withdrawing clean linens. Apparently she thought me incapable of this, for she rushed across the chamber, seized my arm, and would have pulled me back to bed.

When I first stood to approach the chest I feared that my head might swim. I was only a little light-headed as I reached into the chest. But Kate so rushed upon me, concerned that I not fall, that as I stood from the chest with her gripping my arm, I lost my balance. Kate is not a frail lass. Together we tumbled to the planks. I discovered then that my ribs had absorbed a few kicks the day before, which, because of my face, I had not betimes noted.

I stifled a groan while Kate scrambled to rise from my prostrate form, then, for all the aches of face and ribs, I could not but laugh. Kate, I think, thought me mad; that I was deranged from the blows to my skull.

After a few moments she saw that this was not so and a grin spread across her face.

"I apologize, Husband," she said.

"Accepted. Now, assist me to stand and I will change my linens."

My lips were yet swollen and stiff but speech seemed easier than the day before. I am not yet thirty years of age. I have noticed that the young heal more rapidly of wounds and injuries than the old. I am no longer a lad, but I must take care when I am fifty, if the Lord Christ permits me so many years, that I do not so antagonize men that they beat and kick me then.

I drew on clean chauces and cotehardie also. Kate waited whilst I did so, and would not hear of me descending the stairs unless she fixed herself to my elbow like a leech. I protested that 'twould be best for only one of us to plunge down the stairs, not both, but my argument did not impress her.

Our tumble and laughter had awakened Bessie and Sybil, so after Kate saw me safe to the ground floor she returned to our chamber to fetch our hungry daughters.

'Twas not only Bessie and Sybil who were hungry. I had had no dinner or supper the day before. Indeed, had I tried to consume a meal then, I might have soon lost it. I take it for a good sign when a patient has regained an appetite, and I had found mine that morning. But 'twas an ordeal to pass even small portions of a loaf past my lips. Kate promised a thin pottage for dinner.

My stomach wished for more, but my lips said, "Enough." I took some ale, and as I set the cup upon the table I heard hoofbeats approach. Many hoofbeats.

Kate peered at me with a puzzled expression. I guessed who might be approaching and tottered to the door. I opened it to see Lord Gilbert reining his favorite ambler to a halt before Galen House. Behind him was a small army, also mounted. Two knights in Lord Gilbert's service drew their beasts to a halt behind him. Behind them rode their squires and pages, and squires, grooms and pages in Lord Gilbert's service, including Arthur and Uctred. I did not count the company, but there must have been twenty men, all armed and resolute of appearance.

None were more resolute than my employer. He leaned over the pommel of his saddle to inspect me and my swollen, discolored, patched visage.

"You are in no state to accompany us," he said. "Thought it would be well to have you at hand when I confront Sir John, but I see now 'tis not to be. I will tell him that when you are restored to health you may visit Kencott again, and if you do, he is to afford you protection and cooperation. Something about this business stinks."

With that Lord Gilbert drew upon the reins, wheeled his beast about, and set off down Church View Street. Knights, squires, grooms, and pages followed, each taking his place in the queue that rank required.

I watched the riders disappear onto Bridge Street. As they passed from view another form appeared. I recognized the skeletal figure of John Kellet. The priest saw me standing before my door and increased his pace, his bony elbows flailing the air and the scrawny ankles and feet under his black robe raising puffs of dust with each step. 'Twas clear he intended to seek me, so I awaited him at Galen House door.

Kellet stopped before me and said, "They spoke true."

"Who spoke true, and what did they say?"

"Cotters who live about St. Andrew's Chapel. Word has come to us that you were waylaid upon the road and the beating has left you quite loathsome."

"Some men are of loathsome appearance and no man has attacked them," I said. "I will heal. And speaking of healing, how does Thomas Attewood?"

"I made him a crutch from a 'Y'-shaped branch. Pained his ribs an' shoulder to use it at first, but he does well enough with it now. Can visit the privy unaided. Leg aches an' itches, he says."

"He may be tempted to put too much weight upon the broken leg. Tell him he must not for at least another fortnight. Aches and pains are oft the body's way of telling a man he must not do a thing again."

"The men who attacked you... have they been taken?"

"Nay. Come in. I should like to sit down."

The world before Galen House was beginning to tilt, it seemed, and the priest appeared to stand a good deal from vertical but did not fall over.

My way was unsteady and I soon found myself with palms pressed against a wall. The priest saw and grasped an elbow.

Together we entered Kate's kitchen and she looked up from her pot as I dropped to a bench.

"Dizzy," I said as Kate lifted her cotehardie and rushed to me.

"You should be abed," she said.

I thought this a fine suggestion.

"Thirsty," I said. "And a cup of ale for Father John, also."

We drank our ale in silence. This was a relief to my injured lips, and the bench below me and the wall at my back caused the world around me to stop swirling about and fix itself in place.

"Did the felons get your purse?" Kellet finally asked.

"Nay. Didn't seek it. I'd been twice to Kencott, where I'd heard that the bailiff had gone missing."

"Did you think 'twas him in the St. John's Day fire?" Kellet asked.

"Yesterday I saw in Kencott a man hanging from a gallows and was told he'd slain the bailiff."

Kellet's frown told of his confusion. "How'd one man bring another from Kencott to Bampton?"

"A worthy question."

I told Kellet of the bailiff's horse, and the hanged man's attempts to flee from villeinage which the bailiff had thwarted. For my lips' sake I kept the explanation succinct.

"As long as you're here," Kate said to the priest, "you may help me get him upstairs to our chamber."

Kate took one elbow and Kellet the other. 'Twas a good thing the priest was not so plump as he once was, else we would not all three have fit upon the same treads.

I was too sore to sleep well. Each time I moved upon the bed some part of my anatomy reminded me of the attack. Kate climbed the stairs several times to look upon me. I feigned sleep so that she would believe me comfortable, but this may have had an opposite effect. Once when she entered our chamber, through a half-opened eye I saw her place a hand over her mouth and quickly approach our bed. I turned under the blanket to reassure her that I was yet among the living.

Kate woke me about noon. She had brought to the chamber a steaming pot of thin pease pottage flavored with a few small morsels of pork. I sat upon the edge of our bed while she fed me spoonfuls of the meal. My lips would not close properly and so some of the watery pottage found its way down my chin and into my beard. I was too young for this, I thought. 'Tis only ancient grandfathers who must be spoon fed and cleaned up after.

The chamber stayed in place whilst Kate fed me. It did not tilt or twirl, and so I suggested that I might go to the toft and sit there upon a bench in the sun. Kate would not hear of it. I did not much like being treated like an invalid, but I would not have liked to topple down the stairs, either. So I did as Kate required and when I had eaten my fill lay back upon the bed. This time I was soon asleep. What is it about a full stomach and a warm afternoon which makes a man as lethargic as if he had plowed half a yardland?

Some time in midafternoon I awoke to the sound of footsteps upon the stairs. 'Twas Lord Gilbert, and behind him I saw Arthur. Both men were tight-lipped, and as I rose to a sitting position my employer spoke.

"Nay, Master Hugh. Lay you down. We are just returned from Kencott. Sir John claims ignorance of why men would attack you to keep you from the village. I told him that when you are recovered from the blows you were given you may return to Kencott. He knows that I will hold him responsible for your safety whilst in the village, or on the road to or from the place."

"You believe he spoke true?" I said. "That he knew nothing of my assailants?"

"Nay," Lord Gilbert replied. "'Twas his bailiff slain, his hallmote which sentenced a man to hang. Sir John has right of infangenthef, and the villein was found with the bailiff's horse, so he'd the right to hang the fellow. But if justice for murder was done, why did men wish to drive you from Kencott? What did they fear that you would discover? And who would most fear the discovery? The murderer was already dead."

"So we are meant to believe," I said.

"Just so," Lord Gilbert agreed. "When you return to Kencott, take Arthur with you... just in case."

"I will do so."

A day earlier I had considered leaving Lord Gilbert's employ. A peaceful life in Oxford, dealing with men's bodily complaints and injuries, seemed preferable to the insults and contusions I had suffered in his service. But I am stubborn. I dislike men who shirk their duty. If I should flee Bampton Manor I would be such a man. And with Arthur beside me, it is easier to face adversity caused by malefactors. I knew that if I resigned my post in Bampton I would think of my cowardice each night when I lay my head upon a pillow. Which is worse: the pain of wounds incurred in discharging one's duty, or the regret a man may feel later when he looks back upon his lack of valor? Wounds may heal, regret seldom does.

Lord Gilbert and Arthur bade me "Farewell," which would be an improvement, as I had fared ill in the recent past. I heard them speak to others as they reached the base of the stairs and understood that most of those who accompanied Lord Gilbert had also attended him to Galen House.

I heard Kate wish a "Good day" to Lord Gilbert and shortly after she appeared in our chamber with a cup of ale freshly procured from the baker's wife. While I drank we heard a knock upon Galen House door and Kate descended to see what new visitor we had. 'Twas John Kellet.

I heard Kate greet the curate and tell him that I was above, in our chamber where he had left me some hours earlier. Kellet's bare feet slapped the treads as he climbed to our chamber, and when he entered the room it was clear to me that he had hurried from St. Andrew's Chapel to Galen House. He was red in the face and breathless.

"I have news," Kellet said. "You must speak to Thomas."

"The swineherd? Why so? Has he done some further injury to himself?"

"Nay. He is well. 'Tis not his injury which you must learn of. The man knows of Kencott's bailiff."

"What? How so?"

"Thomas is of Broadwell."

I knew of the village. It was half a mile from Kencott, to the south. Like many villages, it had suffered much when the great pestilence attacked twenty years past.

"When I told him of your wounds and the matter of Kencott's murdered bailiff, his eyes grew wide. I saw this and asked of the reason. He would not say, but asked that you come to him. He was insistent that you do so. I told him of your hurt, and that you would not be able to visit him for several days. He stood, reached for the crutch I made for him, and said that being so, he would seek you.

"I persuaded him that this would be unwise, and that I would carry to you his request to speak to you as soon as possible."

"He knows something of the slain bailiff, you think?" I asked.

"He would say no more to me. What shall I tell him? Will you come?"

"Tomorrow. Already I feel better. A walk to St. Andrew's Chapel will not over-tax me tomorrow, I think."

Kate disagreed. I told her of my intention and the reason for it between more spoonfuls of pottage which she brought for my supper. The pottage had thickened. My lips were thinner, so 'twas an even trade. But because it was not so thin I did not drool my meal as at noon.

"You must stay abed," Kate said, "'till you are well. As you now are, if you walk to St. Andrew's Chapel, men will find you next day sleeping in a ditch."

So I spent most of another day in bed. But in the afternoon I crept down the stairs so I could sit in the toft upon a bench and enjoy the sun. Kate frowned when she saw me, but what was she to do? She is not a scold, so rather than berate me, she assisted me in moving a bench into the sun, and sat there with me and Bessie.

I asked for her mirror. I was eager to learn how much my wounds had healed in two days. Kate was reluctant to provide it, and when she finally did I understood why. Both of my eyes were swollen, dark, and purple. My cheeks were much the same, and when I lifted my cotehardie and kirtle to inspect my ribs I saw the same colors displayed. A few bits of dried blood speckled Kate's needlework across my forehead and cheeks. I was pleased to see no pus issuing from the sutured wounds. But little else I saw in the mirror pleased me. I set the glass upon the bench and once again thoughts came to me of abandoning my position as bailiff to Lord Gilbert Talbot. But not 'till I had straightened out the matter of the bones found in the St. John's Day fire. Perhaps I would heal before that day. Perhaps not.

Lord Gilbert, when he offered me the post of bailiff, had not promised comfort. Who is interested in my comfort? Not Lord Gilbert. He desires only my service. Does the Lord Christ wish for my comfort? He did not say so. Rather, He told His followers that they must take up their cross and follow Him. A cross is not a comfortable burden. The Lord Christ, I think, is more interested in my character than my comfort. What kind of man will flee his duty when it becomes uncomfortable? Am I such a man? But how can wounds and contusions contribute to my character? And could not the Lord Christ devise some other way of doing the work than using the clubs and kicks of wicked men? I have too many questions and too few answers. This also I will place in my mystery bag.

Chapter 9

Next day, after a loaf and ale, I set out for St. Andrew's Chapel. The way before me was reassuringly firm, my headache nearly gone, and the chapel less than half a mile from Galen House. John Kellet resides in the tower, but the swineherd could not climb the narrow stairs, more like a ladder, to the chamber. The priest had laid a pallet upon the flags at the base of the tower and there I found the man. Kellet heard my greeting and descended from his tiny chamber.

Thomas struggled to his feet, nearly as unsteady as I had been yesterday. The benches in the porch were the nearest place we could sit, so I suggested we go there. We made a remarkable company: John Kellet, the emaciated, barefoot curate; Thomas, hobbling upon his crutch; and me, of the multicolored face.

"Father John said you wished to speak to me privily of Randle Mainwaring."

Thomas nodded and glanced to the priest.

"We will treat this as confession," I said, "if you are concerned that what you will say should go no farther. Father John will hold what you say in confidence, as if you sought absolution. Is this not so?" I said to the priest. He nodded.

I thought such reassurance necessary not only because of Attewood's glance toward Kellet, but because the day before he had asked to speak to me, but withheld the subject from the priest. Some delicate matter must be on his mind.

The porch faced east, and was well lit by the morning sun. Thomas studied my face and said, "Father John said you was bad hurt. They told you to forget about Randle, he said."

"Aye. You speak as if you might know the men who tried to refashion my face."

"Got suspicions, that's all," the swineherd shrugged.

"Why so? Who are the men?"

"Wouldn't want 'em to learn I'd said."

"They'll not discover such a thing from me," I said, then looking to Kellet, I added, "nor from Father John." The curate nodded agreement.

"Been gone from Broadwell for many years. No future there after plague came. Took Sir Reynold an' 'is sons."

"Sir Reynold?"

"Sir Reynold Penderel, lord of the manor of Broadwell. Lady Alyce wed a knight from Kent an' departed Broadwell. Little enough to hold her there. Left the manor in the hands of a steward, but Simon was drunk much of the time an' when 'e was sober 'e thought of nothin' but when 'e'd get another pot of ale."

"How many villeins and tenants remained in the place after the plague?" I asked.

"First time it come, or second?"

"Both."

"Before the great death first come we was near forty families, I'd say. I was but a lad then, an' took no account of such matters. When plague come again it took mostly children what had been born since first time, but some folk my age perished also."

"That was when the affliction returned eight years past?" I asked.

"Aye, 'bout that. Lose track of the years after a time."

"How many families then remained in Broadwell?"

The swineherd pursed his lips, scratched the nape of his neck, then replied, "Mayhap ten."

"That many were taken of plague?"

"Not all that was gone was dead. Some went to other manors, bein' tenants an' not villeins. An' when I say ten families was left, that don't mean fifty or so folk remained. Many lost father or mother or children. I was the only soul remaining of my family."

"So perhaps thirty folk remained in Broadwell?" I said.

"'Bout that... no more."

"How did you come to Lord Gilbert's service?"

"Broadwell was dyin' an' I didn't want to die with it. Heard from Walter that Lord Gilbert's swineherd was dead."

"Walter Chyld, groom to Lord Gilbert?"

"Aye. Me bein' a tenant an' free to leave Broadwell, I sought the post an' I been in Lord Gilbert's service since."

I had heard Thomas Attewood's name before, but had never met the man 'till I found him in the forest. He had spent most of his time with pigs, and had done nothing to run afoul of his bailiff.

"This is what you wished to tell me but would not tell Father John?" I asked. "What of your suspicions of the men who altered my face?"

"Gettin' to that. Broadwell is but a half-mile from Kencott."

"So you know folk from that place?"

"Aye... know the talk, too."

"It is of this talk you wish to speak to me?"

"Aye. Mayhap just rumors. Folk do like to talk 'bout others an' their misfortunes, 'specially their betters."

"Of whose misfortunes do you speak?"

"Randle Mainwaring."

"He's dead. I suppose most folk would consider that a misfortune," I said.

"Aye, right enough. But that ain't the misfortune I speak of."

"What, then?"

The swineherd hesitated, as if he was reconsidering the conversation and his part in bringing it about.

"Just rumors, you know," he said.

I nodded and waited for him to speak.

"Some folk about Kencott an' Broadwell did say that Randle was higher born than what bailiffs usually is."

"My father was a knight," I said. "I was his fourth son, so was required to make my own way in the world. No manor for me. Why did such a topic cause tongues to wag in Kencott and Broadwell?"

"No offense," Thomas said, "but Randle was maybe higher born than fourth son of a knight."

"Where did you hear such talk, and what has it to do with his death?"

"Rather not say. Don't want to get some other in trouble so men do to 'im what they did to you... or worse."

"How long has this gossip been heard about Kencott and Broadwell? When did you first learn of it?"

"I heard of it but a few years past. But there are old folk what knew of it long ago, I think."

I would have liked to know the source of this rumor which Thomas had learned a few years past. But at the moment I was unsure that such gossip had anything much to do with Randle Mainwaring's bones being found in the ashes of the St. John's Day fire, and thought that Thomas was more likely to tell me other things he knew of Broadwell and Kencott if I did not try to force the information from him.

"You wish to set me upon a path," I said, "but want me to find my own destination."

"Aye."

"Because the men who attacked me would do the same to you if they knew of or suspected this conversation."

Thomas nodded. "Or worse," he said.

I looked to John Kellet, who had remained silent during this conversation. He responded with a finger to his lips.

Thomas Attewood's guarded assertion meant that I would return to Kencott. Whether or not Randle Mainwaring's ancestry had to do with his death I could not then guess, but the proper questions asked of the proper villagers might tell me. And there were at least four men of Kencott who did not want me to ask of this business or any other. If folk given to villainy wish for me to remain ignorant of some matter, 'tis sure that I should do what I can to learn of it.

I left St. Andrew's Chapel after admonishing the swineherd that, if he thought of any other matter involving Randle Mainwaring, he should send John Kellet with the information. And also that he should not walk about upon his leg even if it no longer pained him much.

I saw Kate peering from Galen House door as I walked from Bridge Street to Church View Street. I suspect she had done so often whilst I was away at the chapel. I was sorry to worry her with my absence, yet pleased that there was a woman concerned about my health and safety. 'Twould be a woeful thing to have no woman who cared about my welfare.

The pottage and wheaten loaf which was my dinner I consumed more readily than in the past days. My lips seemed some reduced from their previous swollen size, and the loose tooth did not trouble me while eating soft pease pottage.

Kate watched me consume my dinner and when my bowl was empty took it to the pot and filled it a second time. I did not object, and devouring a second bowl would, I knew, put Kate's mind at ease. A man with a good appetite is rarely very ill.

Returning to Kencott whilst yet purple and bruised with my face sewn together with silken thread seemed a poor idea. I did not wish to be the butt of jokes and ribald jesting. Perhaps I am too proud.

I spent the afternoon at my table, reading from my new Bible. Eynsham Abbey's scribes had created a fair copy, and had embellished it with illuminations. I did not request this, but no doubt the monks' pride in their work drove them to beautify the manuscript. Perhaps this also is a sin? But if a worker did not take pride in the product of his labor we would surround ourselves with poor goods.

I possessed already a gospel of St. John which I had copied from a rented gospel whilst I was a student at Balliol College. As I had read that many times over, I decided to begin with the gospel of St. Matthew.

The afternoon passed quickly. Bessie played about my feet while I read, so perhaps I lost some of the theology of the gospel, but when I reached the tenth chapter my thoughts were arrested. "You will be hated by all men," the Lord Christ told His disciples, "for My name's sake." Did He mean that those who, like Him, attempt to do good, will be hated by those who do evil? It is likely so. So a man may perhaps judge his place in the Lord Christ's kingdom by knowing who it is who hates him. Mayhap the blows and kicks I suffered were a mark of approval. I might wish that there was a less painful way of discovering His esteem.

A few verses later the Lord Christ said, "There is nothing covered that will not be revealed, and hidden that will not be known." Is this a task He has given to me? To make known hidden things? Or did the Lord Christ speak only of Himself? Scholars seek to make hidden things known. Well, some of them do so. I knew some scholars while at Balliol College who delighted in making hidden matters even more obscure. For some folk. If all men knew as much as they, then their place and reputation as scholars would be imperiled. So some men, most men, must remain ignorant to preserve the standing of others.

I had thought 'twas Lord Gilbert Talbot who gave me my position and therefore assigned me the task of making hidden things known. Perhaps he was but the agent of the Lord Christ. Another notion for my mystery bag.

Of one thing I was sure. If the Lord Christ put me in place to do His work in making hidden things known, I would abandon the work at peril of my soul. I could resign from Lord Gilbert's work, but not from the Lord Christ's.

Nevertheless, I had no desire to show my purple complexion in Kencott. So for the next week I remained in Bampton and considered which folk in Kencott I might seek and which questions I should ask them.

Nine days after I was attacked I felt whole enough to set out for Kencott. The color was nearly gone from my face and my ribs ached only when I sneezed, which in late summer I seem to do often. The stitches across my cheeks and forehead remained. 'Twould be another week before I asked Kate to snip them free. But as I healed I became impatient to see justice done, for Bertran Muth, for Randle Mainwaring, and for me. If folk in Kencott stared at my stitches, the notoriety would be the price I must pay to get on with my work.

I found Arthur at the castle and told him that, as Lord Gilbert had suggested, I would have his companionship next day as I traveled to Kencott. Perhaps this request showed a lack of confidence in Lord Gilbert's powers of persuasion. But I had journeyed alone to Kencott with lamentable results. With Arthur at my side, if we were again set upon by four men, the odds, four against two, would be about even. In a fight Arthur is worth three ordinary men.

Bertran Muth's corpse and the makeshift scaffold were both gone when Arthur and I entered Kencott next day. I had decided that this day I would seek Henry Thryng. Why would a villein be in Burford to see Bertran Muth sell a horse he had gained through murder a month past?

I drew my palfrey to a halt before St. George's Church, left Arthur with the beasts, and entered the gloomy structure. The day was heavy with low clouds. Little light entered the building through the narrow windows. The clerk was a dim shadow in the chancel. As I approached I saw that he was hanging a new curtain across the entrance to the Easter sepulcher. He heard me come near and peered into the nave to see who had entered the church.

The clerk was completing his work, so descended to the flags before asking my business.

"How may I serve… ah, 'tis you, the bailiff of Bampton," the man said. "I have heard that you were set upon while returning to Bampton last time you were here."

"You heard true. What else have you heard?"

"About the men who attacked you?"

"Aye. Or any other matter."

"Very little. Surprising, actually. There is, as a rule, much gossip in the town, Kencott being no different from other villages, I suspect."

"There are whispered suggestions of my assailants?"

"Nay."

"This curtain is of fine stuff," I said, holding the fabric between thumb and forefinger.

"The finest velvet. 'Twill see Sir John freed of many years in purgatory, I think."

"DeMeaux? He provided the veil?"

"He did… Italian silk, too."

I wondered for what sin Sir John sought absolution. What

would Holy Church do if men were virtuous? They would then need no pardons nor would they give gifts to churches and abbeys to purchase forgiveness. The more sins men commit, the wealthier the Church becomes. As the Church is very wealthy, men must be great sinners.

"Where may I find Henry Thryng?" I asked.

The clerk did not immediately answer. When he did 'twas not the reply I sought.

"In the churchyard. When you depart the porch look to your left. You will see, near to the wall, a fresh grave."

"The man who saw Bertran Muth with the bailiff's horse is now dead?" I said, rather stupidly. Men are not found in new graves otherwise. "When did he die? What was the cause?"

"'Twas two, perhaps three days, after you were last here. Albreda said he was taken with a gripe of the bowels an' died but a few hours after."

"How old was Henry?"

The clerk pursed his lips and shrugged. "Dunno. Thirty years, mayhap thirty-five. Oldest lad is ten or so. Even young men die if their bowels become twisted."

"Aye," I agreed. "Where does Albreda live?"

"You remember where the gallows was erected where Bertran was put to death? A lane leads to the right. Albreda's house is second on the left down the lane. You think she'll know something of the scoundrels who attacked you? Or of Randle Mainwaring's death?"

The clerk understood why I was a third time in Kencott. But I could not answer his question. After I spoke to the woman I might then reply.

Henry Thryng had reportedly sheared a sheep of Bertran Muth's, and tried to impinge upon Bertran's land. When I saw Albreda Thryng's house I understood why her husband might have resorted to thievery. Daub was peeling from wattles in many places and the roof had needed thatching for many years. Wisps of smoke drifted from the vents and filtered through the thin thatching. Two scrawny chickens scratched about in the toft.

A few spindly onions and cabbages grew aside the house. They would provide poor provender for the coming winter.

The door of the house stood open even though the day was cloudy and cool. Arthur and I dismounted, and while he remained with our beasts I approached the open door and rapped my knuckles upon the doorpost.

The woman who appeared, wreathed in smoke from her hearthstone, was nearly as skeletal as John Kellet, and her cotehardie was patched in some places and frayed in others. It seemed her husband did not or could not provide for her and what children they might have produced.

I introduced myself and saw no sign in the woman's eyes or manner that she had heard of me. As I spoke I saw two children, lads, appear from the smoky gloom of the house. They were as ill clothed as their mother, and as the clerk had suggested, the oldest seemed perhaps ten years old.

"I am told that your husband died about a week past," I said.

"Aye, 'bout that," the woman replied guardedly, as if I had some sinister motive in inquiring. Perhaps I did.

"What was the cause?" I asked.

"Dunno. Came 'ome early one day from hoein' the pea field. Bent double from pain in 'is belly. Gave 'im oil of fennel but did no good."

"He died soon after?"

"In the night."

"What had he done before he went to the pea field with his hoe?"

"Doin' boon work for Sir John. Cuttin' barley."

"This was the day before?"

"Nay. Went to harvest on Sir John's demesne soon as dew was dried, then went to the pea field in the afternoon."

"Where did he eat his dinner?"

"'Ere. Sir John don't feed folk doin' boon work 'less they serve all day."

A man who might tell me of Bertran Muth and a wandering horse was dead. Coincidence? Perhaps. If I had never appeared in

Kencott, would Henry Thryng yet live? Serving as a bailiff has given me a suspicious nature. Many things may cause a man so much pain in his belly that he will bend double in agony. There are poisons which will do so. I had never heard of scything barley or hoeing peas so tormenting a man that he passes from this life to the next.

"Your husband saw Bertran Muth with Randle Mainwaring's horse."

"Aye, he did so."

"In Burford, where Bertran was offering the beast for sale, I'm told."

"'At's right."

"Why was your husband in Burford? Had he some business there?"

"Took capons to sell in the market."

I looked about the toft and saw only two fowl. Perhaps there had been more before Henry traveled to Burford.

"Your husband must have taken your supply," I said. "How many did he sell?"

"Wasn't our fowl," she said, "'though 'twould be none of your business was they ours."

"Whose, then?"

"Sir John's."

"Sir John's poulterer did not take them?"

"Nay. Edgar don't travel about much. All bent with age, is Edgar. When Sir John wants hens or capons took to market he sends another."

"Had Henry performed this task before?"

"Once, two... three years past."

"How many fowl did he take to Burford market this last time, when he saw Bertran?"

"Six."

"Sir John would send a man all the way to Burford for three or four pence?"

"Guess so," the woman shrugged.

"Before your husband died, of what pains did he complain other than a bellyache?"

"Said 'is mouth was burnin'. I remember that. An' broke into a great sweat. Tried to stand but was so dizzy 'e couldn't. Called me Maud."

"Who was Maud?"

"'Is mother," the woman said, and shook her head.

"Did he vomit up his dinner?"

"Aye, not an hour after he ate it."

"Has Sir John appointed a new bailiff yet? To look into matters such as your husband's death?"

"Nay, not yet. 'Twas Sir John's son come by next day. Told 'im as how Henry 'ad perished, what news 'e'd already heard."

"What did the lad say?"

"Said Henry must've injured 'imself cuttin' barley. Twisted 'is bowels from bendin' an' swingin' the scythe... so 'e said."

"I wonder why he would think so?"

"Said Henry was stooped over when 'e left the field to come home to dinner," the woman explained.

"Did you see him bent in pain before his meal?"

"Paid no notice. 'E didn't complain 'till 'e come back from the pea field."

Albreda Thryng was not likely to know more of her husband's journey to Burford, nor was I going to learn more of her husband's death from her. I bid the woman "Good day" – a convention, surely, for she would have few good days in the future unless she could find another husband. She might succeed in this. We have been visited with plague three times, and plague is not selective. It kills women as well as men.

"I 'eard," Arthur said as I approached him and the palfreys. "Never 'eard of a fellow dyin' of swingin' 'is scythe too strong, like."

"Nor have I. I think we must seek the reeve."

"Why so?"

"He'd have been in charge of the villeins doing Sir John's boon work."

"Oh, you think 'e might've seen the fellow begin to suffer from injury?"

"Something like that."

Chapter 10

The reeve, his wife said, was harvesting his own oat field this day, and told us where it could be found. 'Twas along the road from Alvescot, not far from where Bertran Muth's sister made her home.

A man who has been swinging a scythe for several hours, and has become sweat-stained, dusty, thirsty, and exhausted, might welcome respite from his labor. So it was that Kencott's reeve put down his scythe when I approached and gave no hint of displeasure that I had interrupted his toil.

"How may I serve you?" the reeve said, peering at my multicolored face and its sutures. Was that the hint of a smile I saw cross his features?

"Henry Thryng died a few days past, I am told, after doing his boon work on Sir John's barley field."

The reeve said nothing, apparently finding nothing in my words with which to disagree.

"Did you notice anything amiss while Henry was at work with the scythe?"

If one of Sir John's sons said that Henry was bent in pain when he left the barley field, he would surely have learned that from the reeve, or perhaps one of Henry's fellow laborers. It would be unlikely that the son would have been observing the work of villeins harvesting a barley field.

"Why does the bailiff of Bampton want to know of matters here?" the reeve replied.

"Perhaps some day I will tell you," I replied. This reeve was not going to tell me much, I decided. I wondered why.

"Has Sir John spoken to you of Lord Gilbert Talbot's visit a few days past?" I asked.

"Aye."

"What did Sir John say?"

"Said as how 'twas Lord Gilbert's request that all in Kencott answer what questions you might ask."

"Indeed. Though you might better say that 'twas a demand, not a request," I said.

"Beyond me why you involve yourself with business 'ere. We caught the felon who slew Randle."

"So 'tis said," I replied in a tone which implied that I was not convinced that such was true. I did not care if village gossip spread my skepticism. Why else would I return to Kencott?

"But what of Henry Thryng? Did he seem to you in discomfort when he left the barley field and went to his dinner?"

"Nay," he shrugged. "Walked to 'is home with scythe over 'is shoulder, straight as any man."

I had another question, but decided that the reeve would perhaps give an unreliable answer. Any villager might provide the information I sought. I bid the reeve "Good day," rejoined Arthur, and led him and our beasts to the hovel wherein Beatrice would be found.

As in my earlier visit, the woman appeared at her door in answer to my knock in a cloud of smoke from her cooking fire. Perhaps not all of Kencott's villagers knew of my injuries. The woman blinked in the sunlight, saw my face, then drew back as if I was some fiend from the nether regions.

"Good day," I said, which I hoped would reassure the woman, as such a greeting would be unlikely from a servant of Lucifer. "Perhaps you will remember that I spoke to you a few days past."

"Oh, aye. You be the bailiff from Bampton."

"Aye. Have you lived here in Kencott all of your life?"

"Aye."

"Then perhaps you know the place well enough that you can tell me if there be, nearby, a place where wolfsbane grows."

"That which folk call monkshood?" she asked.

"Aye. The plant is known by both names."

"'Tis a terrible poison," Beatrice said with a shudder. "Folk 'ave sickened an' died just from touchin' the leaves, so I've 'eard."

"Is there a place near the village where the plant can be found?"

"Aye." The woman looked over my shoulder, then raised her arm and pointed across the road.

"You see yon copse?"

Beatrice indicated a grove of trees perhaps three or four hundred paces distant to the west. I turned to look at her instructions.

"A small brook flows just the other side of that wood. Folk do say monkshood can be found thereabouts."

The woman's directions seemed reasonable, as monkshood seeks damp, shady places. I thanked the woman, returned to Arthur and the palfreys, and as I mounted my beast turned to glance back at Beatrice. She stood in her door, watching us depart with a mouth hanging open in wonder.

"You think that fellow's bellyache suspicious?" Arthur said.

"Aye. I'd like to see where monkshood grows. Perhaps there will be some sign that a plant has been pulled from the dirt recently."

There was.

Arthur and I rode the palfreys across a meadow, tied the beasts to trees at the verge of the wood, then picked our way through the grove to the low ground on the far side. There were many fallen branches there for Sir John's villeins to gather in the autumn for winter fuel.

We had taken only a few steps along the rivulet which Beatrice had called a brook when we saw the first purple flowers of the deadly vegetation. Twenty or so paces farther was a place where the leaves and mold of a forest floor had been disturbed. Perhaps two or three plants had here been uprooted. The oil pressed from that many roots might kill half a dozen men. I resolved to neither eat nor drink anything whilst in Kencott.

Arthur followed my gaze and spoke. "Suppose some fellows pulled monkshood there? Somethin' was drawn from the ground."

"So it seems," I replied.

"Don't know much about monkshood or wolfsbane or

whatever it's to be called. Does it take a man as Henry Thryng was afflicted?"

"It does. Nausea, burning of the mouth, vomiting, confusion."

"How long does it take to kill a man?"

"No more than six hours, so I've heard. Perhaps less. Depends upon the dose."

Arthur appeared deep in thought, tugging at his beard with thumb and forefinger.

"If 'is wife didn't put poison in 'is pottage, then 'e must 'ave ate it in the mornin', or drank it, whilst 'e was at Sir John's boon work."

"Aye, it does seem so. But why, I wonder? The apostle wrote that 'the love of money is the root of all evil,' but Henry Thryng was a villein, and poorer than most, I'd say. No man would slay him for his wealth."

"Mayhap," Arthur said thoughtfully, "wasn't Henry's money the poisoner was after... if money was behind this business, but someone else's money."

"Perhaps. If money was the cause of the poisoning of Henry Thryng – and we cannot be sure that the man was poisoned..."

"Likely, though," Arthur said.

"Aye, likely. But then, whose money was at risk if Henry Thryng lived? Or Randle Mainwaring? Perhaps Henry sheared another sheep which wasn't his, or stole another man's furrow."

"You think the two deaths connected?"

"Aye, but do not ask me for proof of that."

"Not yet," Arthur smiled. "In a few days perhaps I will do so... If Henry wasn't slain for 'is money, then for whose?" he continued.

"Don't know. But if we can discover why Henry was murdered – assuming he was – we will be well along to discovering who slew him."

"An' who slew the bailiff fellow, also?"

"Aye, the bailiff also."

"Who's got most wealth on a manor such as Kencott?" Arthur said. "Think mayhap Henry's death has to do with Sir John?"

"Follow the money, eh?" I said.

"Most folks do," Arthur replied.

My stomach at that moment growled loudly enough that Arthur could hear. He looked at me, grinned, and said, "Me, also. You reckon Kencott's got an inn? Didn't see one."

"Nay, I think not." I then explained why I had decided to take no food or drink in the village.

"Oh," he said. "Suddenly I ain't so hungry any more."

"We have learned much this day," I said. "We will return to Bampton and visit Kencott again tomorrow. Some man of this place will know we have been here this day, will know why we are here, and will worry about what we have discovered. Perhaps his apprehension will cause him to do some rash, foolish thing which will point him out."

"Like waylayin' you upon the road again, an' this time with worse intent."

"'Tis why you are here."

"Lucky me."

"I've seen you brawling. I know that you relish a fight."

"Only when 'tis thrust upon me. Never start a scrap."

"Aye. You are content to finish it."

"That's so," he grinned.

We retraced our steps through the wood, mounted our palfreys, rode across the meadow to the road, and entered Bampton an hour later, at the ninth hour. Arthur led our beasts to the marshalsea while I walked to Galen House.

At the bridge across Shill Brook I stopped to gaze into the stream. There had been little rain for several weeks, so the brook was not high, and its flow was slow. My stomach again growled, so I did not linger upon the bridge, but hastened to Church View Street and my belated dinner.

My lips were yet some swollen and tender, and this Kate knew, so a soft pottage again awaited me. I would be well pleased to consume something more substantial when I was healed. A roasted capon and wheaten loaf would be pleasant.

Kate held her tongue until I had eaten my fill, then asked of my discoveries in Kencott.

"I went to speak to a man who may have known of hidden things, but discovered that he is dead."

"So if he knew of hidden things, they will remain hidden."

"Aye, unless some other man also knows of secret matters."

"Would such a man also be in danger?"

"You come readily to the point," I said.

Kate smiled. "Perhaps, being wed to a bailiff, I am beginning to think like one."

"Ah, I trust not. One person mistrustful of others is enough for a family."

"You said that the dead man may have known of hidden things. Is there a reason to believe that the knowledge led to his death?"

I told Kate of the circumstances of Henry Thryng's death, and of discovering the boggy place where it seemed likely that monkshood plants had been uprooted. She shuddered.

"I've heard of the poison," she said. "'Twould be an evil way to die."

"There are few pleasant ways to pass from this life to the next."

"Aye," she agreed. "Perhaps that is why men fear death so… not for what may be their fate in the next life, but for the pain of the transit."

I spent the remainder of the day playing in the toft with Bessie and healing my wounds in the setting sun. Kate's stitchery itched less than a day or two in the past, and my face and ribs were fading from purple to a pale yellow. This was an improvement which did not seem so, for neither color is complimentary to my features.

I was not much hungry for supper that day, so after a light meal of maslin loaf and cheese I walked to the castle and sought Arthur. While chasing Bessie about the toft an idea had come to me. It is possible to frolic with a child while one's mind is occupied with other concerns. A two-year-old does not know or care. I told Arthur to have our palfreys ready by the third hour on the morrow.

Next morn my lips were reduced enough in size that I consumed my maslin loaf with little discomfort. I placed two more loaves and a flagon of ale into a sack and when Kate looked to me with a question in her eyes I explained that if the disturbed earth which Arthur and I had found was indeed a place where monkshood had been uprooted, there was likely enough of the plant taken to poison more than one man. If I was to perish in Kencott in mysterious circumstances Lord Gilbert would, no doubt, take vengeance upon the guilty, if they were discovered. That would be of little comfort to me or Kate. When I finished the explanation for why I did not want to eat or drink whilst in Kencott, Kate shuddered and clasped me close. My ribs were yet sore, but I did not care.

Chapter 11

Our palfreys were accustomed to the journey, so required little guidance as Arthur and I traveled again to Kencott. I intended to call first at the church, to again seek the clerk. This also was a procedure with which the beasts were familiar. They turned toward the lych gate and halted where they had been tied the day before.

No priest will tell of what he has learned in the confessional, nor should he. And no clerk would know of the matters his priest had uncovered. But a clerk might know who had recently confessed.

Most men seek absolution a few times each year, no more. But it had occurred to me while entertaining Bessie that a man who had committed a grievous sin might wish to confess it and seek pardon and penance soon after his crime. No man would wish to die with unconfessed murder upon his conscience. How many thousands of years in purgatory might he be assigned – if such a place exists for the unshriven?

I might not learn of any man's confession of murder, of either Randle Mainwaring or Henry Thryng, but I might discover who had sought confession and absolution. The bailiff's death was distant enough that surely many men had visited the confessional box since his demise near to St. John's Day, but Henry was newly dead. Life is uncertain. A man who slays another has evidence of that, and might seek his penance before some tragic event ends his own life.

St. George's Church was empty. Two houses stood directly across the road from the church. I had seen the village priest enter the larger of the two. I guessed that the clerk made his home in the meaner dwelling.

I rapped upon the door of this smaller house and a few moments later it swung open. A woman stared through the opening at me. A child clung to the hem of her cotehardie.

I was temporarily speechless. "I beg pardon," I said when I had found my voice. "I seek the clerk of yon church."

Before I could apologize more for troubling the woman she said, "I'll fetch 'im."

The folk of Kencott, along with priest and clerk, likely spoke of this woman as the clerk's housekeeper. But all know that many such men in holy orders keep women. This is not held against them so long as they are faithful to the woman. Perhaps, should I pound upon the door to the priest's house, a "housekeeper" would greet me there also, I thought.

The clerk approached his door, blinked in the sunlight, saw who stood before him, and greeted me. He showed no sign of embarrassment that I had uncovered his living arrangement. Perhaps the woman really was but a housekeeper. Perhaps some day I will be made chancellor of England.

"I would speak to you privily," I said, and looked both ways to see if any man approached upon the road. "My man will take our beasts to your toft. I'd sooner no man know of this conversation."

The clerk was no fool. "For your sake, or mine?" he said.

"Both."

"Tell him then to do so, and enter."

I did.

Brilliant sunshine passing through the oiled skins of the clerk's windows illuminated the chamber as well as it was ever likely to be. The clerk called to his woman for ale, then pointed to a bench and invited me to sit.

I trusted this clerk more than any other man of Kencott, but was resolved to take none of his ale. But when the woman appeared she held an ewer in one hand and two cups in another. She poured ale from the ewer into the cups, then rested the ewer upon a table. If I was to consume the poison of monkshood by drinking the ale, the clerk would join me in death before the day was done.

I thought this unlikely. The fellow seized a cup and took a great gulp of ale, wiped his lips with the back of his hand, then drank again.

"One moment," I said. "My man will have a thirst."

I took the cup before me to Arthur, who had led the palfreys into the toft behind the house, and explained to him that he need not fear quenching his thirst. I then asked for another cup of the clerk's woman. This I filled from the ewer, then resumed my place upon the bench. I did not ask the clerk or his woman to take ale to Arthur as I did not want the ewer to leave its place.

But the ewer had left my sight whilst I took the cup to Arthur. I drank sparingly. You see what I mean about bailiffs becoming suspicious of all men.

"Of what do you wish to speak?" the clerk said between swallows of ale. 'Twas good ale, not watered. Either the town possessed a good ale wife, or the clerk's woman brewed well.

"Henry Thryng died in some agony," I said.

"So I have heard," the clerk replied.

"I was told where I might find monkshood growing nearby."

"You think..." the clerk exclaimed, and set his cup down upon the table.

"Don't know," I shrugged. "My man and I found the place yesterday. There is sign there that some vegetation was uprooted and not long ago."

"Where monkshood grows?"

"Aye. Many of the plants remain."

"Who would poison Henry? He did not ill treat Albreda... least, not that I've heard."

"Would you have heard?"

"Do you know of Bampton men who beat their wives?" the clerk asked.

"Aye, I do."

"'Tis impossible for a man to do so without others learning of it in villages like Kencott and Bampton. For one thing, the women make such an awful screeching that half the village will hear."

"When does your priest hear confessions?" I asked.

The clerk's eyes narrowed at this change of subject. "You seek absolution here rather than in Bampton?"

"Nay. What days?"

"Monday mornings. You think Henry was poisoned and the felon will have confessed to Father Kendrick? He'll not tell you, even if 'tis so."

"I know. I only wish to learn who has visited the confessional since Henry died."

"Ah, I see. You think amongst those who have sought absolution there may be a murderer?"

"Perhaps. Were you about the church last Monday to see who entered the confessional?"

"Aye, most of the morning."

I waited for the clerk to continue, but he was silent. He stared at the glowing skin stretched across his window. I knew his thoughts. Would he betray the confessional if he told me who had visited Father Kendrick, even though neither of us would know what was said by any of the confessors? Would a refusal to give me names mean that a murderer might go free?

"You must weigh justice against the sanctity of the confessional," I said.

"Perhaps none of those who went to Father Kendrick had anything to do with a felony," he said.

"Then you will do no harm by naming them. Only my time will be wasted seeking a murderer where there is none."

"If you believe that, why ask for names?"

"I do not so think. I say only that it may be so. I know not what to think but that a dead man was found in Bampton's St. John's Day fire and 'tis my duty to seek justice for the slain."

The clerk again fell silent. Then he finally spoke. "Will any man know how you discovered those who sought absolution Monday? Will Father Kendrick know?"

"I will tell no one – not even Arthur."

"Arthur?"

"He who stands in your toft with our palfreys. Even Lord Gilbert will not know."

I felt confident in this assurance. Lord Gilbert seldom troubles himself with matters he has delegated to me. He is interested in the conclusion of such business, but how the conclusion is arrived at is of little interest to him. I suspect the same is true of others of his station.

"Alfred Maskylene was first, I think, then Maud Yardley. Thomas Dyer, Agnes Cribs, Geoffrey deMeaux... Aylmer Smith also."

"Six of the village?"

"Aye... no, Jaket Wheatstone, also."

I waited silently while the clerk rummaged through his memory, seeking any others who might have entered St. George's Church Monday morning.

"Seven, I think. That was all."

"Have any of these quarreled with Henry Thryng?"

"Henry was likely to quarrel with anyone."

"You said that you've lived in Kencott for a year."

"Aye, near about."

"Henry was in dispute with many others in that time?"

"Mostly with Bertran Muth."

"Bertran had accused him of shearing a fleece and stealing a furrow, I'm told."

"Don't know what the issue was. Only that they come to blows an' the reeve had to sort it out."

"In Bertran's favor?"

"Aye," the clerk agreed.

"On another matter," I said. "I was told that Randle Mainwaring was high born."

The clerk was silent for some time. "'Tis a matter best not spoken of in Kencott," he finally said, "but in private."

"Why so? What difference who a bailiff's ancestors were?"

"Not sure. Been here a year, as you know, and in that time I've heard it spoken of but once."

"What was said?"

"Hah... only that such talk must not be bandied about."

"And so it isn't?"

"Nay, but perhaps in the dark, when folk lie abed."

"Are you not curious about why the matter is considered unfit for conversation?"

"Not curious enough to get in trouble for asking improper questions. I've a good life here. I wish to keep it so. Perhaps, when Father Kendrick dies, I will be named to replace him."

"St. George's Church is in Sir John's gift?" I asked.

"Aye."

"You suspect it is he who is opposed to a discussion of Randle Mainwaring's lineage?"

"Who else would care?"

"Who, indeed?"

I bid the clerk "Good day," sought Arthur, and was careful not to depart the toft with our beasts until I saw that the road between the church and the clerk's house was vacant. The reeve had not been hospitable the day before, but what I wished to know I could discover from no other.

"Overseeing boon work," the reeve's wife said when I called at his house. Sir John's barley and oat fields were nearly all harvested. One more day, the reeve had told his wife.

The woman directed us to the field being cut, and when Arthur and I drew near I saw a dozen men in line abreast swinging scythes across the brown, ripened grain. Behind them women with rakes spread the cut stalks so the barley would dry evenly. I did not at first identify the reeve, for he worked with the others. A reeve who was a villein, not a tenant. Sir John did indeed live in the past.

As Arthur and I approached the harvesters I turned in the saddle and saw that we were followed. A lad of perhaps twelve years sat upon a small cart which was drawn by a shaggy runcie. When the horse reached the edge of the barley field the youth guided it from the road, across a shallow ditch, and through a gated opening in the stone wall which enclosed the field.

Behind the lad upon the cart was a large earthen pot. The youth guided his beast around the edge of the barley field, and when it came near the harvesters I saw them lay down their scythes and walk toward the cart. Perhaps my question for the reeve was to be answered before I asked it.

I told Arthur that we would dismount. We tied the palfreys to a bush and leaned upon the wall to watch. If any man or woman saw us they paid no attention. They regarded only the cart and its burden.

The laborers formed a queue, the lad jumped down from his perch and produced two cups, and each man and woman in turn took a cup, dipped it into the pot, then drank deeply of the contents. Sir John had provided ale to quench the thirst of the dusty villeins.

I had meant to ask the reeve if Henry Thryng had consumed food or drink whilst at boon work the morning of his death that his wife would not have known of. It now seemed certain that he had. But no other laborer had died that day. I would surely have heard of it had there been other deaths in the village. If Henry consumed the poison of monkshood, how was it that no other did, if they drank from the same pot?

I watched as all of those in the barley field drank then renewed their labor, and saw no curious behavior which might tell how one man of such a company could swallow poison while the others did not. Perhaps the reeve could tell me if, the day Henry died, the ale had been offered in some other fashion. Perhaps he could, but perhaps he would not.

One of the villeins, then. Perhaps Bertran Muth's brother-in-law was among the laborers. I resolved to wait along the road to the village and see if one of the men walked to Beatrice's door when his day's work was done. I told Arthur, and we led our beasts back from whence we had come.

Two strange men loitering about such a village as Kencott are likely to attract unwanted attention, especially if one is constructed like a wine cask and the other's face is sewn together like a tattered kirtle. I decided to go straight to Beatrice's house, ask of her husband, and await him there if he was among those at boon work. He was.

"What's this about, then?" Beatrice asked. "I know why you're 'ere. Folk in Kencott been talkin' of it."

"What do they say?"

"You ain't satisfied that Bertran murdered Randle."

"Does that trouble your neighbors?"

"Dunno," she shrugged. "Don't trouble me, unless you think my Richard has somethin' to do with murder."

"I do not, but I do wish to speak to him of some matter which he may have observed."

"Be 'ome for 'is dinner soon."

Arthur and I sat upon a crude bench in the woman's yard and awaited her husband's arrival. The reeve must have kept the harvesters beyond noon, for the dusty, sweat-stained fellow did not appear 'till past midday. Perhaps the reeve wished to complete work in the barley field before discharging the laborers. He'd not be chosen reeve again if he did such a thing often.

Richard saw us but paid no heed. Rather, he went straight to a bucket and splashed water from it upon his face and arms to flush away grime. Only when he had completed his ablutions did he turn to me.

"You be the bailiff of Bampton what's been askin' questions of folk about Randle?" he said.

"I am. Now I have questions for you."

"Ask," he said. "I'd no quarrel with 'im."

"Were there folk of Kencott who did?"

"You're a bailiff. You 'ave quarrels with villeins an' tenants an' such?"

"Foolish question," I smiled. "But 'tis not of Randle Mainwaring I wish to speak to you. This morn, an hour and more past, a cart appeared in the barley field where you and others were cutting grain. Did the pot upon it contain ale?"

"Aye. Sir John don't make us work on 'is demesne lands all day, so gives us no dinner... but 'e does give us to drink. Welcome it is, too."

"I'm sure. Cast your mind back to the day Henry Thryng died. Was all as it was today? Men and women formed a queue, dipped from the pot, and drank, one after the other?"

"Aye, just like that."

"There was no difference? Nothing changed?"

The man paused. "Well, one thing was not quite the same."

"Tell me."

"Reeve told us to cease our work when cart came, an' slake our thirst, but when Henry joined the queue reeve called 'im to speak of some matter. Don't know what."

"So Henry Thryng did not drink of the ale?" Here was startling news.

"Oh, aye. Henry had 'is ale – just not right then. When all others 'ad their ale reeve sent Henry to get 'is drink. Right then the horse give a leap like it'd been fly-bit. Upset the kettle, an' what ale was left got poured to ground. Wrathful, was Henry."

"How, then," I asked, "did Henry get his ale?"

"Reeve cursed the lad an' sent 'im back to Sir John's brew house for more."

"When he returned did others also drink more, or only Henry?"

"Only Henry, methinks."

"What of the reeve? Did he drink with the others, or after Henry had had his share?"

Richard tugged at his beard and stared thoughtfully into the distance. "Don't remember Jaket havin' any ale that day."

"Neither with you, from the first pot, nor with Henry, from the second?" I asked.

"Nay. Not that I recall. Soon as Henry'd 'ad 'is fill, reeve sent the lad on 'is way. I'd 'ave liked more ale, was there more in the pot, but reeve sent the lad from the field."

You'd not have wanted more of that ale, I thought. But this I did not say to the man. Not yet. It has always seemed to me that the closer I come to resolving a matter, the more circumspect I must become with the information I have accumulated.

"Do not speak of this conversation with any man," I cautioned Richard.

"Why not? Would it be dangerous to do so?" he asked.

"It might," I replied. Although likely more dangerous for me than for him. But he did not need to know that.

Arthur and I left the man to his dinner and sought our

beasts. A small stream flowed near to the road a hundred or so paces from the church, and we led the palfreys there to drink. Arthur spoke as we walked.

"Reckon we know how Henry Thryng got 'is bellyache."

"Aye. But we need to know why."

"He'd no money to steal. An' seein' 'is wife, I doubt any man would slay 'im so's to wed 'is widow."

"I grant you that," I agreed.

"To silence 'im, then?"

"Likely. He was sent to Burford to sell six capons. Hardly worth the journey. There he saw Bertran Muth selling Randle Mainwaring's horse."

"You suppose that wasn't so?" Arthur said.

"It has crossed my mind."

"Me too. Then you come to Kencott an' begin askin' questions which made some folk unhappy."

"Indeed."

"Unhappy enough that they attacked you on the road an' did away with Henry Thryng before you had a chance to speak to 'im, after Lord Gilbert told Sir John you was to get what help you needed. Same folks, you suppose?"

"Seems a safe assumption. A man would have to be witless," I said, "not to guess that when I returned to Kencott one of the first men I would seek would be Henry."

Arthur looked about him while the palfreys drank. "Closer we get to findin' who them folks is, more likely they'll try to stop you, an' stop folk from talkin' to you."

"Aye. We must be on our guard. 'Tis why I told Richard to speak to no man of what we have now learned from him."

Chapter 12

'Twas convenient for someone that the horse which drew the cart carrying ale to Sir John's boon workers shied enough to upset the cart's burden. This event was surely planned, and if so 'twas no stray insect which caused the beast to bolt. The lad upon the cart would know.

"Come," I said to Arthur when the palfreys had drunk their fill. "We must speak to Richard again."

Arthur looked to me with a puzzled expression but has known me long enough that he no longer troubles himself with my unpredictable ways.

The villein was just finishing his pottage when we reappeared at his door. I thought he might be displeased to have his meal interrupted, but if so, he hid it well. Perhaps his meal was not pleasing enough to demand enthusiastic consumption.

"The lad who brought ale to you this day," I said as Richard wiped his mouth with the back of his hand, "was it the same who did so the day the runcie was startled and overturned the ale pot?"

"Aye. Same as every day."

"Who is it? Where can the lad be found?"

"Walter, Edwin Smith's lad."

"Edwin is the village smith?"

"Aye. Hires out Walter as stableboy to Sir John."

I thanked Richard for this added information, bid him "Good day" again, and mounted my palfrey. Arthur did likewise, and followed as I set off for the smith's forge. We had passed the place several times that day.

We found the smith at work, his dinner apparently consumed. He looked up from his work as Arthur and I dismounted, but continued banging away upon a glowing bar until it had cooled. Only then did he leave his anvil and speak.

"G'day... how may I serve you?" the fellow said in a cordial tone. This was unlike Bampton's smith, who greets all men with a scowl. Especially bailiffs.

"You are Edwin?" I asked, knowing already the answer. Such a village would not have two smiths.

"Aye. An' you be the fellow from Bampton what's nosin' about, seekin' to learn of Randle."

"Aye. I am Master Hugh de Singleton, bailiff to Lord Gilbert Talbot at Bampton. Village gossip has traveled before me, I see."

"Not gossip, so to speak."

"Oh? How did you learn of me?"

"Jaket come by a few days past. Said you might call."

"What else did the reeve say?"

"I was to answer your questions, but no more."

"That will suffice," I said. "Your son, Walter, serves in Sir John's stable, I've heard."

"Aye. Likes beasts, does Walter."

"When will he return from his work at the stables?"

The smith, whose manner had been agreeable, suddenly turned chill. "What have you to do with my son?" he said.

"Very little. But he witnessed an event a few days past of which I seek knowledge. You may listen to my questions and his response."

"Oh." The smith relaxed and his demeanor again became amenable. "Takes 'is dinner with other of Sir John's pages an' grooms, then returns 'ome 'bout the ninth hour."

"Not long, then, 'till he'll appear."

"Aye, not long."

"We will rest ourselves under yon tree," I said, "and await the lad."

This seemed agreeable to the smith, who turned to his bellows and began pumping vigorously.

Arthur and I sat in the shade of a beech tree which overhung the smith's forge and consumed our loaves. Arthur was soon snoring peacefully. I interrupted his slumber when I saw the smith's lad approach.

The child sauntered along the road, idly kicking a twig in

the manner of the young who see before them no impediment to continued days of health and pleasure.

The lad turned to enter his father's forge with Arthur and I close behind. With the keen ears of youth he heard our footsteps behind him. He turned with some alarm.

"Walter," the smith said, "here is a man who would speak to you."

"'Bout what?" the lad said.

"Your work for Sir John," I said.

"Ain't supposed to speak of that."

"Why not? Who has forbidden you from doing so?"

"Jaket... an' Geoffrey."

"The reeve, and Sir John's son?"

"Aye."

"What reason did they give that you must not talk of your work in Sir John's stables?"

"Said some troublesome man was vexing our village. If 'e got no help from lads like me he'd go back to whence 'e come an' leave honest folk alone. You be 'im?"

"Aye, I am the troublesome man. But the reeve was wrong about one thing. I will not return to Bampton and leave murder unpunished."

"Murder? But we hung Bertran."

"There may be other felons about. You can help to root them out."

"But..."

"Not what the reeve said, eh?"

"Nor Geoffrey."

"Your duties have been increased, I've heard, since harvest began. You now take a pot of ale to folk who work on Sir John's demesne lands."

"Saw you watchin' this mornin', leanin' on the wall."

"Indeed, so you did. A few days past your beast jerked the cart and caused the pot of ale to tip."

Walter said nothing, apparently accepting my explanation of the event.

"Why did the beast do so? Old runcies are not usually so quick to plunge about if startled."

The lad was yet silent, offering no explanation for his charge's unpredictable behavior. I decided to offer an explanation and watch his reaction.

"Who was it gave you the sharpened stick and told you to poke the beast in the rump?"

Walter's face became white. He looked to his father, who, as I had agreed, was listening to the conversation.

"Answer Master Hugh," the smith said softly.

"Said I was to do as told an' hold my tongue. Did I not, I'd suffer for it."

"Who said this?" I asked.

"Jaket."

"He told you that he and another man would delay getting their ale, and when they approached, you were to alarm your beast with the stick and cause the pot to overturn? Is that how 'twas?"

"Aye, like that. Jaket said as how he would then curse me, but I was to pay no mind. I'd be told to return to the brewhouse for more ale, an' take it back for them as hadn't got any."

"The ale wife filled the pot again? Did she expect you?"

"Nay. 'Twas Geoffrey what give me more ale to take back to barley field."

"Say nothing of this conversation," I said.

The smith looked from me to his son, then spoke. "Is Walter in danger?"

"He may be if Geoffrey or the reeve knows what he has said."

"Why so?"

"The man who drank from the second pot of ale your son took to the barley field was Henry Thryng."

The smith crossed himself and stepped back as if Arthur had swatted him aside the head. He turned to his son and said, "Was that the day Henry died?"

"Aye," Walter whispered.

"Then peril walks Kencott streets," the smith said.

"It does," I agreed. "I urge you to take no food or drink from

126

any man. Walter, continue your work for Sir John as in the past, but neither eat nor drink anything Geoffrey or the reeve may offer you."

"But... but that's where I eat me dinner, with Sir John's servants."

"Eat only what you see others eat – nothing else. Soup from the same pot as others, bread from loaves you choose, not given to you."

Walter stammered that he understood and would do as I advised. Arthur and I departed the forge leaving a frightened man and his son behind. Well might they be.

Arthur and I had learned much this day. I decided that 'twould be best to return to Bampton, consider what I had discovered, and make plans to return next day. I admit that as we passed through the wood east of Alvescot where I had been waylaid, I glanced about uneasily.

I left Arthur and the palfreys at the castle and walked to Galen House. Again I stopped at Shill Brook to gaze into the stream. The psalmist has told men that they should "Be still and know that I am God." I admit that in the busyness of the day, I had not considered Him nor sought guidance of the Lord Christ. I amended the fault there upon the bridge.

I was sure of the cause of Henry Thryng's death. How to prove a knight's son or reeve was the felon was another matter. And why would Geoffrey or Jaket slay the villein? Because Henry might tell me something of Randle Mainwaring's death? Probably, but what?

Thomas Attewood said Mainwaring was high born. What of it? Folk in Kencott and Broadwell seemed to know of the bailiff's ancestry, but chose not to speak of it. Why so?

My dinner had been simple, so Kate prepared let lardes for our supper. My appetite had increased in the past days as my swollen lips decreased, and my loose tooth did not interfere with enjoyment of the meal.

I told Kate what I had learned that day in Kencott, and she asked a question I should have thought of.

"You think the smith's lad might know something of the dead bailiff's horse? You said the beast must have been cared for somewhere for a month. Who better to do so than a stableboy?"

"I shall ask the lad tomorrow. The reeve and Geoffrey deMeaux seem sure to have planned Henry Thryng's death. Perhaps they did murder of Randle Mainwaring also, and hid the bailiff's horse in the stables 'till they found a way to use the beast to turn men's suspicions to another."

"'Twas one of them, then, who set men to attack you upon the road."

"Mayhap. They saw me coming closer to the truth of Mainwaring's death than I knew at the time, if the bailiff's death was at their hands."

"But why would Geoffrey slay his father's bailiff? Had the man done something to anger him?"

"If so, no man of Kencott has mentioned it. Perhaps I have not asked the proper questions."

As I lay abed that night some of the unasked questions occurred to me, and I was eager for dawn so that I might once again seek felons in Kencott.

Arthur seemed in particularly good humor next day, humming to himself as we set out from Bampton Castle, past Cowley's Corner and on toward Alvescot. When he did not explain his cheerfulness I asked. Travel and seeking felons has never affected me in such a way.

"Agnes told me last night I'm to be a father... again."

Agnes is Arthur's second wife, Cicily having died of plague more than a year past. Arthur's son serves Lord Gilbert as page. I know little of his daughter but that she wed a tenant of Osney Abbey and lives near to Standlake.

"I give you joy," I said. "We must use more care than ever in seeking a murderer. We have now three small children between us which must not become orphans. A man who already faces a noose will not hold back from another murder or two."

"Aye," Arthur said. "Can't hang a man more'n once."

The Kencott church tower came into view and I told Arthur

that we would seek the clerk there again. Walter would be at his duties at Sir John's stables, and for the lad's safety I did not want him to be seen talking to me. So I would wait until he completed his work at the stables and seek him at his father's forge to ask of the bailiff's horse.

We tied the palfreys to the lych gate, entered the porch, and there met the priest. I had wished to avoid him, sensing that he would be reluctant to offer any information detrimental to his patron. But he would know the answer to my question, and perhaps knew of Lord Gilbert's demand that my inquiries receive cooperation. I decided that boldness would serve best.

"Ah, you are well met," I said. "I give you good day."

"You have returned," the priest said. This was obvious, and was spoken in an inhospitable tone.

"Where is your clerk? I have some business at the church for which I require assistance... but you need not trouble yourself with the matter. Your clerk will be able to help me."

"What business is this?" the priest replied.

"I intend to search through your documents chest."

"But that is locked against thieves and forgers."

"Get the key when you seek your clerk. Have him bring it. You need not trouble yourself further."

"What do you seek?"

"If I find it, I will be sure to tell you," I said.

"I must know why you wish to explore my documents chest," the priest insisted.

"No," I said, with my lips as thin as I could make them. "You do not need to know. You need to do as Lord Gilbert Talbot has required, and that is to offer whatever aid I seek."

The priest seemed ready to argue the point, then relented, shrugged, and said, "I will send Simon with the key."

When Arthur and I stood alone in the church he spoke. "What can you think to find in a chest which will tell of Randle or Henry?"

"Nothing much of Henry. He had nothing to leave in a will. Randle, however, may be a different matter."

"Oh? You think the bailiff might have left enough property that some man was willing to slay him to get it? Can't be many folk who'd inherit from a bachelor bailiff."

"Nay. Thomas Attewood said that Randle was high born. I'd like to know who left goods or lands to him rather than the other way 'round."

"Why? A man'd not be slain by an ancestor."

"Might be for an ancestor's decision."

"Ah, a grandfather left 'im somethin' that another wants."

"Something like that, perhaps."

The priest took his time in seeking and sending his clerk. 'Twas near to noon when the man appeared. In the meantime Arthur and I had found the documents chest under the tower and moved it under a window where, when the key arrived, we would be better able to sort through the deeds and wills and other chronicles stored there.

The clerk came near, turned to glance at the door to the porch, then said, "Father Kendrick is displeased."

"I am grieved," I said. "Have you the key to this chest?"

"Aye. What is it you seek?"

"I'm not sure. I hope to learn something of Randle Mainwaring."

"Ah. Let me guess. You believe the rumors of his lineage may be found true or false, and the discovery may add something to... to what? Bertran killed 'im for 'is horse. Didn't 'e?"

"The bailiff's bones were found in the ashes of the St. John's Day blaze in Bampton," I reminded him. "Bertran did not try to sell Randle's beast 'till Lammastide. Where did he keep the animal for that time? How did he feed it? Where would a poor villein get coin enough for oats? No man saw the horse grazing upon a meadow."

"Oh... aye. Well then, I will open the chest and you may seek what you will."

It seemed likely that the chest would hold many records of folk in Kencott. Reading so many documents would be an arduous task, for which Arthur could be of no help. The man cannot read. I hoped to press the clerk to assist the search.

The clerk produced the key, a large iron fixture nearly the size of my palm, and inserted it into the lock. I believe this chest was rarely opened, for the lock did not turn readily, and when it finally did, the hinges squealed when the clerk raised the lid.

Arthur and I had found the chest quite heavy, which did not surprise us much, as it was nearly as long as I am tall, and as wide and deep as my arm is long. But the weight of the chest was greater than the oak of which it was constructed and the iron with which it was bound. It was nearly full of parchment documents, many dark with age and the ink faded. I looked into the opening and felt like closing the lid upon what seemed an impossible task.

"What do you wish for me to do?" the clerk asked.

"There seems to be no order to the documents stored here," I said, "but that the newest are on top and the oldest near the bottom. Take a bundle and sort through, seeking names of gentlemen of Kencott: deMeaux, and also Mainwaring."

"Mainwaring?"

"If Randle was high born, there must be such a name somewhere in Kencott's past."

"Oh, aye."

"What should I do?" Arthur asked.

"Sit in the porch, enjoy the sun, and watch for who may pass the church. The priest is not pleased about this, and he may tell others of what we are doing, who will also be unhappy."

Arthur departed for the porch whilst the clerk and I bent to the chest, withdrew pages of Kencott's past, and rapidly searched through them seeking recognizable names in introductions and preambles.

After an hour of this my back was aching and my stomach growling. The clerk stood, walked to a window, and peered through it. When he saw my curious expression he said, "Sundial. I must ring for the noon Angelus."

He left for the base of the tower and a moment later I heard the church bell sound. When the clerk had completed this duty I told him to go to his dinner, sent Arthur to my palfrey to retrieve our sack of loaves and ale, and sat in the sun of the porch to ponder the misspent morning. I considered quitting what seemed a waste of time. Evidently the sounding of the church bell for the noon Angelus was but a formality in Kencott. The priest did not appear to officiate at the service, nor did any parishioners seek the church.

After consuming my loaf I sent Arthur to water the palfreys at the roadside brook and returned to the church and the chest.

I withdrew another bundle of rolled documents as thick as my forearm and began to sort through them, discarding one after another as I glanced at prologues and titles and headings. Near the bottom of this stack a document caught my eye, and rather than casting it aside I read the first lines.

The document told of the death, in February of 1342, of Amice deMeaux, widow of John deMeaux, who had predeceased his wife by nine years. Amice was the daughter and heiress, according to the certificate, of Sir Roger d'Oilly, lord of Kencott, who had died in 1309. Amice's heir, the document said, was her son, John, born in 1324. This son would be the rotund Sir John whose manor Kencott now was.

But most intriguing was a brief sentence in the last paragraph. Amice deMeaux had been twice a widow. Her first husband had died in 1321. His name was Sir Harold Mainwaring.

The clerk returned from his dinner as I studied the document, and asked what so captured my attention.

"Amice was a wealthy woman, I think," the clerk said. "Heiress to a landed knight, and widow of another before she wed Sir John's father. That's how Sir John came to be lord of Kencott, then: through 'is mother an' grandfather."

"Aye. But what of her marriage to her first husband, Sir Harold Mainwaring?"

"Oh... Mainwaring. I wonder did she have children by that first husband?"

"A worthy question. Do you know of any other man named Mainwaring hereabouts but for Randle?"

"Nay. Never heard of the name but for the bailiff."

"Take another bundle of documents and seek the name Mainwaring."

An hour later, near to the bottom of the chest, the clerk found what we sought. "Here," he said triumphantly. "This parchment says that Harold Mainwaring died upon the fourth day of November in 1321, leaving his wife, Amice, and son, Roger."

The clerk handed me the document and I studied it closely. Roger, according to this record, had been born in 1320 and was but a year old when his father died.

"'Tis no will," I said. "Only a record of the man's death."

In such circumstance the law requires that a man's possessions be left one-third to his wife and two-thirds to his son. But 'twas Amice who had inherited Kencott, not her first husband, Harold. How, then, did the law apply? Was Harold Mainwaring's will gone missing?

Here was startling news. When Amice deMeaux died, her heir was her son, John deMeaux. But before she wed a second time her heir would have been a Roger Mainwaring. Was this man Randle's father? Was this the tangle men spoke of when they said that Randle Mainwaring was high born?

By the ninth hour we had emptied the chest. No more of Kencott's records could be found bearing the name Mainwaring. I replaced the documents, as much as possible, in the chest in the order in which they were removed but for the parchments which bore the names of Amice deMeaux and Sir Harold Mainwaring. These I placed atop the other documents, so that if I wished to consult them again they would be at hand.

I closed the lid and the clerk produced the key from his pouch and locked the chest. The day had not been misspent, as I had at first feared when I looked into the opened chest. I had learned many things. But how this knowledge might serve to identify and convict a felon was yet unclear.

'Twas near the time when Walter Smith would be set free of his duties at the stables. I thanked the clerk for his aid, bid him "Good day," and with Arthur set out for the smith's forge.

I told Arthur of the discovery of the names deMeaux and

Mainwaring, and asked if any man had shown overmuch interest in the church while passing by upon the road.

"Nay, not many folk about. Most is in the fields, either doin' Sir John's boon work or harvestin' their own crops. Saw but three men pass all the while you was in the church, an' they paid little attention but to look at our beasts tied to the lych gate."

Walter had not arrived yet at his father's forge when Arthur and I greeted the smith. The fellow glanced to the sun, then the shadow of the tree near to the forge, and said, "Be 'ere soon. Sir John don't usually keep 'im past time."

Someone did. An hour and more passed, the smith looking up from his hammer and anvil every few minutes to peer down the road, then, when his son was not in view, he would again gaze at the sun and the shadow of the tree as it lengthened across the road.

Arthur and I had sat ourselves beneath the tree to await the lad's appearance. I became nearly as apprehensive as the smith when the shadow of St. George's Church tower reached the forge, yet there was no sign of the child.

The smith removed his apron, set down his hammer and the hinge he was making, then said, "I'm off to the manor 'ouse. See what's keepin' Walter. Mayhap he got kicked, or bit."

"If so, return and tell me of it. I am a surgeon," I said, "and can help the lad."

I might have traveled with the smith, I suppose, but thought for the smith's sake 'twould be best for the man not to be seen in my company. As it happened, my concern was well founded, if too late.

The hour grew late, although the sun was yet high enough above the trees that we should have light to travel back to Bampton. I was loath to depart Kencott 'till Walter was found. I was uneasy about the alteration of the lad's schedule and what it might portend.

A quarter of an hour later, no more, the smith came into view, running. This was no good sign. The man was built like Arthur. Running is for men like me, fashioned like a beech sapling, rather than for men like Arthur and Edwin, who are assembled like wine casks.

"Gone," the smith gasped as he stumbled to a stop before us.

"Who? Walter?"

"Aye," he said. "Sir John said he'd not come to work today. I asked them as work in the stables. No one there's seen 'im all day. Thought 'e was 'ome, sick abed, the other lads said."

"How many pages does Sir John employ in his stables?" I asked.

"Three. I told the others 'e went off to the manor house this morn, as always. But they said 'e'd never come near. Sir John is sendin' 'is lads an' some others out to seek 'im. Ain't like Walter to do this."

"He has never run off before, as lads will sometimes do?" I asked. "'Tis a warm day. Is there a deeper place in yon brook where a boy might splash about on a warm day?"

"Nay. Walter's never shirked 'is tasks before... an' the brook's too shallow to drown in. No place more'n ankle deep."

"Men of Sir John's household are seeking Walter?" I asked.

"Aye. Come back to tell you an' 'is mother, an' now I'm goin' with others to search for 'im."

"Has the lad some hidden places where he and other boys of the village like to conceal themselves from their parents?"

"Likely. Lads'll do such things. But I don't know where they'd be."

"Other youths might. You should seek them and learn of where a lad might go if he wished to escape the supervision of his parents for an hour or two."

"I will do so. 'E'll get a good hidin' when I find 'im, if that's what 'e's done."

I sincerely hoped that Walter was going to receive that hiding, and in the near future. If he did not, it would mean that his absence from the stables this day was no misbehavior of his own but the work of some other man. Or men.

Chapter 13

"**W**hat shall we do?" Arthur said as Edwin hurried off toward the manor house to join the search for his son. "We could search with Sir John's men for an hour an' yet be to Bampton before dark."

"I think not. We do not know the hidden places near the village where lads might go, and I do not want to be seen too often with the smith. Many folk do not want us here, but due to Lord Gilbert's visit they can do nothing to prevent our casting about for evidence of a felony."

"We hope they can do nothing," Arthur said with a wry grin.

"Aye. But no man promised Lord Gilbert to do no harm to the smith, or to the clerk, and if they are thought to be in league with us some evil may befall them."

"Or Walter," Arthur said.

"Aye, or Walter. And if this has happened, you and me searching for the lad will be fruitless. He will be hidden away in some place where neither we nor any other men will find him."

"If Sir John's men is seekin' him, they'll know where others 'ave looked, an' Sir John an' Jaket an' Geoffrey'll know where the lad could be hid so no man will find 'im. You reckon Walter's alive?"

This was a worry I was unwilling to speak. If the child was dead, his death would be upon my hands, for those who wished to silence him would only do so to prevent me learning more of what the lad knew. I wished to find another of the stableboys to ask of the bailiff's horse, but if I did, would that youth also go missing?

I was much conflicted. My heart told me that Arthur and I should follow Edwin and join the search for Walter. My head said that this would be unwise and of no value, perhaps might even be harmful.

I followed my head and told Arthur we would return to Bampton for the night, then come again to Kencott in the morning to learn if Walter had been found.

Kate thought that Arthur and I should have joined the search for Walter. I had told her of the day while consuming a supper of stewed capon, and when I was done, with both tale and capon, she rendered her verdict. Kate has a soft heart for those in peril, which is fitting for a woman, so long as soft heart is not found with a soft head as well.

When I explained the danger which might come to those in Kencott who were seen too often with me, Kate reluctantly agreed that it may have been wise to leave the search for Walter to village residents. Kate might be soft-hearted, but she is also practical.

I was eager to return to Kencott, so when Kate's rooster announced the dawn I hurriedly donned cotehardie and cap, broke my fast with a loaf and cheese, then hastened to the castle.

Arthur was ready with two palfreys. With a sack of loaves and ale over my beast's rump for our dinner, we spurred our horses to quicken their pace and entered Kencott but an hour later. I went straight to the smith's forge. It was cold. Edwin had not begun his day's work. This was not a good sign.

The smith and his wife lived in a house behind his forge. I went to the door and pounded upon it, fearing what I would discover.

A woman, red of eye and with puffy cheeks, opened to my knock. Here, I thought, was Walter's mother. Behind the woman I saw two small children of perhaps nine and five years of age. The older of the two looked up expectantly at me, and I understood that the child knew of his brother's disappearance. Even the youngest child, a lass, seemed fearful.

I asked for Edwin, not really expecting – after seeing his wife's haggard face – to find him at home. He was not.

"You be the bailiff from Bampton?" the woman asked.

"Aye. Has Walter been found?"

"Nay. Edwin's been home to break 'is fast, an' gone back to search for 'im. Been at it all night. Hope they find 'im now it's day."

"Aye, he should be found soon, now that the sun is up," I agreed. But in my heart I did not. A lad would not run off alone, giving no hint of his plan. Some other child in the village would have heard Walter speak of some grievance and his scheme to escape whatever oppression, real or imagined, which afflicted him. When such a youth heard that Walter was missing, would he hold his tongue? Even if Walter had pledged him to secrecy? Perhaps, but I had doubts.

Either Walter had hidden himself, or some man had hidden him. I was becoming convinced his disappearance was due to the latter explanation.

"I and my man will join the search," I said, and bowing to convention, bid the woman "Good day," although it was not.

"Thought you said we mustn't be seen havin' too much to do with the smith or his lad," Arthur said when we passed from the forge to the road.

"We must not," I shrugged, "but 'twill do no greater harm to think two more pairs of eyes are seeking her child. And I do intend we should join the search, but not with the others. We will seek the clerk."

"He may be with those who search for Walter."

"Aye, likely so. But his housekeeper may know where he has gone to seek the lad."

"You think he may know where he is?"

"He may have thoughts about where the lad could be hid, if he has not gone off of his own choice."

"I can think of only two men who would want to seize the lad," Arthur said, "if that's what has happened – Geoffrey or Jaket."

"Or Sir John," I said. "And if they have done so they'll be wise enough not to confine the lad in manor house or stables or barns. The clerk might know of other hidden places."

"Would the clerk not have gone to such a place already?" Arthur asked.

"He might, unless he felt constrained to wait for some opportune time."

"Ah. He did say that he has a good life in Kencott an' don't want to risk bein' sent away."

We reached the clerk's house as Arthur delivered this observation. I left him with the palfreys and pounded upon the door. The housekeeper soon appeared and, as I had assumed, told me that her employer was away, seeking a child missing from his home.

"Do you know where he searches?" I asked.

"Nay. Went off last evening, when 'e 'eard of the child bein' gone. Ain't been 'ome since."

"He has not returned to break his fast?"

"Nay," the woman said, and I saw a slight furrow go vertical between her eyebrows. She thought this odd. So did I. Even Walter's father had returned home for a loaf to strengthen him for continuing the search.

"When he returns tell him that Master Hugh seeks him."

"Where will you be found?"

A good question. I answered honestly. "I'll be about the village, seeking him. If Simon should return before I find him, be sure to tell him I have called and need to speak to him. What is Simon's surname?"

"Hode... Simon Hode."

Arthur and I led our beasts from the clerk's house. I had no more idea of where to seek the clerk than I had of where Walter might be. I decided to seek a thing more easily found: another lad near to Walter's age. We returned to the smith's house.

Walter's mother looked upon us dully. The cares of life will cause the sparkling eyes of youth, lass or lad, to someday lose their luster. To lose a child must surely dim the glow even more. I pray that Kate and I will never discover if this is so.

"Your lad Walter," I said. "Has he friends of his own years with whom he spends time? Perhaps a lad near his age who is also employed in Sir John's stables?"

"None as work in stables," the woman replied.

"Others, then?"

"John Woodman an' Walter's close."

"Whereabouts does John live?"

"House just beyond the reeve's. Mother's dead, an' Thomas'll likely be searchin' for Walter."

"Thomas?"

"Thomas Woodman, John's father. What you want with John?"

"He might know if there is a place where Walter might go."

"My Edwin already thought of that. John named two places but Walter wasn't at either of 'em."

"Mayhap the lad will have thought of some other place of concealment since then?"

The woman did not reply. Hope, if it had ever been strong within her, had become weak. "Mayhap," she finally said softly.

I did not bid the woman "Good day" when I turned to leave her door. It seemed absurd to do so. What, then? Should I have wished her a foul day? Of course not. 'Twas already bad enough without requesting that it become worse. Language fails at such times.

But not completely. I turned again and retraced my steps. The smith's wife stood yet in her doorway. "I pray that Walter will be found soon," I said, "and I and my man will do all we can to make it so."

The woman nodded and I saw a tear trace a path down her cheek. I am not at my best dealing with weeping females, so turned away and this time did not stop until I had mounted my palfrey.

"Where to?" Arthur asked as he also put a foot to stirrup.

"A house just beyond the reeve's house. 'Twill bring us close to Sir John's manor house, but that cannot be helped."

"An' he likely knows what we're about, anyway," Arthur said.

Thomas Woodman was evidently not a wealthy man. His house was small, little more than a hut, the thatching thin where it was not rotting. Daub had peeled from the wattles in many

140

places, and the toft contained only a small patch of onions and turnips and served as a home to three hens. If there was a rooster nearby he kept himself hid.

The door of this house stood open and so I called, "John... John Woodman," into the dim interior. A small, freckle-faced lad immediately appeared, and behind him two smaller children. These lasses peered around their brother to see who stood at their door.

"Is your father at home," I asked, "or does he search for Walter?"

"Lookin' for Walter," the boy said.

"Walter is your friend, so says his mother. I have just come from speaking to her."

I saw the lad's worried expression soften at the mention of Walter's mother. "Walter's father asked you last night, I'm told, if there was any place where you and Walter might hide from others. Some secret place lads like you know of, but no others."

"Told 'im 'Nay,'" John said.

Walter's mother had said that this lad had named two places where Walter might have gone. Why now would he say he had named no such places?

"Have you thought more on it this morning? Has any place come to mind that you might not have thought of last night?"

"Nay... an' I'm not to talk to you."

"Who am I, that you are not to speak to me?"

"You're the bailiff of some other village, 'ere to stir up trouble."

I could not fault the lad. Seeking a felon in Kencott had already brought trouble and was likely to cause more.

"Who told you this?"

"Me father."

"And who told him?"

"Dunno. Seen 'im talkin' to Jaket an' Geoffrey. Them, I s'pose."

"When did you last see Walter to speak to him?"

"Ain't s'posed to talk to you," John said stubbornly.

141

"Do you wish for Walter to be found?"

"Aye," the youth finally said.

"Then what harm can come from answering questions from a man who is seeking him?"

John made no reply. He seemed to be considering the point. I asked again, "When did you last talk to Walter?"

"Yesterday mornin'," he finally said.

"Was he on his way to yon stables?"

"Aye. Like to work for Sir John meself. If Walter don't return, mayhap I can 'ave 'is place."

"Did he say anything about leaving Kencott, or hiding from any man? Was he fearful?"

"Nay."

"What did he speak of?"

"Said as how he couldn't stop. Had to muck out or Sir John would be displeased with 'im for bein' tardy."

"When he left you, did he go to the stables?"

"Guess so. Didn't watch. Had to go to the well for water, so went to me own work."

Here was curious information. From Thomas Woodman's house to Sir John's stables could be no more than seventy or so paces. How could a lad vanish in such a short time and distance? Arthur supplied an answer, for he had heard John Woodman's words.

"Why would Walter come so near to the stables, then turn away? I'm thinkin' the lad didn't go elsewhere of 'is own choice."

"If he did," I replied, "'twas a last-minute decision."

As I spoke two men approached from the north. They had not been in the road a moment earlier. They must have been prowling the wood and fields which verged upon the road, searching there for Walter. Why else would men suddenly appear, carrying no hoes or scythes or axes or any other tool useful in field or forest?

When they drew near I stepped into the road to greet them. The fellows were pale and haggard. Perhaps they had searched for Walter through the night.

"You have explored yon wood, seeking for Walter?" I asked.

"Aye," one replied. "Ain't there 'less 'e grew wings an' is perched atop an oak."

"Run off, if you ask me," the other said.

"Was 'e lost anywhere near, we'd've found 'im by now... whole village lookin' for 'im."

"Can't spare no more time," the first man said. "Got to get me own barley in."

"Have you seen Simon, the clerk to Father Kendrick? I am told he is one of those searching for Walter."

The two men looked to each other, then one said, "'Twas dark last night when we gathered to seek Walter. Not sure was Simon there."

"You've not seen him since dawn?"

"Nay. Heard some folk holler for Walter but saw no one. Sir John sent us to search north, toward Shilton."

"You've searched all night?"

"Nay. 'Bout midnight we come home an' went out again when 'twas light enough to see. Don't know where the lad went, but 'e didn't go toward Shilton, I'll wager on it."

His companion nodded agreement, and the two walked wearily toward the center of the village. There would be little barley harvested this day, I thought.

"Wonder if there's any streams hereabouts deep enough for a lad to drown in?" Arthur said.

"Walter's father said not. And even if 'twas so, how would he be found in such a place when John Woodman saw him walk to the stables, which are not seventy paces from where we now stand?"

Arthur pushed back his cap and scratched his head, which was a way of saying he had no answer.

"'Tis time," I said, "to learn how much influence Lord Gilbert has with Sir John."

Arthur seemed puzzled by this remark. I did not trouble myself to explain. Arthur is no oaf. He would soon grasp my meaning.

For several days I had tried to avoid the lord of Kencott. He had been told to assist me, but I had doubts that his aid would be sincere, and perhaps I was skeptical of Lord Gilbert's influence. Sir John holds his lands of Sir Richard Benyt. I did not know who Sir Richard's lord was, but few men in the realm outrank Lord Gilbert Talbot. I plucked up my courage and led my palfrey toward the manor house. Arthur followed.

I saw men moving to and fro about the manor house precinct. None of these seemed hurried or distressed, as one might expect if a child of the village, and one known to all who labored upon Sir John's demesne, was yet missing. I began to hope that Walter was found, the news not yet generally known.

A groom answered my knock upon the manor house door. His countenance was unclouded, his brow unfurrowed. Had he any cares, his face did not betray them. I introduced myself and asked to speak to Sir John. Upon hearing my name the man's bland expression hardened and his nose wrinkled as if he'd caught a whiff of the pig sty. This was clearly not the first time he'd heard my name.

I had left Arthur with our beast at the hitching rail, but now felt his presence at my shoulder. If I was to beard the lion, he was determined to assist.

"Sir John is at his dinner," the groom said. "Remain here. I will see when he will be free."

"A life is at stake," I said. "I will see him now."

I had seen the groom look over his shoulder toward the open door when I asked to be shown into Sir John's presence. I assumed that Sir John was beyond the opening, so pushed past the groom and made for the next room. Arthur followed.

The chamber was empty but for its furnishings, but as I entered I heard voices and laughter through another open door. I crossed the room, Arthur at my heels, the protesting groom trailing him, and stepped into the second chamber.

Six men and four women sat about a table, chattering and laughing as they consumed their dinner. Sir John sat at the head of the table, a roasted capon leg in his hand. The partially consumed capon, large as a goose, lay upon a trencher before him.

All eyes in the room turned to me, and the prattle ceased. Sir John looked up from his capon leg, frowned, and spoke.

"What means this interruption? Does Lord Gilbert employ such unmannerly louts?"

"Lord Gilbert employs men who believe a lost child more important than stuffing their rotund bellies."

A woman gasped and held her hand to her mouth. I am sometimes not as tactful as might be. With Lord Gilbert's authority, and Arthur behind me, tact is not always required.

The eldest of Sir John's sons – the youth who was unsuccessfully attempting to grow a beard – leaped to his feet. This, I decided, was Geoffrey.

"Leave this house, and Kencott also," the youth shouted, "else Lord Gilbert will be in need of a new bailiff."

We were outnumbered six to two. I began to think that in the absence of Lord Gilbert himself, perhaps I might find more success was I less brusque.

"Has Walter Smith been found?" I asked.

Sir John had returned to gnawing upon his roasted capon leg, allowing his son to defend his pendulous paunch. He looked to me, swallowed, belched, then spoke.

"Nay. Unreliable scamp. Likely run off to seek his way in Oxford or some such place."

"Then you have given up the search for the lad?"

"Aye. My lads sought him last night and this morn. No sign of 'im." Sir John indicated that he wished the subject closed by turning again to his capon leg and tearing away a large, greasy portion.

"Odd, don't you think, that he was last seen entering the curia," I said, "not twenty paces from where I now stand?"

Sir John shrugged and continued his meal. 'Twas Geoffrey who replied.

"Who says so?"

"What difference who speaks if the words be true?"

"They are not," he huffed.

"How is it that you would know? Were you standing before your father's barn yesterday morn to see if Walter arrived?"

"Pages an' grooms about the stables told me. Walter never came to his work."

"Perhaps I should speak to those fellows."

"You call me a liar?" Geoffrey bristled.

"Perhaps only misinformed," I replied. "When did you speak to the stableboys?"

"Uh... last night."

"Before dark, or after?"

"What difference?" he asked.

Of this I was myself unsure, but thought it could do no harm to know when those who toiled with Walter were first questioned about his disappearance.

"I will speak to them myself. Where do your servants take their dinner?"

At Bampton Castle the hall is large enough that all, from Lord Gilbert to the youngest page, dine together. Of course, they do not enjoy the same fare. But the manor house at Kencott apparently had no hall large enough to serve such a purpose. There would likely be a dozen or so grooms and pages dining somewhere near, and their meal would not be roasted capons and wheaten loaves.

"Show this man to the kitchen," Sir John said. As the words were spoken to no one in particular, and Geoffrey was the only man standing other than Arthur and me, the others at the table looked to him. Sir John meanwhile discarded the capon leg which he had gnawed clean and twisted loose the other.

Most who sat at the table seemed to have eaten their fill already. Or perhaps my appearance had impaired their appetites. Whatever was the case, they would not taste the next remove 'till Sir John had consumed what remained of his capon.

These thoughts were interrupted when Geoffrey, after looking about the chamber to see if some other would offer to guide me to the kitchen and discovering no volunteer, pushed back his bench and stalked off toward a door near the head of the table opposite the one by which Arthur and I had entered.

The youth said nothing, perhaps not trusting his tongue, but opened the door so that it crashed against the wall, then disappeared through the opening into the yard. I understood that Arthur and I were to follow. We did.

I trailed Geoffrey across the yard to the kitchen. Before we reached it I heard muffled voices coming from an open door to the structure. Those who spoke did so in little more than whispers, so their words were not discernible. Perhaps they had heard the door strike the wall and guessed that the sound could portend no good thing.

Nine men and boys and two women stared at Geoffrey, me, and Arthur. Some held spoons of pottage halfway between bowl and lips. The eleven servants were crowded about a small trestle table made of two planks resting upon sawhorses. The table could be easily dismantled and propped against a wall when the kitchen was about the business of preparing Sir John's dinner.

"Answer this fellow's questions," Geoffrey said. These words were delivered slowly, in a low and threatening tone. The threat was not to me. I felt certain that these servants had already been warned to disclose nothing of events in Kencott.

If I questioned the servants as a group I was unlikely to learn much. They would not speak before others who could then report to Sir John who had provided information. I needed to interrogate each man alone; women and boys, too.

This I told them. "Perhaps Sir John has told you who I am and why I am daily in Kencott. Randle Mainwaring's bones were found in the ashes of Bampton's St. John's Day fire. It seems sure that he was slain, here or there."

"We know that," one of the grooms said. "Bertran Muth was found in Burford with Randle's horse, tryin' to sell it."

"I know that," I replied. "Does it not seem odd to you that he would slay the bailiff, then wait 'till near to Lammastide to sell his beast? Where did he keep it for that time? How did he feed the animal?

"Now Henry Thryng is dead, him who saw Bertran with Randle's horse. I would have asked him how it came about that he was in Burford the same day as Bertran tried to peddle the bailiff's horse, but now I cannot. Does anyone here think that odd? And perhaps convenient for some man?"

I watched as the servants stole glances at each other, unwilling to say, or even appear to think, that my words created questions about a matter they thought settled and best forgotten.

"I will not interrupt your dinner any longer. Finish your meal, and then I will speak to all of you, one at a time."

A spare bench sat unused along one wall of the kitchen. I pointed to it and said, "I'll move that bench to the shade of Sir John's dovecote, and await you there. I care not which of you will come to me first."

I did not move the bench. Arthur did. When I spoke my intentions he walked toward the bench and hoisted it over a shoulder. Together we departed the kitchen and crossed the yard and adjacent field to the dovecote.

I chose the dovecote as a place where I might speak to Sir John's servants unheard by any other. There are too many places in a house or barn where unwelcome ears might hear a conversation. Sir John's dovecote was sixty paces from the house, and thirty or so paces from the nearest barn, so that the birds would feel safe from harm. No man is likely to hide himself in a dovecote, and Sir John's dovecote is round, as is the new fashion, with no corners behind which a man might hide so as to hear a conversation.

A moment after Arthur set the bench down at the base of the dovecote there came a mad fluttering of wings and a hundred or more birds fled the building.

"Don't much care for guests, do they?" Arthur grinned. "Guess I wouldn't either, if I thought they'd come to make dinner of my children.

"You see Sir John's cap?" Arthur said as we waited for the first of the servants to arrive.

"I suppose. Green, was it not? What of it?"

"You did not see the stain? From where you was standin' you might not."

"Nay. Did he wipe his greasy fingers upon his cap?"

"Nay," Arthur laughed. "He has a belly for that. There was a brown stain upon the cap, an' it seemed wet."

"Didn't see it. Perhaps Sir John is too slovenly to send his cap to be laundered."

"Perhaps... looked to me like it could be blood."

"If some man thumped Sir John upon his head hard enough to draw blood, I'm sure we would have been told of it."

"Suppose so."

We sat upon the bench in silence, enjoying the sun, and one or two at a time the doves returned. A few moments later a figure appeared at the kitchen door, then peered left and right, as if to see if any man watched his movements. No man did so, so the fellow hurried across the open field to the dovecote and sat upon the bench.

"Who are you," I asked, "and what is your duty to Sir John?"

"Oswald... Oswald Rowley. I'm Sir John's falconer. Likes 'is birds, does Sir John."

I asked Oswald of Randle and Bertran and of Bertran's disputes with Henry Thryng. I asked of the bailiff's horse. The falconer claimed to know nothing of the beast or where it might have been for half the summer, nor did he know anything of the disappearance of Walter Smith. And, yes, he had been one of those who searched for the lad last night, and this morning.

I dismissed the fellow, told him to send another servant, asked the next man the same questions, and received the same answers. Either the servants knew nothing or they had been well coached. Or threatened.

The two women left the kitchen and approached the dovecote together. I did not permit this, sending one back to the kitchen. Athelina Blake was a milkmaid, and were it possible, claimed to know less of Randle Mainwaring, Bertran, Henry, and Walter than the half-dozen men who had preceded her upon the bench. The second woman, Edith Ketel, was Sir John's laundress. This I might have guessed from her red, blistered hands. As with Athelina, she knew nothing.

Ignorance reigned in Kencott Manor.

Chapter 14

Older servants had approached the dovecote first. After the two women younger grooms and pages came forth. The first of these was a strapping youth of perhaps twenty years. I could not help but see as he drew near that his eyes went to my forehead and a brief smile twitched at the corners of his mouth. Arthur also saw this. When our interview had ended he said, "That lad seems pleased about your wounds. Mayhap he helped make 'em. If 'e did so, he'll have some of his own to deal with."

The young man disclaimed any knowledge of Walter Smith's disappearance or the deaths of Randle Mainwaring or Bertran or Henry, so after a brief interrogation I sent him to call the next servant. I was determined not to forget the fellow, if it should be that he had been one of my assailants.

The next to visit the dovecote was a lad of perhaps fifteen years who was, like Walter, employed in Sir John's stable.

Henry Lane, for that was the boy's name, knew little of adult matters in Kencott, and after questioning his elders I did not expect to learn much from him of Randle or Bertran or Henry Thryng. But I thought he might know more of Walter Smith than the older servants, as he had served in the stables with Walter.

"Did Walter ever speak of running away to seek a better life elsewhere?" I asked.

"Nay. Always talked of learnin' from 'is father to be a smith."

"Here, in Kencott?"

"Aye. 'Course, I know a good smith can find work almost anywhere. His father'd talked of leavin'."

"Oh? Walter's father is a tenant, not a villein?"

"Aye. Walter once heard 'is father arguin' with Sir John about rent for 'is forge."

"What was said?"

"Edwin said as how if Sir John didn't reduce rent on the forge, he'd go elsewhere. Said Aldsworth has no smith since plague come, an' he could do well there, what with folks havin' no smith to repair hinges and such for many years."

"Did Sir John reduce his rent?"

"Guess so," the youth shrugged. "'E's still 'ere."

The Statute of Laborers was conceived to prevent folk like Edwin Smith using the shortage of smiths and other laborers to better themselves by demanding higher wages or lower rents. Plague made the statute, but avarice has unmade it.

"Was Walter a good worker?" I asked. "Did he shirk?"

"Always done what 'e was told."

"What did his duties involve?"

"Mucked out three times each week. Rubbed down the horses after Sir John or Geoffrey or Andrew come back from ridin'. Fed an' watered the beasts, too. Right fond of horses, was Walter."

"Was? You speak as if he no longer is."

The lad fell silent. "Don't know where 'e is, do we? Or if he yet lives."

"In the past weeks did you ever see Walter quarrel with Sir John or Geoffrey or Jaket?"

"Walter never disputed with any man that I saw."

"Did he ever bring Sir John's wrath upon himself by malfeasance?"

"Nay... well, once Geoffrey bawled at Walter for some wrong."

"When was this?"

"St. Swithin's Day, thereabouts."

"What had Walter done to bring Geoffrey's wrath upon him?"

"Returned tardy from 'is errand."

"What errand was it? Where did he go?"

"Don't know where 'e went, but every day, in the morning, first thing, 'e was sent off. Before I come to stables, but 'e was often 'ere mucking out when I come to work."

"How then do you know that he was sent on early morning errands each day, if you did not see him doing so?"

"Told me, didn't 'e! Said Geoffrey promised 'im tuppence extra each week."

"What was it he did each morning?"

"Dunno. Asked 'im. Would've like an extra tuppence myself each week, but Walter said 'e was told not to say, did any man ask where 'e went or what 'e did there for Geoffrey."

"What do you think he was assigned to do?"

The lad shrugged. "Took somethin' somewhere. On the days I seen 'im return 'e carried a bucket."

"Was it full or empty?"

"Empty. He'd set it down an' I looked in once or twice. Always empty."

Here was interesting news. If Walter returned to the stables each morning with an empty bucket, he must have gone off earlier with the bucket full. There could be no reason to carry an empty bucket from the stables, then return with it in the same condition.

"Did you ever arrive at the stables early enough to see Walter set off?"

"Nay, never."

"When you saw him return, from what direction did he come?"

Henry stood, walked past the dovecote, and pointed to the northeast. "Come across the meadow, just there, where Sir John's sheep is bein' kept this year."

"Perhaps his morning errand had to do with the sheep," I said.

"Dunno," he shrugged. "Sheep don't need much in summer. Nothin' what's carried in a bucket."

"Did Walter continue this work 'till he disappeared yesterday?"

"Nay. Stopped about a fortnight past."

I and Arthur had followed Henry to see where it was that he had pointed. We then returned to the bench, and as we sat, the bench shifted on uneven ground and thumped against the stone wall of the dovecote. A moment later I heard a great fluttering of

153

wings and the doves, which had been returning to their refuge whilst I interviewed the servants, again fled the enclosure with much flapping of wings and the occasional feather floating down.

I suspected that Sir John and his son would be displeased that Henry had spoken so freely, even though Lord Gilbert had demanded that the folk of Kencott were to offer me all assistance.

I thanked the youth for the enlightenment which I had received from him, then required of him that he tell no man, even the other grooms and pages, of what he had revealed to me. I did not know whether or not Walter's errands with a bucket had to do with his disappearance, or the death of Randle Mainwaring, but it seemed possible to me that this might be so.

As Henry stood from the bench I said again that he must hold his tongue if Sir John or any other man asked of my questions or his replies.

"Why so?" he asked.

"Do you wish also to disappear?" I replied. "Folk who speak to me sometimes vanish. One man died before he could answer my questions."

The page shuddered. "Henry Thryng?" he asked.

"Aye."

The look in the lad's eyes told me that he would keep silent. I sent him to the kitchen to tell another servant to seek my bench. He did so, then with a worried glance toward the dovecote, disappeared into the stables.

Four more servants sat upon the bench between me and Arthur, but I learned nothing more of import from any of them. They seemed genuinely perplexed about Walter's disappearance and the death of Randle Mainwaring, which they had thought was a settled matter. The last to come to the bench was an old groom, gone grey and wrinkled in Sir John's service. There was wisdom in his eyes, but I could not pry it out. I even asked of Walter and his buckets, being careful to conceal how I had learned of this, but the old fellow forswore any knowledge of such a thing.

My stomach growled loudly as the old groom left the dovecote to be about his duties. I told Arthur to replace the bench in the manor house kitchen, then rejoin me. We would consume our paltry dinner whilst considering what next to do in the search for Walter Smith.

The stableboy Henry had said that Walter was seen with his bucket returning to the stables across a meadow where Sir John's flock now grazed and manured the soil. I told Arthur that after we had eaten our loaves and drunk our ale we would cross that field and see what lay on the other side.

A harvested field which had been planted to strips of wheat lay beyond the meadow, and beyond that was a wood. I could think of no reason for Walter to be sent to either a wheat field or a forest with a bucket, empty or full. However, things may be hidden in a grove which would be visible in a field of corn.

We came to the edge of the wheat strips and tied the palfreys to the rocks of a low stone wall. 'Twas a simple matter to climb over the wall. A twelve-year-old lad could easily do so, if he was careful to avoid the nettles which found the place to their liking and grew in profusion.

"What we lookin' for?" Arthur said as we entered the wood.

"Whatever might have caused Walter to be instructed to come here with a bucket."

A few branches and fallen limbs, which would soon be gleaned for winter fuel, lay scattered atop moldering leaves. The grove was so dense that little light penetrated to the forest floor, and so few bushes or saplings grew there, and those were spindly and frail as they sought sunlight.

"Suppose folks been here since yesterday, seekin' the smith's lad?" Arthur asked.

"Probably. The two we saw as we spoke to John Woodman came from this direction. But they surely spent time shouting Walter's name, not seeking for something which might be taken to or from a wood in a bucket."

We found nothing which would need transport in a bucket as we prowled the wood, but did discover an anomaly. Arthur and I had penetrated the forest more than three hundred paces when we came upon a tiny brook, hardly more than a rivulet.

"Look there," Arthur said, and pointed to the soggy soil which bordered the small stream. A footprint was clearly visible.

"Some man has been here," Arthur said. "Seekin' Walter, no doubt. Why else come 'ere… unless to gather firewood?"

"Why else, indeed? But I think 'twas no man who made that mark. Place your foot aside it."

For all his brawn, Arthur has small feet – smaller than mine. Smaller than most men, I think. He did as I instructed. The footprint beside the stream was smaller yet than his.

"Hmmm," Arthur said, and pulled at his beard. "Some lad's been 'ere."

"Could be some young friend of Walter's," I said, "helping search for him."

"Or someone using a bucket to draw water from the brook," I said.

"Aye… that also."

I knelt for a closer look at the footprint and saw that it was not fresh. The edges were not cleanly printed in the mud, but rounded.

"Whoever stepped here did so some days past," I said. "See how the mud is eroded, the edge of the footprint not sharp."

"Oh, aye." Arthur then voiced my thoughts. "You think it might've been the smith's lad what stepped 'ere? Could explain the bucket that other lad saw 'im carryin'."

"But why carry a bucket here for water when Sir John has a good well not ten paces from his house?"

Arthur shrugged, which was as good an answer as any I could think of.

"Let's walk on and see what else may be in this wood," I said.

Twenty or so paces farther I began to see more fallen limbs and branches than elsewhere in the grove. One of these in particular caught my eye. Wilted leaves were yet attached to shoots. I bent to pick up the bough from the forest floor and saw that it had not broken from some tree. The base of the limb was sheared off cleanly, as with an axe. Here was a tall, spindly sapling, cut off to make a crude pole, its twigs and leaves left attached.

Oddly enough, this part of the wood had more fallen limbs than any other section. But the debris seemed oddly placed. 'Twas not spread evenly about the forest floor, but gathered in clumps. And why would some man chop a sapling at its base, then leave it upon the ground? And what could this accumulation of branches have to do with a child's footprint? Not much, I decided. I've been wrong before.

Arthur and I picked our way over and through the fallen debris. We were so intent upon our path through the thicket of branches that we nearly missed the dung. Arthur saw it first.

"Look there," he said. "Some fellow's been ridin' 'is horse through here. Why'd he do such a thing? A man can barely get through the bracken afoot."

A brief glance showed another pile of dung, and a moment later, two more. These I pointed out to Arthur.

"Looks like a small army rode their beasts through here. Mayhap they was lookin' for Walter, you think?"

I stood over one of the manure piles and considered Arthur's question.

"Nay," I said. "The horse that left its mark here did not do so last night or this morning. The dung is decaying into the soil."

"Aye," Arthur agreed. "An' all them other dungheaps is the same. Old. How many beasts was 'ere, you think?"

"One."

"What? How so?"

"You see the thicket of vines and branches we crossed to reach this place? See where it continues to the right and to the left, and meets again a few paces before us? The forest floor is nearly clear of fallen limbs but for here, where the boughs form almost a circle."

"Ah... an' the dung is in the midst," Arthur said.

"Just so. Some man made here a pen."

"Not a very good one. We entered without much trouble. If some beast was held here, it would not stay for long."

"Not as the enclosure is now."

"What do you mean?" Arthur said.

"'Tis my belief that some man has been here and pulled down what was built. But he did not take time to scatter the limbs and boughs which he had collected to make a pen."

Arthur looked about, his eyes following the circle of discarded branches. "You think there's enough fallen wood here to enclose a horse?"

"Aye, just."

"Poor beast could move but a few paces in any direction. Wonder it didn't leap over the walls of the pen. Couldn't have been very high."

"Perhaps the pen was also tied. The boughs were likely interlaced from one tree to another so to stiffen the barrier in case the beast tried to push against it."

"How long was it 'ere, you suppose?"

"From just before St. John's Day to near Lammastide."

"That bailiff's beast, then?"

"Aye. And Walter Smith was assigned to take a bucket of oats here each morning to feed the animal, and also draw water from that brook."

"Sworn to secrecy, was 'e?"

"Surely. For tuppence a week. And when he was seen in conversation with me, someone decided that he must be silenced."

"Like Henry Thryng an' Bertran Muth?"

"I pray not."

"Who would do so? Geoffrey deMeaux? The reeve?"

"It has crossed my mind."

But why would Geoffrey or Jaket or Sir John, if it was one of them who instigated the series of murders and a disappearance, do such a thing? Might it have to do with the discovery which I and Simon Hode made in the depths of the chest of wills and documents stored in St. George's Church? If so, how might this be proven and the felon brought to justice? And if Walter was silenced, but not slain, how might I discover where the lad was held and free him?

Walter seemed the key to unlocking this mystery. He could tell me why he came each morning to this woodlot, and who it was had paid him to do so. That would not yet prove the man's guilt as a murderer, but would be evidence. Evidence is not proof, but proof is impossible without evidence. We must find Walter. And not only to solve the mystery of a slain bailiff, but to save the lad's life if his captors thought to silence him permanently. I worried that the closer I came to discovering the felon, the greater would be the risk to Walter's life. If he yet lived.

"Come," I said. "I think we can learn little more here. The village seems to have given up the search for the smith's lad, so perhaps the clerk will be at home. I've a question for him."

We departed the derelict enclosure, clambering through the overthrown foliage, but we did discover one new thing as we withdrew. I stumbled upon some hard, heavy thing covered with leaves and vines and broken twigs. I thought 'twas likely some rotting stump, but kicked at it and saw some wooden object appear. Here was a thing uncommon to a forest floor. I bent to clean debris from it.

A plank trough, nearly as long as my arm, and a hand's breadth deep, appeared as I swept the object clean of the stuff covering it. Arthur had gone ahead a few paces, but stopped and turned when, from the corner of his eye, he saw me kneel and inspect the ground.

"Ah... reckon we know how the lad used the bucket, an' why that footprint was by the stream. Why would it be left 'ere, I wonder?"

"If we were patient we might build a hide nearby and await some man's return to carry this back where it might be needed."

The trough was skillfully made, and with its nails was too valuable to be allowed to remain hidden in a wood. Some day it would surely be recovered. Some day. But Walter could not wait that long. We left the trough where it lay, returned to our palfreys, and retraced our route across the wheat stubble and meadow.

"Where to now?" Arthur asked as we passed between the manor house and the reeve's dwelling.

Shadows were growing long, and after antagonizing Sir John, I did not wish to be upon the road with darkness near.

"I will seek the clerk, then we will return to Bampton."

The clerk was not to be found. His housekeeper answered my knock upon the door with a worried crease between her eyes. Well might she be concerned, I thought, as I heard her tale.

"Ah, 'tis you, what was seekin' Simon. Have you found 'im? Ain't home yet. Has the lad been found? I'm right worried for Simon. Been gone since last eve."

I would find no answer to my question from the clerk. The man had seemed to me one who spent more time listening than speaking, and so I had intended to ask him what he might have overheard from other seekers about Walter's disappearance. Speculation might be folly, but if I could sift through a dozen opinions I might find one or two worth examining.

I left the woman at her door with some platitude that the clerk would soon return, and that when he did so she was to tell him that I would seek him on the morrow. I had no expectation that when I returned I would find him. Not at his house. He had disappeared as completely as Walter Smith, and both likely had vanished because they had been seen in conversation with me.

Arthur had remained in the road, minding our beasts, but close enough that he heard the conversation and saw the anxiety upon the housekeeper's face.

"When we return tomorrow we'll have two to seek," Arthur said. "Be helpful if they're both hid in the same place."

"Aye, so long as it is not a common grave."

"We're not havin' much success with Sir John nor his lads," Arthur said. "Will you tell Lord Gilbert? He might return an' brace Sir John. Mayhap you'd get more cooperation if he did so."

I had considered this, but decided to save Lord Gilbert's influence for such time as all other methods of inquiry had failed. I had already been so incompetent as to allow myself to be accosted and beaten upon the road. To call for more aid from my employer would be to say that I was impotent to discover a felon without assistance.

I worried for the lives and health of Walter Smith and Simon Hode as Arthur and I rode through Alvescot on our way home to Bampton. The Lord Christ said that we are not to worry, but that command was regarding ourselves. I believe He would find worry for the welfare of others acceptable, so long as it is not concern alone, but accompanied by deeds.

My head was on a swivel as we passed through the wood where I was attacked, and I thought I saw Arthur inspecting the foliage with more than just idle contemplation of the greenery. But we passed safely through the wood and I admit to some relief when I saw the spire of St. Beornwald's Church come into view.

I left Arthur at Bampton Castle gatehouse with instruction to be ready next morning at the second hour. The Angelus Bell rang as I walked from Bridge Street to Church View Street and came in sight of Galen House. Here was another reason to discover a felon as soon as possible. When I did so I would no longer need to leave my Kate and Bessie and Sybil each day. Indeed, I feared Sybil might forget me. She was abed most days before I arrived home and not yet awake when I departed.

Kate had prepared a capon stewed in milk and honey, and cabbage with marrow. I was ravenous, so although she was eager to learn of the day, she held her tongue and allowed me to fill my belly. Then 'twas time to put Bessie abed, so the sun was gone and only a glow in the western sky illuminated our toft when finally I drew a bench from the kitchen to the toft and we sat wearily upon it.

I told her of what Arthur and I had discovered, which did not take long, as 'twas little enough.

"'Tis the lord of Kencott's son who has done this, then," Kate said, when I ended the report.

"So I believe. Or perchance the reeve, but I have no proof."

"Which is why the lad and the clerk are not to be found. They might provide the proof."

"Aye. Arthur and I will return to Kencott tomorrow and continue to seek them. We do not know the village, nor its people, so I have little confidence of finding them, but I must do something. I cannot sit in the sun in my toft and wait for the Lord Christ to do justice."

"Will He not do so?" Kate asked.

"Eventually. But I am impatient. Like most men, I think... and women, too. I wish for justice to be done yesterday."

"Patience is a virtue," Kate said.

"Aye, but so is a desire for justice, to see the innocent delivered and the guilty chastised."

"I only hope that doing justice will not gain you more bruises and wounds."

"There we think alike. But you would not wish to be wed to a coward, would you?"

"Nay, I suppose not. But a valorous corpse is of no use to me or Bessie or Sybil."

"Events of the past weeks have taught me caution," I said, and passed a finger over the stitches upon my cheek.

"I am pleased. A man should learn from painful experiences."

"Aye," I agreed. I thought it the wrong time to mention how I had antagonized Sir John and Geoffrey, which I had not told Kate when I had earlier reviewed the day's events.

Chapter 15

When I arrived at the castle next morn two men and three beasts awaited me. Uctred, another of Lord Gilbert's grooms, stood with Arthur in the castle yard.

"Thought the way Sir John an' Geoffrey looked at us yesterday, wouldn't hurt to have Uctred along," Arthur explained.

Uctred is older than Arthur, and not so beefy, but there is strength in his sinewy body.

Another dagger added to my own and Arthur's could not be harmful. A man marching to battle will seldom find added companions unwelcome. Indeed, if a man has enough muscle at his side, it may be that he will have less need of it. Would I have been attacked along the road near Alvescot had Arthur and Uctred accompanied me? Men are not likely to begin a fray unless they are certain of its outcome. A wise man will not begin a fight he believes he might lose, and any man who takes a careful look at Arthur and Uctred will likely decide to avoid offending them.

Sir John, his sons and minions surely knew that I would return this day, so when we passed through the wood I warned my companions to be alert. This proved unnecessary. We traveled the place unmolested. Why is it that evil seems to appear when one is least prepared for it, and when a man is vigilant misfortune passes him by?

I intended to call at the clerk's house first this day. Not that I expected to find him there, but I hoped to be surprised. The question I had for him might also be answered by his housekeeper if he was yet missing.

He was, and the woman was frantic with worry.

"Went to Sir John this morning, when Simon had not returned."

"What did Sir John say?"

"Said as how he was ill, an' not to trouble him about a grown man goin' off. Insulting, 'e was."

All the while she spoke the woman twisted her hands before her. "You will seek Simon?"

"I will," I promised. "Perhaps you may assist us. Who is the oldest person in Kencott?"

The woman likely wondered what age might have to do with her missing clerk, but she did not ask for an explanation. She drew her brows close together and her lips into a thin line, as if the exercise would bring some aged man or woman to mind. The effort was apparently successful.

"Alyce Godswein," she said.

"Where can she be found?"

"Lives with 'er son. Last house on the road to Broadwell."

"Do you know her age?"

"Nay. Don't know that *she* does. Remembers when Mortimer did away with the old king. Was already wed an' a mother when she learned of it, so she says."

The woman was indeed aged. Edward II had been deposed sixty-two years earlier. I wondered if a crone so aged would remember answers to the questions I had for her.

She did. I found Alyce sitting on a bench before her son's house, shelling peas. The woman saw, or heard, as Arthur, Uctred, and I stopped before the toft and dismounted. She squinted in our direction and when I came near I saw that her eyes were white with cataracts. She turned her gaze aside, as folk so afflicted will sometimes do, the better to see through an unclouded part of her eye who it was who approached.

I bid the woman "Good day," and introduced myself, being careful to identify my position as Lord Gilbert's bailiff. I saw her nose wrinkle in disgust, as if a breeze from a freshly manured field had come to her nostrils. This, I was sure, was a reflection of her opinion of bailiffs, not Lord Gilbert. In this she is like most other folk, who regard bailiffs only a little higher than brigands. This reputation is not entirely undeserved. I wondered about her dealings with Randle Mainwaring.

"I am told that you are the oldest person in Kencott," I

said. The woman made no reply, but continued with her peas. I wondered if she heard, so spoke louder.

"'Twas told me that you remember when Edward II was deposed."

"No need to shout, young man. Can't see nor walk well, but I hear you fine."

"Sir John's mother," I said, "was a woman named Amice, I understand."

"Aye."

"And she inherited Kencott Manor from her father, Roger d'Oilly, having no brothers."

"That's so."

"I have also heard that before she wed Sir John's father she was wed to Sir Harold Mainwaring. Did the marriage have issue?"

"Oh, aye… young Roger."

"Was he Randle Mainwaring's father?"

"Aye. A fine fellow, man an' boy, was Roger. Not like Randle."

"Was there talk amongst the villagers when Sir John became heir to his mother's estate rather than Roger?"

"Oh, aye, some. But Father Philip told us 'twas all proper, according to Amice's will."

"Did Sir John's father yet live when Amice died?"

"Aye. Sir Thomas lived on a few years. Died 'bout the same time as Roger."

"Randle would have been but a lad then?"

"Aye. Ten years, mayhap eleven."

"Did Randle or his father ever speak to you or any others about a claim to the manor?"

"Not to me. Who am I that such as him would say the like to me?"

"To others, then?"

The old woman was silent for a time, then answered. "'Tis known about Kencott that some matters are best forgot."

"But did Randle forget his claim?"

"Some say he did, some say 'Nay.'"

Try as I might, I could learn no more from the woman. I asked a few more questions, but she answered all with but an "Aye" or "Nay" and I could not draw from her any more about the complicated title to Kencott Manor.

Had Roger d'Oilly left his estate to a son when he died in 1309, the line of inheritance would be clear. But having no son, the manor fell to his daughter, Amice. When she wed Sir Harold Mainwaring, did lordship of the manor stay with Amice or pass to her husband? I had found no document in the chest in St. George's Church to say. This was odd. Such an important matter should surely have been recorded. Perhaps it was, and was now missing.

Would Thomas deMeaux have wed Amice if he had known that his heirs would have no part of Kencott Manor? He might, I suppose, depending upon his circumstances. Plague had not yet struck at the time, so land was dear and not easily come by. But as matters now stood, Amice d'Oilly's first husband's heir evidently had no claim to Kencott Manor.

In the past fortnight I had developed an opinion of Randle Mainwaring as a peevish fellow. The same might be said of most bailiffs, dealing as we do with tenants and villeins who would cheat their lord on his rents and shirk work on his demesne. But perhaps Randle Mainwaring had another reason for his irascibility. I might be resentful also if I thought I had been defrauded of my rightful inheritance.

In the Singleton family of Little Singleton Manor, such was not an issue. I am the youngest of four sons. My inheritance was a small stipend for my education and then, when that was exhausted, I was meant to make my own way in the world. I believe my father would approve of my course, were he yet alive to see it.

Arthur and Uctred had remained with the beasts, in the road, but that was but five or six paces from where Alyce Godswein sat shelling her peas. They heard the conversation clearly.

"If that bailiff was makin' trouble over the inheritance of Kencott Manor," Arthur said, "then 'tis no wonder he was found burnt to ashes in a St. John's Day fire."

"With his skull dented as well," I added.

"Aye, that also."

It was time to speak to Kencott's priest. Surely he knew by now that his clerk was missing, as well as Walter Smith, and must have some opinion of the matter. I put foot to stirrup and led the way back to the center of the village and the vicarage.

I rapped upon the priest's door and was here also greeted by a woman. Another housekeeper, I supposed. Well, Holy Writ says that it is not good for a man to live alone. I concur.

"In the church," the woman said in reply to my question, and pointed across the road. I led my palfrey to the lych gate and Arthur and Uctred did likewise. We tied the beasts there and had crossed the churchyard nearly to the porch when the priest appeared.

Kendrick Dod looked as if he hadn't slept for a week. Circles under his eyes were as large and dark as muddy cartwheels. He walked slowly, staring at the ground when he left the porch, so he did not see my approach until my feet came in view of his downcast eyes.

The priest looked up, startled, and stopped in his tracks.

"You," he said. Such a word can be phrased in many ways: friendly, questioning, accusing. Dod's tone conveyed the last.

"Why must you continue to torment this place?" he said. "Three men are dead, and now Walter Smith and my clerk are missing."

"You sum up the matter well," I replied. "I am here because three men are dead and a lad and your clerk are missing. You have no idea, I suppose, where Simon Hode might be?"

"None. I know only what Rosamond has told me. He joined those seeking Walter, and has not been heard from since."

Rosamond, I assumed, was the clerk's housekeeper.

"The lad might have run off," I said, "and if it were only him missing from the village, folk might think little of his going. But Simon would not have fled Kencott and his life here. His disappearance speaks to Walter's vanishing... that the two must be entwined. Whoso has taken them made a mistake when they seized your clerk. 'Twas like announcing to all that Walter was also captured and not a truant."

"How do you know Simon would not leave Kencott?" the priest said. "He never seemed joyful about his place here."

"He told me so. I think your clerk is a man who hides his thoughts."

"Hmmm. Well, more than his thoughts are hid now."

"Is it possible that your clerk saw trouble ahead for Walter Smith, and himself, and so has hidden himself and the lad 'till he can see some way of escaping his danger?"

"What danger?" the priest said.

"Trust me, there is danger aplenty for them both."

The priest shrugged. "I've a barn on my glebe."

"Let us search it," I said. "Lead the way."

The priest did so, and as we passed the lych gate I motioned for Arthur and Uctred to leave our beasts and follow.

The barn is not so large as the new tithe barn in Bampton, for Kencott is not so large a village. But it is well formed and the thatching will keep autumn rain from wetting the grain stored there for the church's use, for vicar and clerk and the poor.

"Wait here," the priest said as we walked behind his house. He disappeared into the dwelling and a moment later reappeared with a large iron key.

The barn was twenty paces behind the vicarage and I could see as we came near the structure that its door was fastened against thieves with an iron bar and lock. "Will a man rob God?" Holy Scripture asks. It seems that men might at least rob their village priest, although some might not consider such theft an offence against the Lord Christ.

Dod turned the key in the lock, loosed the bar, and swung open the door.

"Does Simon Hode have a key to this lock?" I asked.

"Nay."

"Then we waste our time here," I said.

Nevertheless, the priest entered the dim barn and shouted the clerk's name. I was not surprised that there was no answer.

But seeing as we were already through the door, I told Arthur and Uctred to inspect the place, and did so myself, peering behind sacks of barley and rye and peas and beans. The priest and his housekeeper would not lack for sustenance this winter. Village tithes and his own glebe lands would provide well for him and his clerk. If the clerk could be found.

The priest seemed disappointed that his clerk had not been discovered crouching behind a sack of barley. He closed the door behind us and fastened the lock, his shoulders slumped in failure.

"I know not where he might be, either hid on his own account, or held by some other."

"Who would seize him, I wonder," I said.

I thought the priest might suggest a name or two, but he did not reply. Rather, he stared off past the vicarage to his church.

"St. George's Church is in Sir John's gift, I think," I said. "And if you speak ill of the man and he learns of it, you will be seeking another place."

Dod did not reply. He did not need to. His silence was answer enough.

"My father was a villein of this place. Paid Sir John well to allow me to seek my living as priest."

"You are a younger son?"

"Aye. But now I'm the only son. My father an' sisters died when the great pestilence first come. Then my brother an' wife and all their children perished eight years past when plague returned. I've half a yardland from my brother. Rent it to John Stobbe."

"Did Randle Mainwaring perform his duties as bailiff to Sir John's satisfaction?"

"Suppose so. Never heard Sir John complain of 'im. And folk of the village weren't much pleased with Randle. Probably because he served Sir John's interests too well, rather than theirs."

"Did you ever quarrel with Randle?"

"Nay. I'd no cause."

"But Bertran Muth did?"

"Aye. Bertran sought some other place but Randle found 'im out an' brought 'im back."

"Twice, I'm told."

"Aye."

"Sir John would have been pleased."

"That's so. Sir John's got land not under plow, for too few souls on his manor."

"So Bertran slew his bailiff and tried to steal his horse."

"So 'tis said."

"You never wondered why Bertran waited more than a month to sell the beast, or where or how he kept it?"

"I'm not employed to question such matters," the priest said.

"And to do so might bring you trouble," I said. "Does the Lord Christ ask you to seek comfort or justice?"

"The Lord Christ has no need to live in harmony with the lord of Kencott. Sir John said Bertran was a murderer and thief and had evidence of it."

"I have found a place in a wood north of the village where a crude pen was built, and has since been dismantled. There is evidence that a horse was kept there."

"You think Bertran hid Randle's beast there?"

"Nay, not Bertran."

"Who, then?"

"Walter Smith was seen many mornings early returning from the place... with an empty bucket."

Dod again stared across the road to his church, perhaps wondering how he could find another position if he allowed his mind to follow the path I had set for it.

"Sir John employed Walter in his stables. Knew how to care for horses," the priest said.

"Do you also know that Randle Mainwaring's grandmother was Sir John's mother?"

The priest straightened as if I had prodded him in the ribs with my dagger.

"Who told you that?"

"What matter, if it be true? And it is true, is it not?"

Staring at his church seemed to be the priest's way of avoiding unpleasant considerations, for he did so again, which was answer enough.

"Your clerk and I investigated the documents kept in the church," I said. "We found several wills which relate to Amice d'Oilly and her heirs."

"What has this to do with Walter and Simon gone missing?"

"I spoke often to them."

"Now you speak to me," Dod said, and glanced nervously about.

"Aye. So, to prevent you going missing as well, it would be wise for you to offer me all aid."

"I have done so. What more can you need from me... that I know?"

"You are sure that you could not guess where Simon Hode may have gone, if he is away for his own reasons, not under compulsion?"

"Grown men do not go sneaking off to hidden lairs like children at play," the priest said.

"I suppose not. But sufficiently threatened, they might."

"You think that Simon saw danger and hid himself?"

"Nay... but 'tis possible."

"Then why ask this?"

"Because I must sort through all possibilities, even those which seem unlikely, 'till I find the truth."

"Then you believe he is held somewhere against his will – him and Walter?"

"That is my hope."

"Your hope?"

"Aye. If not held, they are slain."

Chapter 16

I bid the priest "Good day," but I believe he did not consider it so after I had planted in his mind the seed of danger to those seen too much in conversation with me. I bid Arthur and Uctred follow and together we led our palfreys to Sir John's manor house. I had exhausted other sources of information, so, little as I wished it, I saw no other course but to confront the fellow.

There is a slight curve in the road between vicarage and manor house, and as we rounded it I saw a man leave the distant dovecote. Sir John would have squab for his dinner this day, I thought.

It seemed unlikely that a man of Sir John's girth ever lost his appetite, but I intended to ask of him questions he would prefer not to answer, and which might put him off his dinner. So I thought.

We tied the palfreys to Sir John's hitching rail and I bid Arthur and Uctred follow. Some man had observed our approach, for as I neared the manor house door it swung open. A beardless page stood in the opening.

"If 'tis Sir John you seek, he is unwell," the lad said.

"Master Hugh is a surgeon," Arthur said with a chuckle. "Mayhap he should sharpen his blades an' slice away some of Sir John's troubles."

To my surprise the page did not frown at Arthur's wit, but rather said, "Wait 'ere. I'll see does Sir John want a surgeon."

I looked to Arthur, astonished at this response. He grinned and shrugged. Perhaps Sir John really was ill and not simply choosing to avoid me.

The page ascended a stairway at the end of the chamber and a moment later I heard voices from the upper floor of the manor house. This conversation was too muted to understand, but a moment later I heard rapid footfalls as the youth descended the stairs, and when he spoke the muffled conversation became clear.

"You are truly a surgeon?" the page asked.

"Aye. Surgeon and bailiff to Lord Gilbert Talbot." Sir John might have need of a surgeon, but 'twould do no harm if from his upper chamber he heard a reminder that I served a man more powerful than he.

"Come," the lad said, and led me to the stairway. I motioned for Arthur and Uctred to follow.

Sir John lay abed, his blanket mounded over his belly as if some man had placed on the bed a wine cask. The knight turned his head upon his pillow to watch as we entered the chamber. This obscured his complaint, for 'twas not his gut which troubled him.

"The lad says you are ill," I said.

"Aye. He says also you claim to be a surgeon," Sir John replied.

"Studied in Paris," Arthur said from behind my shoulder.

"What malady keeps you to your bed?" I said.

"My head," Sir John replied, and turned away as if to gaze at the wall opposite his bed. The bed curtains had been drawn open, so I could see clearly what was uncovered when the knight looked away.

A reddish-brown stain as large as my hand discolored his pillow. Sir John's greying hair was plastered to his scalp, crusted with a mixture of blood and pus. Here was the cause of the stain which Arthur had seen upon Sir John's cap, and perhaps a cause of his surly disposition, although I have known peckish men who had no wounds to blame for their vile temperament.

"How long have you been so afflicted?" I asked.

"Since Candlemas, thereabouts."

"Have you sought treatment?"

"Aye. Went to Oxford a fortnight after Easter."

"What did the physician say?"

"Said 'twas a scrofulous sore an' needed the king's touch. I'd no wish to travel to London, an' who knows when Edward might visit Woodstock, him bein' aged an' ill?"

"The physician provided no salve?"

"Oh, aye, he did so."

"You have not returned to Oxford?"

"To what purpose? The sore remains and has grown larger. More pus issues from it now than before I was given the salve. Can you do aught for me, or will this grow and take me to my grave?"

"Ask me in a year and I will give a better answer. If the wound is a cancer, you must be sure of your will. If some other malady is the cause, I can perhaps cure it. But 'tis no scrofulous sore."

"What? You know more of illness than an Oxford physician?"

"Did that physician cure you?"

"Nay."

"Then I can do no worse, eh?"

"Unless your prescription kills me."

"It will not... but to treat an ulcer like yours will cause you some pain."

"Why so?"

"The sore must be cut away, the wound cleansed and then sewn together, much like my face you see before you."

I saw the knight shudder as he considered my words and face.

"If this is a cancer, your surgery will be in vain?" Sir John said.

"Aye. But perhaps 'tis not. When the wound appeared, was there a cause?"

"Aye. Struck my head upon a low branch riding through the wood, hunting."

"You were lacerated even through your cap?"

"Aye. Threw me from my horse. Ribs an' back so tender for a week, I gave little thought to my head."

"'Tis not likely that such an injury will result in cancer."

I saw relief flood the knight's fleshy face. "Why does my head yet ache so?" he asked.

"The corruption has grown, I think, and will continue to do so 'till it is cut away. Evil is like that. The cutting away is painful, but if 'tis not done the corruption will grow and kill."

I watched to see if Sir John would react to these words, for I spoke not only of his disease but also of the wrongs which infected Kencott Manor. Perhaps I was too subtle. The knight made no expression nor said any word to betray that he might think I spoke of anything other than his carbuncle.

"When will you do this?" Sir John asked.

"Tomorrow. I must return to Bampton for my instruments."

"Can you not do so today? 'Tis not so far to Bampton."

"Nay. I have other business in Kencott today. Walter Smith and Simon Hode are missing and no man knows where they might be. Well, some men may. You have given up seeking them."

"We were unsuccessful. Walter has run off, I'm sure, else we'd have found him."

"What of the clerk? He would not run from Kencott. He was pleased with his situation here... told me so himself."

"Don't know where he might have gone. 'Tis a puzzle."

"There is another puzzle in Kencott I'd speak to you about. Three days past Simon Hode and I opened the documents chest in St. George's Church and discovered a wondrous thing."

"What did you find?" the knight said guardedly.

"'Tis not so much what we found which was curious, but what we did not find."

Sir John frowned in puzzlement. I enlightened him.

"Your mother's first husband was Sir Harold Mainwaring."

Sir John said nothing. I continued.

"Sir Harold left no will. We found in the chest only a parchment telling of his death. Does it not seem odd to you that the lord of Kencott Manor would not leave a will advising his heirs of how he wished his possessions to be disposed of?"

"Surely he left his lands and chattels in the normal way of things," Sir John said.

"Then why did you inherit Kencott Manor? Common law says that your mother would receive one third of the estate, and her son, Roger, two thirds. But Roger evidently received nothing, his mother all."

"There was an enfeoffment," Sir John said.

"How so?"

"What difference to you?"

"Because if you wish for me to deal with your canker, you will explain cloudy matters upon this manor... and because Lord Gilbert has demanded this of you."

"'Tis not his estate," Sir John muttered.

"Randle Mainwaring was found dead in Bampton. How he died, and why, has thus become Lord Gilbert's concern."

Sir John lay silent for a moment. "Before Sir Harold Mainwaring died, so my mother said, he called her to him and said he wished to have a charter of enfeoffment drawn, to escape fees and the manor falling to wardship, his lad Roger being but an infant, and great lords willing to pay the King for wardship of the child."

"But Roger was no orphan. His mother lived."

"When did such a detail ever impede a greedy lord with a king who needed money?"

An enfeoffment would escape not only fees due to the king but also laws of primogeniture. "Your mother, Amice, received the enfeoffment?" I asked.

"Aye," Sir John said. "The document was kept here; not in the chest at St. George's Church."

The feoffee, in this case Amice Mainwaring, was to hold property and chattels for another. I wondered who was named in the enfeoffment. Surely not Amice's second husband, as her first was not yet dead. Her son, Roger, would likely have been named. No difference from the normal order of things, except that enfeoffment could keep the king's hands from Amice's and Roger's silver, and prevent some greedy lord from seeking wardship of the child, claiming Amice's incompetence.

But if the document existed and was written as I thought likely, how did Sir John deMeaux become lord of the manor of Kencott rather than Roger Mainwaring, and after him his son Randle? Perhaps the document might explain.

"I would like to see the enfeoffment," I said.

"Alas, 'tis gone, in the blaze."

"What blaze?"

"Many years past," Sir John sighed, "sparks from the chimney set thatching afire. My men pulled down the burning thatch and walls, so most of the house was saved."

"But the enfeoffment document was kept in the part of the house which was consumed?" I asked.

"Aye, it was."

How convenient for Sir John and his sons, I thought. And this explained why half of the manor house seemed new. It was.

Did Randle Mainwaring know of the enfeoffment which his grandfather had made? This seemed likely. Why else would his inheritance be in some other's possession? Had he ever demanded to see the document before it burned, to learn if it named his infant father as the beneficiary of the enfeoffment? I had one last question for Sir John.

"The wood to the north of your meadow... have you gone hunting there recently?"

"The wood just across the wheat field and beyond my sheep?" Sir John replied.

"Aye."

"No man has gone there since Whitsuntide."

"Why so?" I asked.

"My command. There are fallow deer in that wood. No man nor beast is permitted to enter the wood from Whitsuntide to Michaelmas. 'Tis fence season."

"Ah, Lord Gilbert has made much the same rule for his forests."

I had wondered how, if a beast had been hidden in the wood, the animal could go undiscovered for many weeks. Now I knew. I had seen Sir John return from hawking with his sons. I thought the knight an eager huntsman, strict in preserving game, and therefore likely known for enforcing heavy fines against those who might interfere with his sport. A man might hide a horse in such a place with little fear that it would be discovered by some villein gathering fallen limbs or pannaging his pig.

Although I would need my instruments to deal properly with Sir John's canker, there was something to be done for him this day before I left his chamber. I told him to call for a servant, and have the fellow bring two egg whites, wine, and linen torn into strips. This Sir John did, and half an hour later a page set before me a bowl with the egg whites within, a cup of wine, and the linen strips.

I told Sir John to turn onto his belly – not an easy task, considering the size of his paunch – then folded one of the linen strips into a patch. I dipped this into the wine and cleaned blood and pus from the sore, then with a clean bit of linen I spread the egg white upon the wound as a poultice.

It is my practice, following the teaching of Henri de Mondeville, to leave wounds open, not covered with salves and bandages. But in Sir John's situation I thought it best to wrap his head with linen strips so that the egg white would work to draw contamination from the canker and not be swept away by movement of his head upon the pillow. When I was done the top half of Sir John's head was swathed in white.

I bid Sir John "Good day," told him that I would return on the morrow with my instruments to better deal with his ailment, then departed his chamber. There was nothing more to learn from the man regarding either the death of Randle Mainwaring or the disappearance of Walter Smith and Simon Hode. Perhaps he knew no more of these matters, or, more likely, what more he knew he would not tell to me. And what he knew of Bertran Muth and Henry Thryng, if anything, he would not divulge, either.

The page showed us to the door and to reach it we passed through Sir John's hall. Grooms and valets were preparing his table for dinner, and before his place I saw a roast of pork. No squab.

It then occurred to me that an hour past I had seen, from a distance, a man leave the dovecote. His hands had been empty. I was near enough to see that. Why would a man enter, then leave the dovecote empty-handed?

Twice birds had noisily fled the safety of the dovecote when Arthur and I sat upon a bench beside the building to interrogate

Sir John's servants. Why would doves desert the place when they were safe inside and the only threat they might perceive came from without?

I turned from the palfreys and walked across the field to the dovecote. The door was sturdy and secured with an iron lock as large as my hand, as I expected it would be. Gentlemen who own such structures prefer to keep them secure so as to preserve the fowl for their own table rather than provide meat for light-fingered villeins.

Arthur and Uctred saw me walk from our tethered beasts and followed. I put a finger to my lips to silence any question they might have, and quietly approached the dovecote door. A few birds came and departed the place, as would be a normal order of things at midday.

I stood silently at the dovecote door, then lightly tapped my fingernails upon the planks. I wished to make enough noise that anyone inside the dovecote would hear, but not so much that the birds would be startled and abandon the place in a flutter of wings because of the loudness of my rapping.

I waited at the door for some response to my gentle knock. When nothing immediately happened I lifted my hand to tap the wood again. Before my fingernails could contact the door I heard the fluttering of hundreds of agitated wings and saw above me a cloud of doves escaping their shelter in a torrent of feathers.

Neither Arthur nor Uctred have any responsibility for Lord Gilbert's doves, but they know enough of the creatures' behavior to understand that the response to my light taps upon the dovecote door was not proportional to the threat. A man who knows what he is about may quietly, slowly, enter a dovecote and take squabs for his lord's dinner without causing fright or flight.

"What was all that about, then?" Uctred said when the last of the birds had fled the dovecote.

"Return to Sir John," I said, "and request the key to open this door. If he refuses, tell him I will send you to Bampton this day to fetch Lord Gilbert while I remain here before the dovecote door. And his sore will go untreated. Arthur will remain with me. Hurry."

Uctred hastened to the manor house as rapidly as his short, stumpy legs could carry him.

"You reckon somebody's in there?" Arthur said.

"Mayhap. Something caused the doves to take flight and I didn't strike the door hard enough to do so, I think. Do you remember when we sat upon the bench and questioned Sir John's servants just there? Twice birds fled the place. I gave it no thought at the time, but I don't remember that we made enough fuss to cause all that mad fluttering."

"What did so, then?"

"What if someone is inside the dovecote, bound and gagged, able to hear folk outside, but unable to call for help? Perhaps all they may do is thrash about, hoping somehow that the sound of a struggle against their bonds might be heard outside the stone wall of the dovecote."

"Ah," Arthur said. "We heard nothing, but the doves was frightened an' fled the place. An' with all the flutter of wings, if there was anyone inside tryin' to be heard, we'd hear only the doves."

"Just so." Then, turning to the door, I said in a loud voice, "'Tis Hugh de Singleton. Walter, Simon, if you are there, we will have you out soon."

Arthur and I fell silent to hear any response, but there was none. At least none that could be heard through limestone walls nearly as thick as my forearm is long and a heavy oaken door.

The wait for Uctred's return was long enough that I began to consider attacking the door with some tool from the nearby stables. But eventually he appeared, accompanied by a groom in whose hand I saw a key.

"Couldn't find the key," Uctred said by way of explanation for his tardy return. He rolled his eyes to indicate disbelief. The location of the key had been known an hour or so earlier. Why it should be difficult to locate now seemed odd.

Arthur and I stood aside to allow the groom access to the lock. He fitted the key and attempted to turn it, but was unsuccessful.

"Been havin' trouble with this lock," he said.

"Strange," I replied. "I saw a man leave the dovecote an hour or so past. The key must have worked well then, unless there is another key to this lock. Is there?"

"Nay. Key works sometimes, an' sometimes don't."

"Too bad. We shall have to break down the door, then. You are sure that this is the proper key?"

"Geoffrey gave it to me. I don't have much to do with the dovecote," the groom said.

"So you would not recognize the proper key, or know if this is it? How then do you know that the lock is sometimes difficult to open?"

"That's what Geoffrey said when 'e give it to me."

"Return to him and tell him to provide the correct key. If he will not, go then to the barns and return here with an axe. And be sure to tell Geoffrey that those are my instructions. Make haste. Uctred, accompany him."

Uctred and Sir John's groom touched forelocks and walked swiftly back to the manor house. I thought it likely that Geoffrey would provide another key rather than see the dovecote door battered down, as he would know that I was determined to enter the place and so, with Lord Gilbert's authority, could not be kept from seeing what was beyond the door.

What I believe to be likely is not always so. Uctred and the groom reappeared with Geoffrey and four others following. A key was in the groom's hand, as before, and as he came close it seemed to me that it was the same key he had before tried in the lock. Of course, one key looks much like another.

"Why do you trouble us to enter the dovecote?" Geoffrey said when he drew near.

"Why do you wish to keep me from it?" I replied.

"You will annoy the doves."

"I think you are more annoyed than the doves. Is that the proper key?" I said, and pointed to the key in the groom's hand.

"Edwin has told you that the key often fails to open this lock."

181

"Aye, he did so. 'Tis no wonder, as it is surely the wrong key."

The youth bristled at this and I saw his companions sidle close behind and about him. I glanced down at that moment and saw that one of these wore a patched shoe. The sole had become detached from the upper part of the shoe and some time not long past the tear had been crudely sewn together. I recognized the repair. The last time I had seen it, I had an intimate view as the foot within the shoe directed a blow to my head. The stitches in my cheek began to itch.

The groom with the mended shoe saw my eyes travel to his foot, then rise to his face. This did not seem to cause the man any worry. Rather, I thought a smirk flashed briefly across his face.

"Why would I try a key for this lock which will not serve?" Geoffrey said.

"Why, indeed? There can be but one answer. There is something, perhaps someone, within which you do not wish me to see. But I will open this door, either with the proper key or with an axe. You choose. Send your servants for one or the other."

"No man will hack through my father's dovecote door with an axe," Geoffrey said.

"The key, then."

"Are you so dull that you cannot understand?" Geoffrey said. "There is no other key."

There is a rule amongst soldiers that a commander must not divide his forces. For a moment I considered sending Arthur or Uctred to investigate Sir John's barns for an axe or some other sturdy tool which could be used to smash through the dovecote door. But then it came to me that we were three facing six, which were unfavorable odds already. Two opposed to six would be much the worse, even though Arthur is worth two in a brawl. What, then, to do to end this impasse?

Chapter 17

Alvescot is but two miles from Kencott. Gerard, Lord Gilbert's aged verderer, lives there with his sons and I knew that he would surely have more than one axe. I turned from the dovecote and, feigning disgust, stalked away from Geoffrey and his grooms. Arthur and Uctred, puzzled, followed. When we were far enough from Geoffrey that a whispered conversation could not be heard, I instructed Arthur to go back to the dovecote to see that no man opened the door until Uctred and I returned. We would make haste to Alvescot, I told him, and would be back anon. I mounted my palfrey, motioned to Uctred to do likewise, and spurred my beast away from Geoffrey, the manor house, and Kencott.

When we had passed from the village I explained our departure. We spurred our palfreys to a trot and soon arrived at Gerard's door. We found the man limping about his yard, directing two laborers in the sawing of a timber into planks.

"Axes?" he said. "Aye, got as many as you'd want."

One axe would have been enough to demolish the dovecote door, but if two men with axes upon their shoulders and resolute scowls upon their faces stood near whilst a third man attacked the door, Geoffrey or any of his grooms who came running to the sound of splintering wood might be persuaded not to interfere with the work.

Armed with three axes – and Gerard had kept them sharp – we returned to Kencott and tied the palfreys to Sir John's hitching rail. Arthur stood alone before the dovecote, arms folded, looking formidable. None of Sir John's household seemed to pay him any notice. That would change with the first blow upon the door.

While Arthur and Uctred stood watch, frowning blackly in case any man should offer resistance, I delivered a blow at the door near to where the hasp was bolted. Instantly the feathered inhabitants fled the dovecote in a tumult of beating wings. But the door held fast. I swung again, and two of the bolts tore free.

As I gathered myself for a third swing of the axe I saw from the corner of my eye a hurrying figure approach. The man did not appear from the manor house, but rather came from the road, beyond our palfreys. I did not wait for the fellow, but with all of my strength delivered another stroke against the door and was rewarded by seeing the door bang open.

I turned to face the approaching figure and saw 'twas the Kencott reeve. The man was not pleased. His face was red and distorted with rage. Arthur also watched him come near and raised his axe in what even the dullest man could see was a threat to life and limb. This did not improve the reeve's scowl but did slow his approach considerably.

Meanwhile three men tumbled from the manor house. None of these had axes, but it seemed likely they could find some quickly.

Battling Sir John's servants was not the reason I broke down the dovecote door. What, or who, might be inside was my purpose. I motioned to Arthur and Uctred to follow me into the dim interior of the dovecote, then told them to take position at the door so to deny entry to any who would follow.

There is little light inside a dovecote – only that which penetrates the place through the holes created to allow the birds entry and egress. But there was enough light to see two trussed, gagged, blindfolded figures upon the filthy straw. I laid my axe aside, drew my dagger, and hastened to the bound figures. I immediately stumbled into a pile of pigeon droppings which had not been cleared. The stink was profound. I regained my feet and began hacking at the cords which restrained the two, the smaller one first.

'Twas Walter Smith, and the other was Simon Hode.

I dimly heard the clamor of angry voices as I cut the fetters, gags, and blindfolds which had shackled Simon and Walter, then assisted them to their feet. They were unsteady, and unsure, I think, of what was happening. I was somewhat confused myself. I had found Walter and Simon, but what I was now to do about it was a new puzzle.

With Arthur and Uctred at the door, axes ready to cleave the skull of any man who would attempt to enter the dovecote, we were temporarily safe. On the other hand, the dovecote had been a prison for two but could now become a gaol for five. The dovecote, like many things in life, might prove to be easier to get into than out of.

I wanted to know who had imprisoned Walter and the clerk in the dovecote, and why. This I could reasonably guess but wished to be certain. But other matters forced themselves into my thoughts; namely, how to leave the dovecote without requiring more stitches.

Arthur and Uctred stood on either side of the door with axes poised to strike. I walked between them and saw the reeve standing just outside the dovecote door. He had assumed a crouch, as if considering whether or not he could force an entry between two upraised axes. He saw me, gradually stood erect, and folded his arms across his chest.

"Go seek Geoffrey, or Sir John. Tell them I have questions for them."

"Sir John is abed," Jaket said. "Ill."

"So he is, but it will be best for his health if he comes here. Geoffrey also."

"Do you threaten Sir John? You have broken down his dovecote door. I am newly made bailiff here, and 'tis my duty to see justice done."

"Oh? Then why were Walter Smith and Simon Hode held in this stinking place? Such incarceration does not seem just to me."

"They disobeyed Sir John."

"How so? Was it that they spoke to me of secret matters? Lord Gilbert will be interested to know that his command was disobeyed."

"If he ever learns of it," the new Kencott bailiff said with a smirk.

"How do you intend to prevent it? Will you wall us in here? Folk in Bampton know we are in Kencott. When we do not appear this night Lord Gilbert will be told and by midday tomorrow he and a dozen or so knights and grooms will arrive here seeking us."

The fellow seemed lost for words, and stepped back. Apparently the thought of facing a company of well-armed and unhappy knights was distasteful. Perhaps the alternative was also.

I spoke again. "Sir John was told to give me all aid in my investigation into the murder of Randle Mainwaring."

"The felon was caught, and hanged."

"A man died upon a gallows here in Kencott, I know, but 'twas not the man who murdered Randle Mainwaring.

"Sir John, I think, will not want to run afoul of one of the great barons of the realm. If you persist in blocking our departure Lord Gilbert will blame Sir John. What, then, do you imagine Sir John's view of your actions will be? My guess is that since you will have brought Lord Gilbert's wrath upon Sir John, Kencott will soon have another new bailiff. Now, are you ready to bring Geoffrey or Sir John here?"

I saw Jaket turn and speak to one of the others who had been drawn to the sound of splintering wood. The fellow turned and walked to the manor house. I spoke no more, nor did the reeve made bailiff. We awaited Sir John or, failing his appearance, his son.

'Twas the son who soon trotted across the field. Geoffrey slowed his pace when he neared the dovecote and I saw him exchange a knowing glance with his father's new bailiff. *What is it that these two know?* I wondered.

"You did not seek a missing lad or clerk very thoroughly," I said.

Geoffrey shrugged. "Who could know they would hide in such a place?"

"They tied and gagged and blindfolded themselves?"

"That is how you found them?"

The young man's voice seemed genuinely incredulous. He was either an accomplished player or was surprised. My guess, given the wordless exchange with Jaket, was the former.

"You are in violation of Lord Gilbert's command that I be given all aid in seeking Randle Mainwaring's murderer. Do not tell me that the felon has already paid for his crime. We both know 'tis not so. You are in danger of Lord Gilbert's wrath already. How much more of his choler will you tempt?"

I saw the youth grow pale and again look to Jaket.

"I am to return to Kencott tomorrow with instruments and salves to deal with your father's injured head. If the wound is not dealt with it may fester and bring him to an early grave."

Another look passed between Geoffrey and Jaket. The youth shrugged. "Then I may come the sooner to my inheritance," he smiled.

"Perhaps. But if your father lives another day – and unless some man slips a blade between his ribs, he surely will – Lord Gilbert and his knights will be here seeking me. He will turn his wrath against your father. Upon whom do you think your father will turn his anger?"

The time for words had ended. I fell silent and allowed Geoffrey and Jaket to consider their situation. The two men moved out of hearing and whispered, their faces close together. I did not need to hear to know that they discussed their options. These were few.

The day had been long and I was hungry. I thought of the loaves in the sack across my palfrey's rump, and the ale in the flask carried by Arthur's beast. If we were not soon released from the dovecote my growling stomach might be heard through the open door.

Geoffrey held his palms up and ended the conversation with Jaket. I saw Jaket scowl. Whatever Geoffrey had decided did not meet with his companion's approval.

The grooms who blocked the dovecote door stepped back when Geoffrey came near. He stopped but one step from the door and said, "You may go... and take Walter and Simon with you. They are no longer welcome in Kencott."

"Your father may have an opinion about that," I said.

"And do not return tomorrow to treat my father's scalp."

"Sir John will have an opinion about that, as well."

"He is abed, and not here to know what has been said and done. He will be abed tomorrow, also, but I will not. If you approach Kencott on the morrow you will discover how unwelcome you are. Now go, and take Walter and Simon with you."

We five cautiously departed the dovecote, Arthur, Uctred, and me with axes at the ready. Our apprehension was unfounded. No man attempted to interfere with our departure. Perhaps they were pleased to see Walter and Simon gone from both dovecote and village.

Silently we crossed the field and manor yard, mounted our palfreys, and made for the smith's forge. Walter rode behind me, the clerk behind Uctred. Arthur's palfrey had work enough with only him mounted.

The stink of the dovecote and the dried bird droppings was intense upon Walter and Simon. And upon me also, due to my tumble into the pile of droppings. But this would have to be borne for a few hours. At Bampton Castle Walter and Simon might bathe away the stench and find clean clothes. I could do likewise at Galen House. What they now wore should be burned.

"Will we take Walter an' Simon from Kencott, as Geoffrey demanded?" Arthur asked.

He said this with a peevish tone to his voice, as if he'd rather do battle with his axe than acquiesce to Geoffrey's command.

"Aye, for now. We will visit the forge and the clerk's house, explain why Walter and Simon must accompany us, and then make for Bampton."

These things we did, and shared the loaves and ale after we left the clerk's housekeeper weeping in the doorway.

By the time we had reached Alvescot I had heard Walter's and Simon's tales. Geoffrey had paid Walter extra to arrive early at the stables and take a bucket of oats to a runcie confined in a crude paddock in the wood. He was to water the beast also, and make certain that the horse had not broken down any part of the enclosure. He did not know whose the beast was, but the duty stopped when Bertran Muth was found in Burford with the bailiff's beast.

Then two days past Walter had entered the stable, expecting nothing but a normal morning, when a sack was dropped over his head. Men silently trussed his arms and legs tight, then carried him off. He knew not where he was taken at first, but when he heard cooing and the flapping of wings he knew he was in the dovecote. The sack was lifted from his head, but light in the dovecote was dim, and a cloth was instantly wrapped tight about his eyes so he saw nothing of his captors. Then a wadded cloth was stuffed into his mouth and another strip was tied so as to keep the lad from spitting out the gag.

Next day the clerk was treated in the same manner. "I heard you speak to Sir John's servants," Hode said, "and thrashed about hoping you would hear."

"Ah, that's what drove the doves away from the dovecote in fright," I said.

"Were you given to drink?" Arthur asked.

"Aye. Our legs were freed, and the gags were taken from our mouths each night. But the blindfold remained and our arms were never freed. We were given water and a loaf and warned that if we cried out no man could hear us and we would be beaten. We were allowed to relieve ourselves on the far side of the dovecote. When I asked what our captors intended, one said we would be held until you no longer came to Kencott asking of Randle Mainwaring."

"Did you recognize Geoffrey's voice, or the reeve's, when men spoke to you?"

"Nay. Neither Geoffrey nor Jaket, but some of Sir John's pages and grooms were among the men who held us."

"You knew their voices?"

"Aye."

"This may be of use to us," I said.

"Surprised they didn't slay 'em," Arthur said.

"One spoke of it," the clerk said, "but another said they were told there had been enough killing and there would be no more unless it proved necessary."

My stitches began to itch again when we rode through the wood wherein I was attacked. But no men tried to block our way, Geoffrey and Jaket and their minions being pleased to see us away from Kencott and having no mind to interrupt our journey to Bampton.

I took Walter and Simon straight to the castle. The first man I saw after passing under the portcullis was John Chamberlain. I dismounted, told him briefly of matters in Kencott, and asked that he see to preparation of a chamber for Walter and Simon.

"Will they be Lord Gilbert's guests for many days?" he asked.

"A night or two, I think... I hope. No more."

I am an optimistic sort of man.

I found Lord Gilbert with his guests in the solar, having only just returned from hunting, and readying themselves for supper. I saw Lord Gilbert wrinkle his nose as I drew near, so I kept my distance while I spoke. My employer knows my moods, and after a brief glance at my face guessed that much was amiss. He asked what was troubling me and I told him.

Before a valet announced that supper was ready in the hall Lord Gilbert had organized an expedition to Kencott for the next morning. Peace with France meant that Lord Gilbert's guests were bored, hunting being less stimulating than combat, and were, to a man, eager to set off on the morrow with swords buckled about their waists.

I was eager as well, but not to return to Kencott. Rather I was keen to return to Galen House and my family. They were not so ardent to see me, however.

It was the smell. Bessie ran to me when I entered my house, then skidded to a stop when an arm's length away and peered at me strangely. My own nose had become inured to the odor of aging bird droppings. Not so Kate and Bessie's.

Kate followed Bessie, managed a weak kiss, then drew away in disgust. "What causes this awful stink?" she said. "Lord Gilbert's goats are not so rank."

I laughed and chased Kate to the rear of Galen House where

I caught her and held her in close embrace. Bessie laughed and clapped her hands to see such sport.

"Nay," Kate squealed. "Let me go 'till you have washed away that abominable smell."

I did so.

My bowl of pottage I consumed in the toft. Kate would not have me in the house. I cannot blame her. Walter rode behind me from Kencott to Bampton, so I well understood her disgust.

I set three kettles filled with water near the fire and waited in the toft for the water to warm while Kate put Bessie and Sybil into their beds. From a corner of an unused chamber in Galen House I dragged my bathing barrel close to the fire. This was a wine cask sawn in half, reinforced with an extra band of iron about the top. When I last traveled to Oxford Kate requested that I return with, among other items, two cakes of Castile soap. Spanish soap is not so harsh as that made from ashes and lard, Kate says. At four pence a cake it should not be.

I poured the kettles of warm water into my bath barrel, disrobed, and with the Castile soap scrubbed away the scent of dovecote. Kate reappeared as I was concluding my ablutions and grinned.

"What is funny?" I demanded. "Have you never seen a wine cask sawn in half before?"

"Of course. Do all surgeons bathe as regularly as you?"

"They do if they have recently toppled into the manure of a dovecote, else their wives will have nothing to do with them."

Kate lifted the cake of soap to her nostrils, sniffed, and said, "Much better. You will not have to sleep this night with the hens."

I dried myself with a length of linen cloth, donned fresh kirtle, braes, chauces, and cotehardie, and felt once again presentable. The day was near done, but enough light remained in the western sky that I drew a bench to our toft and Kate and I sat there until the stars glimmered and Kate's head rested upon my shoulder.

Kate was drowsy, but I was not. Later, in our bed, I reviewed events of the past days and planned for the morrow. I made a list in my mind of instruments and herbs I must take to deal with Sir John's abscessed scalp. I thought of three dead men and who might have slain two of them. I thought of enfeoffment and fires and documents consumed in a blaze. I considered Geoffrey's threat that I would discover how unwelcome I was in Kencott should I return.

I thought I knew why Randle Mainwaring, Bertran Muth, and Henry Thryng had died. But how to prove it?

Some time before Kate's rooster announced the dawn a scheme whereby I might prove the who and why of the bones in the St. John's Day fire came to me. The plan entailed some danger, and for some time I lay considering why I might risk more stitches, or worse, to uncover felonies in Kencott. 'Twas not my bailiwick, after all.

Because, I decided, I am, for good or ill, a stubborn man. And I dislike murderers who leave the result of their felony in Bampton.

I had said nothing the night before of returning to Kencott, but Kate knows me and was not surprised that I intended to do so.

"Be careful, husband," she whispered at the door as I set off with a sack of instruments and herbs thrown over my shoulder.

"A dozen men will accompany me to Kencott today. What harm can come to a man so well defended?"

I did not speak to Kate of my plan, else she might have replied. But even though I would seek some danger this day, I walked to Bampton Castle with some joy in my heart. I saw, if my scheme prospered, a conclusion to matters this day, and an end to journeys to Kencott. So my joy was due not to ease or riches or the praise of my employer, but to doing something worthwhile and seeing it near an end.

Lord Gilbert was in the castle hall, breaking his fast with cheese and a loaf with those knights, squires, and grooms who would accompany us to Kencott. When he rose from the table I drew him aside and outlined the scheme by which I hoped to sniff out proof that Geoffrey deMeaux was guilty of three murders.

"Arthur, Uctred, and I will ride ahead of you by half a mile or so. If Geoffrey lies in wait, as I believe he will, for he is a worried man, he will sooner try to attack three men than a dozen. And he expects no more than we three."

"You wish him to make an attempt on your life?"

"Aye. If he appears we will turn and gallop back to you, shouting for aid, so you must keep close enough to hear."

"But why take such a risk? If we succeed in taking Geoffrey, he will not slip a noose about his own neck by admitting to three murders."

"Aye, he will not. But the pages and grooms with him might be persuaded to tell of what they know if they believe their punishment for attacking me – and you, if it comes to that – might be the less. There is a groom who wears a mended shoe that I believe can be persuaded to speak."

"You think Geoffrey deMeaux did not slay the Kencott bailiff alone?"

"Could one man have brought the corpse to Bampton in the night and hid it in the makings of the St. John's Day blaze? I believe he had help... perhaps the Kencott reeve who is now bailiff had to do with the business."

"One man?" Lord Gilbert said. "Nay, not likely. So you believe whoever aided Geoffrey in moving a dead man from Kencott to Bampton will also be with him today?"

"Aye. 'Twould be a man he trusts. And when the fellow is threatened with a noose for what he might attempt to do this day, his tongue may be loosened."

"To save his neck," Lord Gilbert laughed. "Very well. We shall ride to Kencott, as you suggest. What if no man, Geoffrey or any other, attempts to do you harm upon the road?"

"I shall need to think of another scheme," I shrugged.

And so we set off for Kencott: me, Lord Gilbert, five knights, six grooms, and Simon the clerk. Walter Smith we left in Bampton.

The knights enjoying Lord Gilbert's hospitality were pleased to be hunting something more hazardous than a stag, jesting with one another as schoolboys set free from their studies to play.

At Cowley's Corner Lord Gilbert raised his hand and all halted but for Arthur, Uctred, and me. Whilst we rode from the castle Lord Gilbert had explained my plot, so all understood this separation.

I expected that the attack, if it came, would be at some place where a wood came close to the road so as to camouflage the approach. There was no better place than the wood near to Alvescot where I had been scarred for life. I thought now of the place as being the site where retribution might be mine, and was some disappointed when we passed the grove and no men appeared.

Arthur must have entertained the same notion. "Thought for sure Geoffrey'd set upon us here, if he's of a mind to do so." He sounded disappointed.

There was one other place, near to Kencott, where a wood came close to the road. Beyond that lay fields, and then the village. We could not be surprised by horsemen coming at us across harvested fields, so when we came near the copse I warned Uctred and Arthur to be alert, then turned in my saddle to see if Lord Gilbert and his company were in view.

They were, having just then ridden past a bend in the road. If we needed to turn our beasts and spur them back along the road Lord Gilbert would not need to hear our cries for aid. He would see us galloping headlong toward him. I thought it likely that Geoffrey would believe our flight a natural result of fear, and not look beyond the haunches of our fleeing beasts to see others thundering up to do combat. So it was.

The copse which sheltered Sir John's son, bailiff, pages and grooms was small – the road entered and was through to the other side in less than two hundred paces. Half a mile beyond lay the village of Kencott.

Trees grew so close to the road that men hidden amongst them could not see behind us along the road. So when Arthur, Uctred, and I came into view Lord Gilbert and the others were veiled from our attackers' sight. Of course, this meant also that we could have little warning of our assailants' approach until they were nearly upon us.

A wise man once said that he who fears God need not fear any man. That may be so, but I suspect the fellow had never had half a dozen mounted men brandishing daggers plunge toward him.

We three yanked upon the reins of our palfreys, got them turned about, and spurred the frightened beasts into flight. The shouting men close behind so alarmed the horses that the spurs might not have been necessary, but this was no time to take chances. My scheme seemed at for moment to be succeeding, but I admit to some trepidation about the final outcome of the matter.

Much confusion followed, so the melee remains tangled in my mind. Our assailants were but a few paces behind, and gaining upon us, when we met Lord Gilbert's band. I dared not draw my palfrey to a halt, nor did Arthur or Uctred, for fear of receiving a blade in the back, so we swept through our rescuers, we three going east, Lord Gilbert's eleven galloping west.

I would like to have seen the faces of our attackers as the nostrils of eleven charging horses replaced the haunches of our fleeing beasts.

Once safely past Lord Gilbert, his knights and grooms, I pulled hard upon my palfrey's reins and the misused beast skidded to a halt. Arthur and Uctred did likewise, and from the corner of my eye I saw Arthur spur his beast back along the road to join the brawl now thirty or so paces distant.

It was over before Arthur could strike a blow, which disappointed him, I think. Swords conquer daggers when the two are tried against each other. There were six attackers: Geoffrey, Jaket, and four of Sir John's servants. Two of these lay wounded in the road, three stood surrounded by Lord Gilbert's knightly companions, and another galloped away toward Kencott, having escaped the brief combat. Two of Lord Gilbert's grooms, Roger and Fulk, spurred their beasts after the fleeing man.

The escapee was a servant. Both Geoffrey and Jaket were within a circle of knights with drawn swords and grooms with daggers. Geoffrey stood, along with two servants, but Jaket was one of the assailants who lay bleeding in the road.

I dismounted, handed my beast's reins to Uctred, and hurried to the wounded men. I came first to the injured groom, who had raised himself to a sitting position and had his left hand pressed tight to his right forearm so as to staunch a flow of blood. This was mostly unsuccessful. Blood oozed between his fingers. I had silken thread and needle with me, their use being necessary to the surgery I intended to work on Sir John's pate. I could stitch this man's wound closed there in the road, although if the King's Eyre decided to hang the man for this felony, my skills would be wasted.

I next knelt over Jaket, who had made no attempt to rise. When I saw his wound I understood why. He had been stabbed in his gut.

Men who have been in battle and seen wounds know when a sword thrust will be fatal. Jaket's eyes told me that he knew his life would end in the dust of this road. He knew other things as well, and it was this other knowledge I hoped to pry from him before death took him.

"Ride to Kencott," I said to Arthur, "and fetch the priest. Take Simon with you. Jaket must be shriven."

I watched Jaket's eyes as I spoke, but they registered no surprise at my words. More evidence that he knew death was near.

I was of two minds regarding Jaket and the slashed servant. A wounded arm will not usually take a man to the next world, so long as a competent surgeon is available to deal with the cut. But the wound was great enough that no time should be lost in dealing with it.

On the other hand, if I took time to stitch up a lacerated arm, Jaket might die before I could seek information from him. He was going to die. Only the moment was in doubt. Such may be said of all men.

I turned back to Sir John's new bailiff and bent over him. The anger which I had seen in his eyes at the dovecote was gone. Fear was there now.

No blood issued from Jaket's lips, so the sword thrust had not penetrated his lungs. And had the thrust pierced his heart, he would have been dead already. This observation gave me hope that he might live long enough to illuminate the obscure happenings in Kencott village.

"I have sent a man for Father Kendrick. Did you hear?" I said.

Jaket nodded.

"So you know that you will die soon?"

He nodded again.

"Father Kendrick will ask you seven questions. If you are to be properly shriven you must answer them truthfully."

Jaket neither nodded nor spoke. He knew I spoke true.

"One of the questions is thusly: 'If God grants that you live, will you confess your sins and amend the evil you have done?' Will you answer, 'Aye?'"

Jaket again nodded.

"But you will not live. You will have no time to make amends. Will you die with guilt upon your soul? Or will you tell what you know of Randle Mainwaring and Bertran Muth and Henry Thryng?"

"He knows nothing," Geoffrey bellowed.

"We shall see," I said.

"Do you wish this man silenced?" Lord Gilbert said to me while looking at Geoffrey deMeaux.

I nodded. Lord Gilbert turned to Sir Philip Dodwell, one of his visiting knights, and said, "If that fellow speaks another word, bind him." Then he pointed to the road and said in a voice loud enough that Geoffrey would surely hear, "And then shove a handful of that horse dung into his mouth."

Geoffrey would not interfere further, I thought.

"Did Geoffrey deMeaux slay Randle Mainwaring?" I asked the dying man.

"Nay," he whispered.

This was not the reply I expected.

"Then who did so? Do not say 'twas Bertran Muth. I know better."

"I did," he said.

Another reply I did not expect.

"You? Why so? I know of the enfeoffment which has led to this conflict. What had that to do with you?"

Jaket opened his mouth to speak but no word came forth. His eyes rolled back in his head, he shuddered, then lay still. Dead. Had the man indeed slain Randle Mainwaring? Why? Or did he, knowing death was near, seek to protect Geoffrey deMeaux?

I looked up from the dead man and my eyes fell upon a mended shoe. It was upon the foot of one of Sir John's grooms who had been unmarred in the fight. 'Twas the man who had delivered the kick which opened my cheek. Perhaps, I thought, he knew of secret matters in Kencott and could be persuaded to speak of what he knew. Being threatened with justice at the hands of the King's Eyre for attacking Lord Gilbert's bailiff might loosen the fellow's tongue.

It did. I stood. All those about me were silent, crossing themselves in the presence of death.

Chapter 18

The man who had lacerated my face stood opposite Jaket's fallen form. I stepped around the corpse and approached the fellow. In similar situations in the past I have found it profitable to approach such miscreants closely, and did so this day. I was some taller than the man, and so looked down upon him from little more than a hand's breadth from his forehead. He had a clear view of Kate's excellent stitchery.

"What is your name?" I barked.

"Uh, Elkin," he stammered.

"You are in much trouble, Elkin. You have attacked a great lord, and before that you and some others set upon me upon this very road. My cheek will forever bear the mark of that shoe."

I looked down and pointed to Elkin's feet. Others followed my gaze and the man shuffled back as if he might somehow escape the regard of so many hostile men. The mended shoe was peculiar enough that all who looked upon it knew that I could not have mistaken it for some other.

"Upon whose command have you done these felonies?" I asked.

The man did not reply, but looked about him as if measuring the distance to the wood and considering if he might run and hide himself there.

"Master Hugh asked you a question," Lord Gilbert said. My employer had dismounted and followed me to confront Elkin, and I heard his growling voice from just beyond my shoulder.

"'Twas Jaket required me... us, to aid him."

"You helped him slay Randle Mainwaring?" I asked.

"Nay, he did so. But he demanded that John an' me help 'im take Randle to Bampton."

"If Jaket truly murdered Randle, why not bury him in some forsaken place in a wood?" I said. "Why take the corpse to Bampton?"

"Jaket said if Randle was consumed in the St. John's Day blaze, 'e couldn't rise when the Lord Christ returns. An' he'd be consumed so no man would know 'e was dead."

"Jaket hated Randle so much that he wished to prevent him rising from the grave when the Lord Christ returns?"

"Aye, he did so."

"Why?"

"All men disliked Randle. 'E was a bailiff."

Elkin did not explain. Likely he thought identifying Randle as a bailiff was enough reason for the man to be hated.

"But what had Randle done to antagonize Jaket so? Why did he want him dead?"

"'Cause Sir John an' Geoffrey did."

"Silence, you oaf," Geoffrey roared. The youth's face was purple with rage.

Sir Philip bent to the road and with a gloved hand picked up a yet-warm dropping from one of our beasts. Geoffrey raised his hands and backed away, but two other of Lord Gilbert's knights moved to stop him. Each seized an arm, held the youth fast, and Sir Philip stepped resolutely toward the cringing lad.

"Nay," Geoffrey cried.

Sir Philip looked to Lord Gilbert. My employer can grin and appear stern at the same time. Perhaps this is a talent which only powerful men possess. I've known few others who can do so.

"Not yet," Lord Gilbert said. "But keep you ready. If his mouth opens again, fill it."

Geoffrey looked to the wad of manure in Sir Philip's hand and tightened his lips.

This diversion now concluded, I turned back to Elkin.

"Why did Sir John and Geoffrey want their bailiff dead?"

I thought I knew the answer to that question, but too many times in the past I have assumed that which was not so.

"He contested their right to the manor of Kencott."

"Because of the enfeoffment?" I asked.

The groom gave me a startled glance, as if he thought knowledge of Kencott Manor's past was better hidden than it was.

"Aye," he finally said.

"Had he brought suit? Or had he threatened to do so?" I asked.

"Tried."

"Tried? What do you mean?"

"Don't know for sure."

"Then what do you know which is unsure?"

Elkin looked toward Geoffrey as if seeking guidance. I followed his eyes to see if the young man shook his head or nodded or gave any other sign which might influence the groom. Geoffrey glanced from Elkin to the fistful of manure Sir Philip held before him and remained impassive.

"Folk do say," the groom began, "that Randle bribed a clerk of Chancery Court to hear 'is claim to the manor. The clerk told Sir John of what Randle was about, an' Sir John bribed 'im to dismiss Randle's suit."

"So that was the end of it?" I said.

"Nay. Randle saved 'is coin an' bettered Sir John's bribe."

"And Sir John learned of this?"

"Aye. Clerk wanted more coin to set Randle's suit aside."

"And Sir John paid?"

"Nay. Said 'e was not going to allow some corrupt clerk to plunder 'is purse."

"So Randle's suit was to be heard in Chancery?"

"Dunno," Elkin shrugged. "Guess so."

"How did you learn of this? Did Sir John share this with you and other of his servants?"

"Nay, never spoke of it to the likes of me."

"Then how is it you know of the matter?"

"Like I told you, don't know for sure if 'tis all so."

"But how did you learn of what you have just told me, true or not?"

"Sir John's valet."

"A friend of yours?"

"Aye."

"What is his name?"

"Henry Cadogan."

A knight's valet knows much of his lord's business. I thought Elkin likely spoke true, and Randle Mainwaring was surely angry at being swindled of his inheritance. Angry enough to bring suit to recover what he believed was rightfully his. A clerk at Chancery Court could not be bribed with but a few pence, or even a few shillings. The bailiff of a small manor like Kencott would find it difficult to accumulate enough funds to sway a clerk at Chancery. And even Sir John would find matching Randle's bribe with one of his own a costly business. Death would be less dear. Unless, of course, some meddling bailiff from a nearby manor interfered.

"What of Bertran Muth?" I asked. "He was deemed guilty of Jaket's felony."

"Stole the horse," Elkin replied.

"Randle's beast, hid in the wood?"

"How'd you know that?" Elkin said.

"Never mind. Why do you say Bertran stole the horse of a murdered man?"

"Jaket didn't know what to do with it, but thought to sell the beast when folk 'ad forgot about Randle. Worth ten shillings, Jaket knew. Sir John 'ad banned folk from the wood during fence month, so he hid it there."

"And Geoffrey put Walter to work feeding and providing water for the beast?"

"Aye. Jaket thought to sell it in some nearby town when 'e could."

"How did Bertran find the beast?" I asked.

"Poachin'. Good with snares, was Bertran."

"He entered the wood against Sir John's decree?"

"Must've, else 'e'd not have found the horse."

"What then? How did Henry Thryng discover him trying to sell the animal in Burford?"

"Dunno."

I thought it likely that Elkin spoke true, but if *he* did not know why Henry Thryng happened to be in Burford at the same time Bertran tried to sell Randle Mainwaring's horse there, I thought another in the company might. I turned to Geoffrey.

"You hanged a man for a murder he did not do, you and your father," I said.

"A man may hang for stealing a horse," he replied.

"Aye, but how did you know he did so? Albreda said your father sent Henry to Burford to sell six capons. That would fetch three pence, no more. Why would Sir John send a man to Burford for but three pence return?"

"Dunno. Father doesn't tell me of all he does."

Perhaps the lad spoke true. But I was convinced that Henry Thryng was sent to Burford for more than the sale of six capons. And that Sir John knew Bertran Muth would on that same day be in the town with a horse to sell.

"Henry Thryng's death was convenient, wasn't it?" I said.

"Don't know what you mean," Geoffrey replied.

"He could not tell me of who sent him to Burford on such an unprofitable errand, or what else he was expected to do whilst in the town. Perhaps your father can explain."

"He is ill."

"Aye, and I have the tools and skill to make him well again. I will seek him now and deal with his complaint as soon as he tells me what I wish to know of Bertran and Henry."

I had no sooner spoken the words than I heard in the distance a ringing bell. 'Twas Arthur and Simon returning with Father Kendrick. The clerk, as was fitting, had abandoned his horse and walked before the priest, ringing his bell. Father Kendrick wore surplice and stole and carried a small sack wherein was the blessed sacrament.

Simon ceased ringing the bell when he and Father Kendrick and Arthur came near. The priest saw our company standing about Jaket's prone form and guessed the man's fate. He knelt over the corpse, crossed himself, and began to quietly whisper a prayer for the dead.

When he was done, and standing, Lord Gilbert commanded that Jaket's corpse be raised from the dust and laid across his palfrey. This was done, and the company began the short walk to Kencott.

Sir John's valet answered my knock upon the manor house door with wide eyes. Well he might, for before him he saw one of the great barons of the realm, several well-armed knights, and a half-dozen resolute-appearing grooms surrounding his master's son and a corpse.

The valet's eyes flashed about, then returned to me. He knew of my promised return this day, and said, "You have come to mend Sir John's wound?"

"Aye... perhaps."

"I will tell him you have come."

The valet was so addled that he did not invite Lord Gilbert or me to enter the house, but fled to seek Sir John, leaving us standing in the yard. While we waited I pointed across the road to Jaket's house and told two grooms to take his corpse to his wife. They did so as Sir John appeared at the door.

'Tis a remarkable thing that a man so arrogant in the company of underlings can become so humble when in the presence of a superior. Sir John removed his cap and bowed in greeting to Lord Gilbert. His head, however, remained partly covered by the linen strips I had bound about the wound.

The knight saw beyond the group at his door to Jaket's corpse being taken across the road. At that distance he could not identify the dead man, and so asked.

"'Tis your new bailiff," I replied. "He died trying to slay me upon the road to Alvescot."

"Jaket? Do murder? Surely not," Sir John protested.

"While he lay dying in the road he also admitted the murder of Randle Mainwaring," I said.

"Randle? Bertran Muth slew him."

"Jaket said not. And I suspect you have known this."

"Me? Why would I know of such a thing? And why would Jaket slay Randle?"

"Because you told him to do so, or he knew that you wished it to happen. I know of Randle's suit to win back Kencott Manor, which he believed rightfully his. Mayhap you thought that he could be appeased if you appointed him bailiff, so he could use his position to cheat you of some of the manor's profits, as bailiffs are known to do. But Randle was not content with occasional larceny, was he? He wanted more, and was ready to sue to get it. He bribed a clerk at Chancery with coin he had taken from you."

"Bah," Sir John scoffed. "You speak foolishness."

"Makes sense to me," Lord Gilbert said.

"How did you learn that Bertran Muth had discovered Randle's horse hidden in the wood? Did Jaket tell you of this?" I asked.

"A horse? In the wood?" Sir John replied incredulously.

"You sent Henry Thryng to Burford with six capons to sell," I said. "Why would you send a man on such an errand for so little return, unless you knew there would be a greater profit than just a few coins?

"Bertran had to die, you decided, because I had come to Kencott asking of Randle. If I somehow learned from Bertran of the bailiff's beast being hidden in your wood, I might then guess that Randle was not away visiting a brother, for he had none, but was dead and nearly consumed in Bampton's St. John's Day fire."

"Bertran stole Randle's horse," Sir John muttered.

"And for that theft he might hang," I said. "But that was a convenient excuse to do what you wished, which was to silence the man so I could learn nothing from him."

"You said that you would return to deal with my wound," Sir John said. "Why has Lord Gilbert also come?"

"Many men of Kencott knew I was to return this day. Some did not wish me to do so. Lord Gilbert traveled with me to see that I arrived here safely."

"What will you do to relieve my injury?"

"Nothing, 'till I have the truth from you. You can go to your grave with the wound, for all I care."

"This hurt will kill me?" Sir John asked.

Such a wound as he had suffered was not likely to end his

life, even though it might make his days unpleasant, but I saw no reason to reassure him of that.

"It may," I said.

"And you can deal with it so I will live?"

"I can, after you have told Lord Gilbert the truth of matters here in Kencott."

Sir John stood yet in the manor house door. He looked from me to Lord Gilbert to the others standing before his door.

"I will speak privily to only you and Lord Gilbert," he said. "In my chamber. The others may wait in the hall. I will send ale."

Sir John directed a groom to lead the others to his tiny hall, then motioned me and Lord Gilbert to follow him to the stairs. Two chairs and a bench, as well as his bed, furnished the chamber. Knowing my place, I stood before the bench and waited to sit until Lord Gilbert had taken the best chair.

"Now, then," Lord Gilbert began. "Master Hugh has fit together pieces of this sorry business. I will hear it all from you, with nothing omitted. Your bailiff was found consumed in the flames on my lands, and I will know why and how."

Lord Gilbert's tone left no doubt that Sir John would face disagreeable consequences if he did not comply. The knight sat heavily upon the other chair, which he would have done even was he not under duress, then began to speak.

Sir John told of the enfeoffment which placed Kencott in his mother's hands, free of wardship, and how, rather than comply with the enfeoffment, his father, following Lady Amice's death, had claimed the manor as his own. Randle Mainwaring's father was too young when this happened to know that he had been cheated of his inheritance, and a few years later a convenient fire destroyed a part of the manor house and the enfeoffment document with it.

"What of the documents chest in St. George's Church?" I asked.

"My father saw that relevant records of Mainwaring and deMeaux were removed."

"And the priest at that time was willing to do so for a few well-chosen gifts?"

"Aye," Sir John agreed.

"How did Randle discover that he was rightful heir to Kencott Manor?" I asked.

"Don't know. Some old folk with long memories and loose tongues, I suppose."

"Did he not come to you and complain that you had usurped his rights to Kencott?" Lord Gilbert asked.

"Aye, he did so."

"And when you disdained his claim he decided to seek redress at Chancery Court?" I said.

"He did so. Bribed a clerk."

"As did you," I replied.

Sir John looked at me from under raised eyebrows, certainly wondering how I could know this. I did not enlighten him.

"Jaket, before he died, claimed that he had slain Randle. Why would he do so? 'Twas not his manor to lose if Randle won his suit."

"Randle an' Jaket didn't get on," Sir John said.

"So you told Jaket of Randle's suit, knowing that if Chancery decided for Randle, he would not permit Jaket to remain reeve. Did you hope that Jaket, to save his position, would remove your troublesome bailiff?"

Sir John did not reply. Lord Gilbert spoke for him. "It surely crossed your mind, did it not?"

"Aye," Sir John finally said.

"Did Jaket ask your permission to keep Randle's horse in the wood?"

"Aye. 'Till time had passed an' the beast could be sold. Should've slit its throat an' fed it to the hounds," he muttered.

Sir John was adamant that he had had the right to hang Bertran Muth, as the man had stolen a horse. That the beast had been stolen from Jaket, a murderer, seemed to him of no consequence, and I could see in Lord Gilbert's puzzled expression that this matter of law confused him. Lord Gilbert is a good lord, but he does not deal well with complex issues. I thought it best to let the business rest. Nothing but the return of the Lord Christ would raise Bertran Muth from his grave. A hanging cannot be undone.

"Did Jaket tell you why he poisoned Henry Thryng?" I asked.

"He what?"

"The man who saw Bertran with Randle's beast, in Burford, died after consuming poisoned ale."

"How do you know this? Jaket said he died of twisted bowel or some such thing."

"Jaket lied. Whose idea was it to send Henry to Burford to sell six capons?"

Sir John was again silent. "Well?" Lord Gilbert said. "Answer Master Hugh."

"Jaket's," he finally said. If this was so, I wondered at his reluctance to say. Perhaps Geoffrey, or he, had devised this plan for Bertran to be caught with a dead man's beast, the scheme designed to end my investigation into Randle Mainwaring's death. But I had no way to pry truth from Sir John if his answer was untruthful.

"How did Jaket know when Bertran was taking Randle's horse to Burford?" I asked.

"Kept watch on 'im. When Bertran asked to travel to Burford, Jaket guessed what he planned to do."

Lord Gilbert looked to me with one raised eyebrow, as if to ask, "What more do you wish to know?"

"You lied to me when you told me that Randle had gone to visit a brother," I said.

"So I did. Will you ask the sheriff to hang me for such a lie?"

The sheriff of Oxford would not hang a knight for lying to a bailiff, even Lord Gilbert's bailiff. Nor would the King's Eyre convict a knight of such a felony. I knew this, as did Lord Gilbert. And Sir John knew that I knew this. So he smiled.

"Nay," I said. Then, to Lord Gilbert I said, "I am done with Kencott and hope never to return to the place. Let us be off."

"Wait," Sir John cried. "My wound. You said 'twould kill me if you did not treat it."

I had not said this, but had hoped that Sir John would believe it so. And his smile of assurance that no sheriff or court would side against him for lying to me caused me to seriously consider leaving him with his festering sore, to deal with it as best he might.

Sir John had done evil. But would I be guilty also of evil if I refused to help him in his distress? Should a man take pleasure in the troubles of the wicked? It seems fitting to do so. But Holy Scripture says there is a way which seems right to a man, which way leads to death.

I had brought my sack of instruments and herbs with me to Sir John's chamber. I told him to send a groom for an ewer of wine, then laid out my tools upon a table. In normal circumstances I would have given Sir John a cup of ale containing crushed hemp and lettuce seeds to dull the pain of surgery, then waited an hour for the herbs to do their work before I began to repair his injury.

But this was not a normal circumstance. I wished to be gone from this place as soon as possible, and if Sir John felt pain as I worked, 'twould be but his due for his duplicity and felonies. So I thought. Perhaps this was a sin. When I next see Master Wycliffe I must ask his opinion.

I told Sir John to lay upon his bed upon his stomach, his head to one side toward me. The groom soon appeared with the wine which, after I had removed the linen strips from about Sir John's head, I used to wash his wound.

Using my sharpest blade, I trimmed away corrupted flesh and skin down to the skull. With a fresh scrap of linen I again washed the wound with wine, then with needle and silken thread I closed the cleaned cut. To his credit, Sir John did not jerk his head nor thrash about while I did this, although I admit that I was not dainty while at the business, and wine applied to such a wound will bite.

When the new laceration I had made was properly sewn together I washed the stitches again with wine, then told Sir John to wear no cap until Michaelmas. When that day arrived he might have his valet use a sharp blade to cut and remove the stitches.

Sir John nodded understanding and reached a tentative hand to his scalp to touch the needlework I had done there.

"What is owed for this?" he said.

"A shilling," I replied.

Sir John's eyes widened, but he said nothing. He left the bed, walked to a chest in the corner of the chamber, and from it withdrew a pouch. He counted out twelve pence and handed the coins to me with a scowl. I had charged the man thrice what I would have asked another. Perhaps this also was a sin. My own stitches were itching at the time and I thought the charge fair. Only later did my conscience begin to trouble me, but not so much that I returned eight pence.

"Walter Smith has remained this day in Bampton Castle," I said. "He will be returned to his family tomorrow. I have heard that Edwin Smith would like to leave Kencott and seek his living in some new place. Allow him to do so."

"But Kencott needs a smith," Sir John protested. "And the Statute of Laborers..."

"I'm sure that Lord Gilbert would agree that the statute does not apply in this matter," I interrupted. "You and your son have shown that you cannot be trusted to deal justly when you think your interests threatened. The smith's family will not be safe so long as they remain upon your manor."

"But..."

"Do as Master Hugh requires," Lord Gilbert said.

Sir John said no more, which was reply enough.

I replaced my instruments in the sack, which was a wordless way to tell Sir John and Lord Gilbert that my work was done. We left Sir John standing in his chamber door and thumped our way down the stairs. Lord Gilbert's knights and grooms heard us descend and appeared at the opening to the hall as we reached the ground floor.

"We are done here," Lord Gilbert announced, and led the way from the house to the rail where his beast was tied. A few moments later we passed the church and from his house I saw Simon Hode appear. He had clearly been watching for us. The clerk raised a hand when he saw that he had caught my eye and hurried from his door.

He bowed to Lord Gilbert, then approached me. "I am done here," he said. "Sir John will demand that Father Kendrick dismiss me. I know not what will become of me. Is it possible that the vicars of Bampton might need a clerk?"

I looked to Lord Gilbert, who has some influence in Bampton even though the Church of St. Beornwald is under the authority of the Bishop of Exeter. "See to it," he said to me, and spurred his ambler to a trot.

I smiled at the clerk and said, "I believe you will find a place in Bampton." The clerk gave a sigh of relief and stood watching as our company set off for Alvescot and Bampton.

"Will Sir John retain Kencott Manor?" I asked Lord Gilbert when I caught up to him.

"Who else will have claim to it? Randle Mainwaring was not wed... had no heirs. Nor had he a brother, you said. Some injustices cannot be righted."

"Not in this world," I said.

"Aye," Lord Gilbert replied. "The Lord Christ will have much justice to dispense from His heavenly throne to make up for what is impossible below."

Next day I sent Arthur and Uctred to return Walter Smith to his father, and to tell the smith that he was free to depart Kencott and seek another place.

I walked then to St. Andrew's Chapel to learn how Thomas Attewood mended.

Perhaps I had not made the swineherd's leg as straight as could be when I fixed the break with a fence of reeds, or mayhap he walked upon the leg before the break was truly knit. One of these was likely true, for when I examined the man I saw that his left foot pointed out at an angle which did not match his other foot. Thomas did not complain of this, and when I asked to see him walk he did so with no more limp than any other man recovering from a badly broken leg. The fellow was eager to resume his work with Lord Gilbert's pigs, although not with the old boar which had sent him plunging into the gully. That animal was now, he said, made into ham and bacon and was hanging in Lord Gilbert's smokehouse. A capricious temper will cause trouble for both man and beast.

Next day Kate and I celebrated the end of my travels to Kencott. With my smallest blade she cut the stitches she had made to close my lacerations, then set about preparing a dinner of mushroom tarts, capon farced, and cabbage in marrow, all dishes she knows I enjoy. Of course, there are few dishes I do not enjoy.

Late in the day Arthur came to Galen House to report that Walter was safely returned to his parents.

"When I told 'im 'e was free to leave Kencott," Arthur said, "the smith dropped 'is 'ammer an' left off plyin' 'is bellows. Stopped work right then, so I think. Wouldn't be surprised was 'e packin' 'is belongins into a hand cart an' away tomorrow."

"He may be pleased to be upon the road," I said, "but I am pleased not to be."

No man can see the future. Arthur and I and many others would set off from Bampton not many months hence. All because of a bungling bishop.

Afterword

Since the key to wealth in the medieval period was land ownership, disputes regarding property were common, and a good source of income for lawyers, clerks, and judges. The manor of Kencott was indeed inherited by female descendants in the early fourteenth century, although the dispute I created is entirely fictional.

Bampton Castle was, in the fourteenth century, one of the largest castles in England in terms of the area surrounded by the curtain wall. Little remains of the castle but for the gatehouse and a small part of the curtain wall, which form a part of Ham Court, a farmhouse in private hands.

Many readers have asked about medieval remains and tourist facilities in the Bampton area. St. Mary's Church is little changed from the fourteenth century, when it was known as the Church of St. Beornwald. Visitors to Bampton will enjoy staying at Wheelgate House, a B&B in the center of the town. The May Bank Holiday is a good time to visit Bampton. The village is a morris dancing center, and on that day hosts a day-long morris dancing festival.

Village scenes in the popular television series *Downton Abbey* were filmed on Church View Street, and St. Mary's Church appears in several episodes.

The Bampton town library building, now 400 years old, was transformed into the Downton hospital for the television series. The building needs extensive repairs and the town would surely appreciate contributions to help maintain this historic facility.

Schoolcraft, Michigan
April 2015

Lucifer's Harvest

An extract from the ninth chronicle of
Hugh de Singleton, surgeon

Chapter 1

When I first traveled to France I did not rue the journey. I was a student, and like most lads eager to see new lands and learn new things. I was then on my way to Paris to study surgery at the university.

I was less eager to cross the sea in the year of our Lord 1370 when Lord Gilbert Talbot, my employer, required it of me. France was no longer a new land to me, and perhaps I had lost the desire to learn new things. I learned anyway. Knowledge is not always desired or intended. It is, however, often useful, even if unwanted, and accumulates like the grey whiskers which Kate occasionally finds in my beard. At least for this journey I would ride a palfrey rather than walk.

Three days before Whitsuntide I awoke to a pounding upon Galen House door. My Kate was already from our bed and called out that Arthur must speak to me. Arthur is a groom to Lord Gilbert Talbot and has been useful to me and his employer in helping untangle several mysteries which fell to me to solve. The fellow is made like a wine cask set upon two coppiced stumps, with arms as thick through as my calves.

I am Hugh de Singleton, surgeon, and bailiff to Lord Gilbert Talbot at his manor of Bampton. I assumed that Arthur's early appearance at my door meant that someone in the castle required my surgical skills.

This was so, but not in the manner I expected.

I drew on chauces, donned my cotehardie, ran my fingers through my hair, and descended the stairs. Arthur stood dripping upon the flags at the entrance to Galen House. The day had dawned grey and wet with rain. Arthur would not, I thought, be about in such weather unless propelled by some important matter.

"I give you good day," he said, and continued before I could ask his business. "Lord Gilbert wishes to chat with you this morning. 'Tis a matter of import, he said, and asks for you to wait upon him without delay."

"Is m'lord ill, or injured? Or some other in the castle? Shall I take instruments and herbs?"

"Nay. Lord Gilbert's well enough, an' all others, so far as I know. Didn't tell me why he wished words with you; just said I was to seek you an' give you his message."

"Which you have done. Return to the castle and tell Lord Gilbert I will be there anon."

I splashed water upon my face to drive Morpheus from me, hastily consumed half of a maslin loaf, and swallowed a cup of ale. Weighty matters should not be addressed upon an empty stomach. Half an hour later I walked under the Bampton Castle gatehouse, bid Wilfred the porter "Good day," and set my path toward the solar where I expected to find Lord Gilbert.

But not so. John Chamberlain was there, and told me that my employer was at the marshalsea. I descended the stairs to the yard, crossed to the stables, and found Lord Gilbert in conversation with Robert Marshall and a gentleman I had not before seen.

"Ah, Hugh, you have come," Lord Gilbert greeted me. "I give you good day. Here is Sir Martyn Luttrel with news from France. Hugh, Sir Martyn, come with me. We will speak in the solar."

News from France which must be discussed in the solar could not be agreeable. I had no hint of Lord Gilbert's topic, but assumed the conversation would have something to do with the burly stranger who had appeared at Bampton Castle. So it did.

When we were seated Lord Gilbert explained his reason for calling me to him.

"Sir Martyn has brought disquieting news from France," he began.

'Twas as I feared. News from France is often troubling. Much like news from Scotland.

"King Charles has announced that he is confiscating Aquitaine, in violation of the Treaty of Bretigny. No matter how many times we vanquish the French, they will not remain subdued. The Duke of Berry has even now an army approaching Aquitaine. Prince Edward has sent for knights and men at arms from England to assist him in opposing the French king. I am his liegeman, and am required to provide five knights, twelve squires, and twenty archers and men at arms. My chaplain will accompany us, and I wish to have a surgeon as a member of my party."

So far as I knew Lord Gilbert had but one surgeon in his employ: me.

I was speechless at this announcement. Lord Gilbert saw my mouth drop open and continued before I could voice the objections which were forming in my mind.

"You have crossed to France once already," he said, "so you know that the passage is not arduous in summer."

When we might return no man could know. Returning to England in December did not bear thinking about.

"And I am not so young as I once was," he continued. "I am yet fit for battle, but 'twould be well to have you at hand should some French knight strike a lucky blow. Or unlucky, depending upon one's loyalties," he laughed.

"But what of folk here?" I finally stammered. "If I travel with you to France there will be no bailiff to see to the manor. Who will serve in my place to collect rents at Michaelmas?"

"John Prudhomme has served well as reeve. I intend to appoint him to your post 'till we return. Your Kate I would have oversee the castle," he continued. "'Tis not a duty beyond a woman. Lady Petronilla did so when I was at Poitiers and she was then younger than Kate. I have no one to leave in charge of Richard but his nurse, and 'tis not meet for a woman of such station to supervise a castle. John Chamberlain will deal with most matters. Kate will not be much troubled."

I knew what Kate's opinion of this move would be, but before I could explain my wife's loyalty to Galen House, Lord Gilbert continued.

"Kate will lodge in Lady Petronilla's chamber. It has been empty since the Lord Christ took her from me, but I will see that it receives a good cleaning. 'Tis a large chamber. Plenty of room for Bessie and Sybil."

Lord Gilbert had considered that I might object and answered my protests before I could voice them.

But for one matter.

"Warfare is a perilous business," I said. "What if I am slain in battle or captured and held for ransom? Who will care for my family? I am not wealthy. Kate would find few resources if I was taken and held for ransom."

This assumed that a French knight would believe that a poor surgeon's life was worth the trouble of sparing for a trifling ransom.

"Oh," Lord Gilbert said, pulling at his beard. "Just so. I pay your wages, so have some thought as to your value. What say you, Hugh? What are you worth?"

"To you, or to Kate and Bessie and Sybil?"

"A fair question. Would one hundred pounds serve for ransom if you are taken, and ten pounds each year to Kate if, the Lord Christ forbid, you are slain? Neither is likely, mind you. 'Tis my thought that if this expedition comes to a battle, you will be far from the field, prepared with your instruments and physics to deal with wounds."

"What if you also are slain?" I said. "Or seized? Who then will provide for Kate?"

"I will see an Oxford lawyer and have drawn up a document which will serve as your security in this matter. Does that satisfy you?"

The tone of his voice told me that Lord Gilbert was becoming exasperated with my objections. I decided that I must make no further protest. If a great lord wishes a man to accompany him to France, it is best for the fellow to see the journey as an opportunity rather than an obligation and make the best of it. After all, France is not Scotland, although priests often assign travel as a penance, and for good reason.

Sir Martyn was present for this conversation, but he took no part in it other than to turn his head from me to Lord Gilbert as we spoke in turn. Lord Gilbert's conversation now turned to his visitor.

"Where are you bound this day?" he asked.

"I am to seek Sir John Trillowe, then Sir Richard Coke and Sir Ralph Lull on the morrow."

"How many knights and men at arms has the prince called for?" I asked.

"Three hundred knights are bid come to France," Sir Martyn replied. "With a thousand squires, pages, archers, and men at arms."

"We are to assemble at Dover on St. Thomas's Day," Lord Gilbert added, speaking to me, "where ships are even now being assembled to carry us to Calais."

"This being so," Sir Martyn said, "I must be away to complete my task. You and the others have but to prepare and make your way to Dover. I came first to you."

"Stay for dinner," Lord Gilbert said. "You can easily travel to East Hanney this afternoon to inform Sir John of Prince Edward's command."

Throughout the realm other messengers were informing knights and their men of this requirement for their services. Many, perhaps most, would welcome the summons. Peace can be boring and war may be profitable – if a rich castle can be plundered or a wealthy French knight captured and held for ransom.

Lord Gilbert invited me to stay for dinner that day at the castle. The meal was of five removes, regardless of the king's requirement that two removes be the limit. If Edward should learn of Lord Gilbert's violation I suspect he will permit the transgression to pass.

The announcement of my forthcoming journey did not harm my appetite. Very little does. I stuffed myself with parsley bread and honeyed butter, fruit and salmon pie, sole in cyve, aloes of lamb, and pomme dorryse. So when I departed the castle I was well sated. Kate knows that upon occasions when I am called to the castle my return to Galen House is uncertain, so she had fed herself and our daughters rather than await my return.

Rain had continued, so I shook my cotehardie free of as much water as possible, stamped mud from my shoes, and thereby soiled Kate's clean floor. Here was no way to begin an account of the morning's tidings which would likely trouble my spouse. But I thought of this too late. 'Tis impossible to unstamp a foot and replace mud upon a shoe.

"What news, husband?" Kate said from the kitchen, then appeared in the doorway. She looked from my sodden cap to the muddied flags and frowned. My announcement did not improve her expression.

"Lord Gilbert is called to France," I began, "and bids me accompany him. He will have you occupy a chamber in the castle to oversee his son and the lad's nurse."

"And leave Galen House? What of Bessie and Sybil?"

"You and they will have Lady Petronilla's chamber in the castle. It has remained empty since she died. Lord Gilbert promised to have it put right before you move to the castle. The walls of Lady Petronilla's chamber are hung with many fine tapestries," I added by way of persuasion.

"When? How long 'till this is to happen?"

"Not long. A week perhaps. We are to be in Dover to take ship for France by St. Thomas's Day. I think Lord Gilbert will require at least to fortnight for the journey to Dover, or near so."

Next morn I was busy with my instruments, sharpening blades with an oiled stone I keep for the purpose, when Arthur again thumped on my door with his meaty fist.

"Lord Gilbert says we will leave Bampton Tuesday morn," he said. "I am assigned to help you move Kate to the castle. I'll bring a cart an' runcie on Monday at the ninth hour, that bein' acceptable."

"The ninth hour will serve. We will make ready."

We did: Kate packed our largest chest with clothing for herself and our daughters, and I filled a smaller chest with my own garments, and bags of crushed hemp and lettuce seeds, and betony. I also placed a jar of St. John's Wort ointment in the chest, for I was likely to see wounds aplenty before I returned to

Bampton. My instruments chest I keep ready for use, so nothing of preparation was necessary but for the sharpening of blades.

On Sunday, after mass, as this was to be our last meal together in Galen House for many months, Kate used her supply of eggs to prepare an egg leach for our dinner. That night, after dark, when the fowl would be roosting, I intended to send pages from the castle to collect Kate's hens and cockerel from the coop and add them to the castle poultry, 'till those of us off to restore King Edward's privileges could return.

Arthur was prompt, and we soon had the cart loaded. I lifted Kate and Bessie and Sybil to the cart, watched as Arthur led the runcie down Church View Street, then turned to Galen House to affix a lock to the door. The rear door I had already barred from within.

This was the second house on the site to bear the name of the great physician of antiquity. My first house, a gift from Lord Gilbert, had been burned to ashes by Sir Simon Trillowe, he being furious that I, a slender surgeon with an equally slender purse and a large nose, had won Kate Caxton for my bride. His father had been, at the time, Sheriff of Oxford, and he a handsome young knight who had little experience of failure or denial. When Kate chose my suit over his, he was enraged. Fortunately a new sheriff took office, a friend to Lord Gilbert, and when 'twas proven that Sir Simon had set my house ablaze, he required of the knight ten pounds to rebuild Galen House.

Last week Sir Martyn was to call Sir John, Sir Simon's father, to join the force summoned to aid Prince Edward in France. The son would surely accompany his father on this expedition.

Sir Simon was no longer so handsome as he had once been. His left ear protruded from the side of his skull in a most unbecoming fashion. A brawl upon the streets of Oxford had left the fellow battered and bleeding and with an ear hanging from his head by but a wisp of flesh. I was in Oxford and nearby at the time and was summoned to stitch the dangling ear back to Sir Simon's bruised skull. I did so, but such a repair is difficult, an ear being all gristle and nearly impenetrable by even the sharpest needle. And I had no experience at such a reconstruction.

Sir Simon did not lose his ear. My surgery was successful, mostly. But when the injured appendage healed, it extended from the side of his head. For this asymmetry he blamed me, not understanding how difficult it is to remodel an ear, nor realizing that without my effort he might now have no ear at all. Ungrateful wretch.

To this disfigurement add his choler at losing Kate to me, and his arson is understandable, if wrongheaded.

As I followed the cart down Church View Street to Bridge Street I resolved that for the next few months I would avoid turning my back to Sir Simon Trillowe. As it happened, 'twas Sir Simon who should not have turned his back to another.